the one true ocean

the one true ocean

by Sarah Beth Martin

SOURCEBOOKS LANDMARK™
AN IMPRINT OF SOURCEBOOKS, INC.®
NAPERVILLE, ILLINOIS

Published by Sourcebooks, Inc.
P.O. Box 4410, Naperville, Illinois 60567-4410
(630) 961-3900
FAX: (630) 961-2168
www.sourcebooks.com

Library of Congress Cataloging-in-Publication Data

Martin, Sarah Beth.
The one true ocean / by Sarah Beth Martin.
p. cm.
ISBN 1-4022-0143-5 (alk. paper)
1. Young women—Fiction. 2. Widows—Fiction. I. Title.
PS3613.A786O64 2003
813'.6—dc21
2003006750

Printed and bound in the United States of America
QW   10 9 8 7 6 5 4 3 2 1

First Edition

This book is dedicated to my parents,
Janet and Jack Martin.

acknowledgments

For their contribution to this book I owe a word of gratitude to the crew at Sourcebooks: Jennifer Fusco, for her vision and editorial finesse; Laura Kuhn, for her enthusiastic support; Vicky Brown, for friendly guidance; Megan Dempster, for pure artistry; and Dominique Raccah, for giving me this wonderful opportunity. Thanks for taking me in.

I also would like to thank my agent, Stacey Glick, for her devotion and perseverance, and for seeing the light in this book from the very beginning.

A special thanks goes to those who witnessed the evolution of this book, whose support I treasure: to my family and friends, for welcoming all the chronicles and excerpts; to Jim, for listening, always; to Dad, for passing down his love for stories; and to Mom, whose memory still guides me as I write them.

And to a little yellow house in Maine that sparked this one.

CONTENTS

the one true ocean

part one
aftermath

{renee

one

"Women are capable of horrendous deeds," Renee McGarry reads from the textbook in her hands, while stunned, pubescent eyes stare up at her. She feels significant, powerful, speaking the words to her students; this aspect of the female mind is something many of them may not realize. They might not learn it in a physical science class, perhaps not even in history. The words might only appear to them in sensational headlines about violence and madness, murder. But sensational headlines are not what she is talking about.

She looks out the window to the courtyard, to the transition from winter to spring: melting, dripping, dirty ice and snow, the waterlogged branches and soggy leaves left over from fall. It's hard to believe it's the same courtyard, the same thick lawn and colorful trees from autumn. And what about winter, she wonders; was there even a winter? The transition to spring was a blank, cold blue space of nothing. A post-death vacuum.

It was autumn when her daughter's husband died. It had been the most beautiful of autumns, with bright foliage that procrastinated and clung to limbs; beautiful, until temperatures dropped and light rain froze on roads, and the afternoon sun simmered the ice to a slick, invisible black. It all ended in autumn, at four o'clock on a bright, gauzy afternoon, perhaps at the same exact time that odd, circular wind blew the freshly raked leaves back onto the lawn.

Looking out this bleak, gray courtyard window, Renee waits for spring—when dead things come alive again, and she thinks of all the things and people that won't be coming back. This oncoming season—all this growth and regrowth—mocks her.

Soon the russet and gold shreds of leaves will sift through the soil in mica-like flakes, and green will sprout from the hard, cold earth. Insects will twitch and flicker in the sunlight, and there will be that smell of green and dirt and wet—the smell of life. And the birds will return, the sparrows and goldfinches, arriving sooner than many realize—not yet showing themselves, not yet singing. Then the chickadees, who never left, but whose song changes with the seasons: they, too, will hesitate to chirp their spring song in case winter decides to return.

An early robin perches on a naked branch, above the dew and flickering life below, barely supporting itself in the strong wind that smells of ice and metal. Acorns are on the ground, some with their tops and bottoms together, even after the winter.

A young Renee, who loved spring and trees and living things, would paint faces on the acorns with hats. She would place them on top of tiny mud piles to give them bodies, something to balance their heads on. She would think about human bodies, designed by God, the way babies' heads could not stand properly on necks, how heads had to be trained. Why did acorns have hats? she wondered. Perhaps she could ask her big sister Adeline, because she knew about living things.

Renee would one day learn about living things too—not the green life, but human life—the insides of heads and why one wears hats. But she would learn from real life first, from the kind of reality others would not know for ten, twenty years, maybe never. And she was barely sixteen.

So she knew what she was talking about when, years later, she would speak the same words to her daughter that her sister Adeline once had spoken to her.

A baby will change your life.

jenna}

two

What happens to the dead?

I am seven when I think of this, when I first experience death: my aunt, a woman who was gentle and velvety like a butterfly, whose life ended with the clatter of metal and the shock of cold salt water, and perhaps with fear and pain. But I do not think of fear and pain when I am seven; death is simple—it means only that one has gone to a better place, a place that is peaceful and pastel-colored, where there are no heartaches, no unexpected storms. I have no doubt in my mind that Aunt Adeline is at rest.

Now I am not so sure.

My adult life has been invaded by death, infected by chaos. My world is not the same. Whenever I look up at the night sky, I wonder how many more times I will see the full moon, how many Thanksgivings and Christmases will pass before my time. Probably fewer than I once imagined; the number had once seemed so infinite.

Life is taken for granted by the living, is my conclusion.

I don't know if Seth lived this way—if he counted down moons and holidays. Better if he hadn't; better if he never realized it was his last drive home from work, and that there would be no more night sky.

The veneer-bladed ceiling fan spins above me, its hum rhythmic, buzzing like a big mosquito, reminding me that I am made of blood. With my eyes closed I see only mottled, veiny, red-black, but as I open them just slightly there is the flickering above: the shadow of the fan blades, propelled by air destined to go somewhere. Blades destined to turn, like age.

Like life.

Life with Seth started with geology. It was in physical geology that we had our first class together, where we first made eye contact. How Seth loved the science, the explicitness of it; because it was all about rebirth, he had said, about shifting—the upheaval of land. And in life, death is just another part of that shifting—the bones and cells becoming part of the land, the rock. Thinking this way helped Seth to not be afraid.

I didn't know it at the time, but I also would need to be fearless, as one day Seth suddenly would be gone, and I would be sitting on a church pew before the shell of his body, while voices told me to pray.

Pray, they said, as I looked up to a great vaulted ceiling of ornate ivories and golds, to colored glass of amber and blue. The New England sun burned through, turning October cold to a hot, blinding glare, mocking me, while voices told me where my husband was. *He's with God now*, they said, *with Jesus*. A simple solution, I figured, for all who loved Seth, and needed to know he did not simply vanish into nothingness.

As the voices echoed through the chapel, I imagined his low, softish voice, remembered his dark chocolate eyes looking down at me. But I saw only the copper of his coffin up ahead, open like a museum display, exposing a gauzy white pillow of a bed on which his neatly dressed, miraculously unscarred body lay. My head felt fuzzy, a stuffed, cottony feeling. The muscle relaxants had kicked in, softening sounds and muzzling emotions—just enough so I could still respond *loved you too*. I was like a machine reacting to signals, to each button pushed—perhaps reacting better than I normally would, my brain void of the usual questions and analysis, that mirage of morality.

And how strange it was—how surreal—to display his body in such a way; but Seth had wanted the open coffin when his time came. "It's healthy for people to see," he once said. "The body is just a shell." Of course not realizing his own death was so near.

I had seen a dead body before. Aunt Adeline's, twenty years ago, another young body stitched and painted and plumped with preservatives. But in contrast to my aunt's, Seth's body looked more alive on this day, as if he might just open his eyes and laugh, tell everyone he was kidding. As if this terrible thing could never have happened to a sweet, funny man like Seth.

This was not real.

In the front row pew Dad sat on my left side, holding my sweating hand. I could barely feel my own fingers, only my father's cold, wet palm cupped with mine, and the tiny pockets of air where our skin did not touch. I imagined the lines on his palm, crossing over my own, but not like rivers exactly; more like bridges over rivers—like our genes. He is a dad connected to me in a different way, a special way. A dad who came along years after I was born, who saved me from illegitimacy, and saved Mom from shame.

Natural child Elisabeth sat to my right, turning her head toward me several times during the ceremony. When I looked back I saw the tiny pale face, harder somehow—without its usual delicate cast, a face refraining from grimace, perhaps experiencing horror for the first time. Horror, I thought, when a young person learns that untimely death is possible. With the exception of thirteen-year-old Elisabeth, the whole family had been there, many years before.

Especially Mom.

I couldn't see her—she was sitting to the left of Dad, but I could feel the wall with which Mom had surrounded herself for this very occasion. I figured that when she looked ahead to that coffin, she was seeing her sister Adeline again. Aunt Adeline, who had left this world too early for things between them to be resolved. I thought of Seth, of the things we never resolved, never even spoke about again.

A tap on my shoulder surprised me. I turned and saw old friend Paula sitting in the pew behind, her over-rouged face bloated in sorrow, the blonde hair slicked dark and conformed to a bun. Paula, from my pre-Seth college days, now married and back in Maine, now tidy in her navy two-piece pantsuit with white piping—a Halloween sailor, I thought with my fuzzy head; so reserved, so not her. Sitting next to her was husband Gerard, his eyes dull and yellowy, the cheeks and nose blotchy, a too-much-drink look. He had met Seth only twice—seven years ago at Paula and Gerard's wedding, then again at our own, just months later. But then even Paula's friendship with Seth was limited to one beer-induced gathering with us on campus, before she became pregnant and was seduced back to Maine. It all happened so quickly; before Paula left I didn't have the chance to tell her that I had become pregnant, too.

It was a year since I last saw her—when Paula's second of two was born and I visited her at the hospital in Portland. It was the time I took the long way home just so I could drive by the old house in Cape Wood. When I got there it was too dark to see anything except the outline of a roof behind the creepy silhouettes of spruce trees.

Paula reached over from the pew behind and wrapped her hand around my upper arm. "We'll pray for him," she said. I could try to pray, but God wouldn't be there, not after years of my not knowing what to believe.

———

Sometimes I think about other ways he could have died—more horrible ways, so that the way it happened doesn't seem so bad. A slit throat, a gunshot wound.

More horrible.

The truck came out of nowhere, supposedly, a jacked-up blue Dodge on steroids, hurling into his lane from the right, cutting in front of him. Seth must have seen it coming; he must have looked death directly in the eyes. But perhaps it happened quickly; maybe there was no time for fear, and his oncoming death was purely accepted. I hope so; that Seth passed into that dimension of peace and tranquillity without a breath, without the chance to feel any regret, any sorrow or guilt or shame.

A death with dignity. Perhaps one thing all living beings hope for: a life that ends without wronging or without being wronged. In my dreams, the man in the blue truck is still alive, his face intact—not guilty. But in real life, he has crushed his body, his identity, and has taken my husband with him.

Now sirens wake me in the night, and early each morning. I didn't use to notice them; they are common in Cambridge, and I used to sleep right through. Now when I hear them I think of ambulances, police cars, and hospital emergency rooms. I go back in time, back to what Seth's last vision may have been: the colors of October—late afternoon, orange and brown leaves across the dark road, followed by flashes of metal, a blue truck in front of the windshield coming toward him in slow motion. The rescue lights are there—perhaps he never saw these—the blinding red bulbs of the fire truck, blue lights of a police car. I hear the sounds: sirens approaching, wobbling in and out of my ears, the same sounds that resonated through my sleep while I napped cozily on the couch, waiting for him to return from a quick trip to work. I must have thought that these were everyday sounds, that they were nothing. Now I wonder if those sirens I heard were sirens rushing for him, and if they were, if he ever heard them. Or was he dead already? At what precise moment did Seth leave this world?

It is difficult to not know, to not have seen it. To hear only that he was unconscious when witnesses reached the car. Unconscious or dead, they did not know. They didn't say *dead* until he reached the hospital.

So I can only imagine. Each morning I see crumpled metal, the crashed windshield—all those pictures I saw in the paper of his smashed car after they removed him. I see the clusters of orange and brown and wonder if he saw leaves before he died.

I live this way. For a few minutes of every hour, of every half or quarter-hour, I am Seth—seeing what he may have seen, feeling what he felt. I make his experience as painful and terrifying as possible, so that I know it could not have been as bad as I imagine. It feels strange—this solemnizing, this penance, because putting myself in Seth's shoes is something I never bothered to do when he was alive.

I remember his body at the hospital, the nightmare beneath the white sheet. When they lifted the sheet his sweet face and hair were clean, his body remarkably intact. I reached out, touched his still-warm head, and in my half-conscious mind sighed, because for a second, he was alive. He was not the bloodied, dismembered body I had imagined and feared as a policeman drove me to the hospital; he seemed whole. But this lie, this fantasy lasted only for a second, and the truth was what the officer had already told me at my front door: inside this perfect body Seth was dead, his bones were crushed, his organs liquefied. But it was quick, the emergency room doctor comforted. "Yes," the policeman added, "he didn't know what hit him."

But how did they really know?

I had awaken from my nap to this police officer's face at my front door, to the horrible news. As he spoke the words I choked, gagged on my own breath, and my stomach turned inside out. I hunched over, curled my body like a shrimp, then crumpled into the doorway, and he had to pull me up and walk my shaking body to the couch. As I sat down I heard sounds coming from my own mouth—a scraping, guttural cry, like a baby does after screaming for hours. Now when I cry or see anyone else cry, or especially when I hear a baby cry, I replay the words the officer spoke as I opened that door.

"Are you Jenna McGarry, the wife of Seth Morton?"

Wife of Seth, I keep hearing, along with the strange noises throughout my building. Floors creak with life and walls tick with water pipes, making me jump. The dim hallways seem unusually hollow, echoing, and voices floors below resonate through the house. Then there is the traffic outside—the engines and horns of anxious commuters, the distant groan of the subway. Never before have such slight sounds been so painful.

And I can hear the leaves. Outside the living room window on the street below are the rotted, recycled leaves from fall, dark and drenched with melted snow and exhaust. The sound they make is different from the crisp, autumn leaves that scratch against the sidewalk in an elegant sweep, like the crackle of a fire. These late-winter leaves are lower-toned and sluggish as they scour the pavement, making way for spring.

The oncoming spring terrifies me. I will have to emerge then, to come out from hibernation. In winter I was not expected to get better, to be happy; I did not have to grow, or even face the sunlight. I could hide from the world, from reality. Some people I don't have to hide from; many avoid me. But from those who stare and scrutinize, I have to look away. It hurts—this surveillance, this waiting for them to ask me how I'm doing. I wait, knowing exactly what they are going to say.

Sometimes in the morning I feel stuck to my bed, heavy and immovable, like a piece of iron pressed into the soft cotton. I lie there for hours sometimes, wondering if someone will find me that way. I don't like going anywhere—the agency keeps calling, asking me if I'm ready for more work—fruits this time, they say, line drawings. Coloring books. "Another week," I keep telling them.

The telephone rings and it frightens me. I'm not sure if I fear bad news or just voices in general, but I don't answer it anymore. I let the machine pick up, the machine with the message that must confuse people, make them wonder about my state of mind. I haven't changed the message on it. After five months it still says in Seth's deep sandy voice, *We can't come to the phone right now…*

And I know that all are listening and thinking how I need to get over this: *When will she be over this?*

———

I awaken from one of my Seth dreams, in which I hear his voice on the other end of a phone line, talking from far away. I can see him, but he's cloudy, two-dimensional almost, as if on a movie screen that's far away. He tells me that he's going somewhere—he doesn't say where, and I want to tell him to be careful, to take a different route, but when my mouth opens to speak, only a strange gasping sound comes forth. I exhale gasping sounds but I cannot form words, while his voice says *are you there, are you there?* I can barely make out his face on the screen with its gauzy layer in front of it; I can't tell if the gauzy layer is in front of the screen or in front of my eyes, like a cataract. He is ready to hang up, but still I try to speak, to yell. There's so much I want to tell him, but it's too late.

So *this* is why so many believe in God and heaven and afterlives, I realize. With God and heaven, there is no *too late.*

His breath still floats around this apartment and this room. When I lie in the stillness of my bed I can feel it whisper against my cheek, my bare arm. But with this fan spinning above I know the air and his breath will move past quickly, and not stay too long. Still, as I drift off to sleep I feel waves of air sweep warm and soft over my face, and I feel him near me.

I'm still here.

Each morning in bed I think I'm done crying. Every day is the last day I'll cry, then each day following. The dreams I'm having are wearing me out. I'm drowning in his memory. My soul is dehydrated.

And there is this apartment: this tiny, attic third floor of a house with colored layers stacked like Legos, where each level pretends to live in private, to feel safe and anonymous. I feel stifled up here, hot—even in this early March, while I lie static below the spinning fan blades. I am smothering in this apartment—no longer anonymous or safe.

Leaving here would be difficult. It would be leaving him behind. *But this place is just a shell,* I remind myself daily, as if taking a vitamin; like his dead body, it is a shell. To stay would not be a symbol of my love for him; to go would not indicate a too-early recovery.

I am not to feel guilty for leaving.

It would only *feel* like I'm leaving Seth, because the place is alive with him. His skin, his dust, lies in the thinnest, unseen layer on top of the furniture and upon the walls. It lives in the cracks and corners of floorboards, within the bedroom rug. There are invisible hairs in the corners of drawers, the fine powder of fingernail on the dresser. Traces of his fluids permeate the mattress pad. He is here still—remnants of him.

Move on.

three

The aftermath of death was not what I had imagined it might be. It was like a dream—a blur of faces and condolences, and I endured the pain the way one endures the extra mile when running uphill. A gush of adrenaline was perhaps what it took, a different, dreamy kind of adrenaline to make it all okay.

Even the after-funeral gathering was surprisingly endurable, not the nightmare I had anticipated. Mostly because it was not *me* wandering amongst family and friends, telling everyone I was okay. It was someone else—someone able to answer, able to smile. I had not imagined that I would be able to smile on such a day.

What I had imagined was a confined, bottled-up feeling, and that I could not wait for them all to leave and just let me explode. But having all those people around me for those two, three hours ended up being exactly what I needed. On that afternoon, Seth's parents' house had been transformed into a diorama of sorts, a façade, and being there was like watching a movie with me in it. And with all those faces, all those stories told only during such occasions, surrounding me like a cushiony wall, a big blanket.

And just hours later those faces and stories suddenly were gone, and sorrow hit me like a wave, knocking me over so I could not move or breathe.

I am drowning.

The waiting room of *Brookline Psychological Health* is air-conditioned, even in March. The air is stale and bland, and there is the smell of year-old dust, hot metal, cold plastic. On the wall above the couch is a watercolor print—a farm field and country farmhouse, with a mauve-colored plastic frame to clash. The waiting room furniture seems to match the frame; there is the same mauve color in the chairs and a couch, both in a hard, scratchy nylon. The room could use some comfort, I think, some warmth. Maybe some earth colors—a little red, the color used in film to imply danger, in restaurants to increase the appetite. Any new sensation to smooth out the edges.

When a loved one dies tragically, there sometimes are social workers and doctors to help, to surround like bees—ready to comfort, console, whatever. I am lucky to have my private meetings, that I'm not just on some survivor's roster at the emergency department, the next one in line. I wonder if Mom had that kind of help after the police found Aunt Adeline's waterlogged car.

Dr. Chase reminds me of Mom. She is slim and tidy and conservative-looking, with the same high brunette bun on her head, the wispy bangs cascading onto her forehead. She wears thin-rimmed glasses that outline her small raisin-eyes, and clutches a clipboard to her chest the way doctors do in movies. Her office is warmer than the waiting room, with a thick plush carpet in emerald green, a shiny mahogany desk. An English ivy crawls up the back corners of the room to the ceiling, then over the window. I take one of the heavy wood chairs in front of the desk, wondering if anyone actually lies on the black vinyl sofa against the wall.

Dr. Chase positions her glasses on the end of her nose, looks down to the stack of papers in her hands, and begins. "Let's talk about the accident again."

I take a breath and repeat the details, the story I've gone over so many times now that I wonder if the words are the same each time they emerge from my mouth: *The driver of the other car was speeding…roads were icy that day, one of those rare, black ice days in October…*

Such an ominous autumn day, I think, cloudy but luminescent; a soft, velvety gray. It was startlingly cold, too; I could feel my eyes drying—freezing open in the coldness, and I could see Seth's breath in the air as he spoke those last words to me outside of his car.

Love ya.

Dr. Chase flips through her paperwork. "You and Seth never had any children," she says.

"No."

"But you miscarried once."

The words feel foreign, intrusive. I've forgotten about all this information she has on me. "Yes," I say. "Seven years ago."

"Seven years," she says, perhaps doing the math in her head. "Were you and Seth married then?"

"No. Not yet." I look to a blank spot on her desk, see the reflection of the window in the shining wood. The bare branches outside the window are moving in the reflection and seem clearer the more I stare at them, as if it's not a reflection at all.

"And," Dr. Chase's voice wakes me up, "was it Seth's baby?" She seems nonchalant about this question, as if the answer could very well be *No.* Then I think, how many women does the doctor talk to who have several men in their lives?

"Yes, it was," I say.

"Did you marry because of this pregnancy?"

"No. Well, yes…originally, yes." The wooden chair feels hard beneath me; I feel rigid, aware of my stiff back and neck, the exact position of my arms and legs. "Then after I lost it we married anyway."

Dr. Chase looks beyond me for a moment to the wall, perhaps skimming the list of possibilities in her head. "Was there ever any question," she asks, "about whether you still would marry—after your miscarriage?"

Of course Seth would marry me; there was no question. That was one thing I would never have to worry about from him: duty, dedication, a lifetime of love. But there also had been so many tense conversations between us during that time, so many unspoken assumptions that led to unspoken decisions. So much of those days are fuzzy now; I can't pinpoint any real conclusion. "No," I say. "We never talked about it. But we did *stay* married, after all." My voice sounds defensive.

"How did you feel after you lost the baby?"

"Terrible, of course. But you could almost say it was for the best. I wasn't ready for a baby."

"Did you ever try again?"

"No."

"Why not?" Dr. Chase's eyes move over my face, scrutinizing, it seems.

"I don't know."

She crosses her fingers and rests her hands on the desk. "And how do you feel about this today, in relation to the accident?"

"I don't. All I think about is that damn accident."

"Do you feel guilty?"

"About the baby?"

"About the accident."

"I guess so," I say. "I feel guilty about being alive. I feel it every morning when I put my feet on the floor, when I drink a glass of water or brush my teeth, whenever I feel like smiling or enjoying life. When I breathe." It feels good to tell her this, like I have just come up for air. "I feel like part of me is missing."

Dr. Chase smiles. "Part of you is not missing, I assure you," she says. "But it does feel like that, because there's a part of you that was devoted to Seth. That part of you doesn't know what to do anymore. That part won't let you move on."

I've heard this before. "I know."

She lowers her glasses and looks up at me. "Did you ever think," she says, "that it's possible you've already begun to recover, and that this is what you feel guilty about?"

Heat rushes within my chest and up the sides of my neck, to my temples. I wonder how she can think this, how she can say such a thing. How many mourning people does she say this to? "No, I don't think so," I say. I look out the window beyond where she sits, through the valance of green plants and polished glass, see the street a half-story below where cars are rushing, rushing to nowhere.

I'm getting nowhere too.

———

After the session ends and I step out of Dr. Chase's office, the tears come. This is how it happens each time, the gush of tears I don't let others see.

On my way out I pass through the waiting room and stare at the mauve-framed watercolor again. A lame attempt at style, I think with my artist's eye, but as I inspect it more closely I notice the illustration within: a yellow farmhouse within an open field, a white picket fence and clothesline in the back yard. Typical, I think, like many paintings of country farmhouses, yet familiar. A little bit like the old house in Maine, where I spent my first few years.

I exit the building and run down the front steps and get into my car. Traffic rushes past, so fast, it seems. I try to pull onto the street and I can't; each time I'm about to press my foot to the gas I anticipate the crash of metal-against-metal, and again think of Seth buried in the ground.

And I think of something else: a voice over the telephone— *Pregnant, you're pregnant,* and remember my tense, upright posture on Seth's living room couch, listening, thinking about the year to follow. We would be married, most likely, living in the same tiny third-floor apartment. And I would be sitting in the same living room, feeling the summer sun through the window, the heat from the pavement two stories below. And with a sticky, screaming baby in my lap, my cleavage and forehead sweating, my full hands unable to wipe. And stuck to that corduroy couch, the milk-spotted, veneered coffee table in front of me.

I wasn't ready.

But in the end I didn't have to experience any of those fears I had, fears I now know were selfish, inconsequential. I lost our baby, its body barely a shell. A body not even big enough to bury, someone at the hospital must have decided.

I look back up to the big stone building and think of how cold the polished granite must feel in this raw wind, yet how indestructible it must be—so different from my tiny apartment in the city that now feels so fragile and so temporary. I feel raw, penetrable. Stripped of my skin. Seth would want me to forget about this terrible thing that happened to him. He would want me to take a deep breath and erase everything from my memory.

And I can do this if I try hard enough—if I think of something else, something that takes me away from him. I close my eyes and see the waiting room watercolor, a painting that does not seem so tacky, so inert as when I first looked at it. Now there is something sunny and comforting about this yellow farmhouse that reminds me of my life before this one—before Seth, when my aunt was alive. Aunt Adeline, who, unlike my own mother, did not seem so far away.

part two
the origins of things

{renee

four

There are times when she begins to remember. The wind will blow from a particular angle at her face, bringing with it the salty mist from the coast twenty miles away, and she will see Maine. Water, waves, sand, and rock ledges. She can't escape it; she should have moved farther away from the coast if she really wanted to escape. But it must be in her blood to be near some kind of water—not the static, buggy inland kind of water but the fresh, regenerative kind. She settled for this west-of-Boston inland that lets her breathe but doesn't smell like Maine.

Renee looks out the front doorway, sees where Bill has just cleaned the winter grit and salt from the walk, a sweep of mud across stone. Clumps of gold and rust peek out from the dirt— the soggy oak leaves from fall, her favorite season.

She thinks of autumn in Maine, especially early autumn, before the first frost, when the smell of apples permeated the cool air. She remembers how sumacs and maples ripened like fruit, and forest floors were covered with brittle brown needles and fallen acorns with their tops removed. Rain was hard and cold as it soaked fields full of pumpkins and squashed, late-summer tomatoes. Spiders came inside and mosquitoes melted away; birds flew south and automobiles followed, towing boats and bicycles. And then suddenly, the yellow school buses appear out of nowhere.

Here in the Bay State, one hundred miles away, autumn looks much the same. Even the coastal cities become speckled with fall—the reds, browns, and golds that thicken toward the suburbs, then explode into color to the west. But in the summer Renee feels safer here than in Maine. She feels secure in her western suburb well inland from the coast, within the plush collar of trees that protects her from the ocean she no longer loves.

She used to live for the summer—for gardens and sun and warm, glistening sand, for the sharp, reflective ocean waves. But she no longer loves those waves of dark, blue-green, or that foamy edge that splashing creates. Her Maine summer waves were lost long ago, when summer evaporated, turned to death. So she turned to autumn, "ironic in its deathly beauty," as she might describe to her social science students. Because she likes irony—that incongruent bridge between what is expected and what actually occurs.

And now, with Seth gone, autumn may be lost too.

On the shelf next to the door stands his picture in which he hovers close to Jenna, his head tilted down to hers, his shadowy eyes looking intensely into the camera. The outline of his shoulders, the deep eyes and dark crown of hair have always reminded Renee of someone else. It is an unsettling memory—not good, not bad, just unsettling—a feeling she longs for and, at the same time, deplores. A face from long ago.

She opens the door and looks out to the mud and melting, smells the oncoming spring towing summer behind it—her faraway Maine. The moment and memory will pass, she thinks, like they always do.

jenna}

five

I chase after butterflies and the fuzz of dead dandelions, then fall into rubbery, cushiony grass. At the center of the lawn, within the fresh dirt and green, is Aunt Adeline, her arms outstretched like wings. She floats through the garden in her blue seersucker dress, her dark hair reddish in the sunlight, her skin ivory white. As she wipes the flyaway bangs from her face, her features are a blur: a hairline and nose, the dark hollows for eyes, a long female hand sweeping across.

Aunt Adeline lets me play while she bends and sifts through the soil, and when she is done we compare dirt spots on our bodies. I ask her if we can show Mom, too, but she always tells me the same thing.

"Your mom is resting."

Mom was always resting, either lying in bed or sitting in a chair—sometimes reading or knitting, but usually just resting. There were some days when she'd get up and walk around, even days when she went out into the yard; but mostly she just stayed in her room. I'd ask Aunt Adeline if Mom might be getting better soon, and she'd say yes, it was a possibility. But she had said this before.

On these days when Mom wasn't well, Aunt Adeline would clean me up and we'd go out in her big brown car to buy ice cream or Popsicles, or to picnic on the town green. Sometimes we'd go to the pebbly beach down the street—my favorite because Mom never liked to go there, where the water was cold and the sun blinding against the sand. There we collected mussel shells to punch holes in and string into chains.

There were some days we didn't go anywhere, and I'd play in the thick green woods behind the house, just beyond the edge of the lawn where Aunt Adeline could still see me. On rainy days I'd sit at the table with my crayons or paints while the smell of cookies baking filled the kitchen. Aunt Adeline would talk to me while she stirred batter or washed the dishes—telling me stories about when I was a baby. She'd recall how she would tuck me in at night and speak to me until I was almost asleep, then shut my little yellow night light out. Sometimes these stories confused me, because when I remembered this fading yellow light in my bedroom, I had always thought it was Mom standing above it.

"Your mother was around," Aunt Adeline once assured me. "But she always needed help, and I was always there to help her."

At that moment I looked over at Mom, who was sitting in a chair before the living room window, not too far from us. Did she just hear what Aunt Adeline said? Probably not, I figured, as she'd been sitting there for hours, silent, the entire time Aunt Adeline had spoken to me. I wondered if Mom always had been like this—present, yet so far away.

Today Mom is forty-two, but the wrinkles at the corners of her eyes and mouth could let her pass for forty-six. Sometimes I wish I could tell people she was older, to void out the sympathy she gets when people discover she was a mother at sixteen.

Even with her tired eyes and bitter mouth, Mom is beautiful. Her hair shines a deep sepia, and her eyes are a pale warm hazel, ranging from gray to topaz. She looks especially thin today in her pleated slacks that billow in front, and her fitted ivory sweater that reveals the concave posture, a defeat in her body. Her slender neck seems bowed, shameful somehow; the delicate gold crucifix that Dad gave her hangs low between her collarbones. And lately she has been a tense, white pale—that perpetual look of just having seen a ghost.

She is especially pale now, as if the miniature rosebush I have brought her might take a bite out of her. "It's pretty," she says, her voice limp, her eyes avoiding. "But cut flowers would have been fine."

That's right, I think. *Cut* flowers, because they're *dead*. Or at least on their way to being dead. If it still has its roots, she doesn't want it.

Mom is not fond of living things. The last time I gave her anything alive was back in fourth grade, a rubber plant from my science class. I remember approaching the front steps, balancing the shiny, jiggling plant in my tiny hands, and looking up to see Mom's blank face through the glass of the front door. She gave a quick smile when I handed her the plant, but then her face suddenly looked milky and dry, as if the blood had left it. It was then I realized just how much Mom didn't like plants, and when I first wondered if these green, living things reminded her of her no-longer-living sister.

It was Aunt Adeline who introduced me to plants. Flowers and greenery surrounded the house in Maine and filled the second-floor bedroom she had converted into a greenhouse. She gave me plants she knew I could handle—ones less likely to die on me: herbs and ferns, the occasional cactus. These plants were special because she had grown them all from seed, and because the green world was her life. But not Mom; on that day in fourth grade when I brought her home the rubber plant, she never did thank me; she only commented.

"It looks like a big green hand."

Today, however, she does thank me. "I appreciate it," she says, her eyebrows dipping, a look of both curiosity and disapproval she manages to wrap into one. "It's just that real plants carry mold and bugs," she adds. "And watering them is a nuisance."

"Whatever, Mom," I say. " I just thought it would be a nice change from all those fake plants you've got all over the place."

"I like my fake plants," she says, raising her chin in pride, carrying the rosebush around the corner into the pantry. I imagine where it will end up: in a dark corner of the den or sewing room, the plastic blinds closed. "They look real," she calls, her voice muffled by the wall between us. "And they're low-maintenance."

"Well, I'm afraid this one will need some maintenance," I call to her, hearing sarcasm in my voice. "It might even need some love."

She appears from around the corner. "What did you say?"

"Nothing. Happy birthday, Mom."

Dad comes into the kitchen, saving us. He looks wearied, a bit shadowy around the eyes. He seems much older lately; I recall his shoulders seeming broader when I was young, without the sloping, that weightiness they have now. Mom and Dad both appear to feel the way I have during the past few months. It is as if my depression has rubbed off on them. Or perhaps it is something else.

"Hi, Jen," Dad says, then turns to Mom, who now is making clatter in the silverware drawer. "Renee, can I help you with anything?"

"I'm all set," she says.

"On her own birthday," he chuckles. "She won't even let us help her on her birthday. Are you sure, Renee?"

"I've got it, Bill." She moves into the dining room, drops the silverware and napkins on the table and rearranges her centerpiece of fake flowers and eucalyptus. She begins to set the table, folding a napkin with geometric precision, flattening it with a perfectly centered fork. She adjusts the cloth so it is parallel with its matching placemat edge, then aligns the placemat with the edge of the table, and finally places a shining plate on top. The arrangement is tidy and shimmering—sparkling stainless and simple-patterned china, the inert bouquet in the center. There is no clutter, as there's no clutter on the living room end tables or on the windowsills. There is only an occasional accessory—a framed photograph, a decorative bowl or print. Unlike my place, with its dusty antiques and trinkets, the dirt-speckled rocks in every corner. Of course, Mom has made sure to comment the few times she came to visit.

Don't you ever dust? she would say about the furniture, and *It's a jungle in here* about the plants that trailed over the living room windows like valances. Then her most popular, about the accessories I had so carefully arranged on shelves and on the coffee table: *When are you going to put this stuff away?* Luckily I don't have to hear the comments anymore; Mom hasn't been to my place since Seth died.

Dad has, though. He drops by to bring me discount art supplies and magazines. I just don't have the heart to tell him I can't even seem to hold a paintbrush or pencil anymore.

Mom looks up at both of us. "Bill, why don't you show Jenna some of the projects you've been working on?" This is the routine with Mom. It's the same every time.

"Jenna doesn't want to look at my models again," Dad says, but I wink at him and he stops.

"It's okay, Dad. Sure I do."

We go down to the basement, where gliders and B-52 bombers hang from the ceiling, and model cars fill the shelves. On the workbench are pieces of a plane-in-progress—the curved shell of the body, the square and triangular sections of wing, pieces of rubber wheel and plastic windows. The pieces are spread out like a wreck, as if his creation has nose-dived into the wood. This is a different Dad, I think, the one who can talk without being interrupted, the one who's allowed to be messy. Probably the one Mom fell in love with in the first place.

The first time I ever saw Dad he was just a big shadow to me, a shape at the edge of the lawn where I was playing. First he was behind the fence, then the next day by the mailbox, and next by the maple tree within the yard. Every day he moved closer and closer to the house, and every day Mom would come out and say hello, and soon they were both moving up the driveway toward the front steps. Then one day he was sitting in the big white rocker on the front porch, drinking Mom's lemonade. "This is Bill," Mom said to me, and I saw him up close—all tall and dark like a movie star. I thought of how this man named Bill was the first person who had come to the house to see Mom, and how it usually was Aunt Adeline who made lemonade. Suddenly Mom had come alive again.

I hear Elisabeth's young voice chattering on the stairs two floors above us. "Your sister's on the phone again," Dad says.

"When is she not on the phone?" I laugh, remembering how I wasn't on the phone as much when I was thirteen, how I didn't have as many friends as Elisabeth has. She is so different than the teen I ever was, with her bright confidence and coltish energy. How did she and I turn out so different? I wonder. Sometimes I wish I hadn't spent my younger years so burrowed into my own skin, my little hole.

"Yes, she is quite the popular thing," Dad says. "Not that you weren't, Jen," he adds quickly, and I frown at him, jokingly, to assure him his doesn't have to be nice, he doesn't have to comfort me about this. He reaches out his arm and touches me. "How are you doing?"

"I'm okay." I feel the rush of emotion filling my head. I can't look at him; it will make everything come out. But he knows this.

"Are you back to work yet?" he says, changing the subject.

"Not yet."

"When you're ready."

"I'm thinking of getting out of the commercial stuff," I say, "and doing some freelance. Maybe portraits, even." I inspect a *Titanic* model on the shelf, notice the paint detail he's put into the tiny people on the deck. "How's your job?"

"Ugh," he sighs. "People complaining about the five dollar service charge on their five million dollar accounts."

"Rather be doing something else?" I joke.

"I'd like to be building these." He picks up a gray plastic shell of an aircraft carrier, holds it delicately up to the light. "Only *real* ones." His eyes squint as he tilts the model back and forth. "Did I ever tell you that I'd wanted to go into the Navy?"

"Why didn't you?"

"Things don't always turn out the way you plan."

"True," I say. "Seth's friend David never ended up going into the Navy...after all that talk."

"And your cousin Joey," Dad says. "He's too old now, but he still talks about it."

I think about another man who wanted to join the Navy, the man Mom once told me about. "I wonder if Montigue ever ended up going in," I say, and Dad suddenly stops his carrier in mid-air. I realize the magnitude of the name I've just spoken by the look of bewilderment in his eyes. "Mom once told me he wanted to," I add. "A long time ago she said it. But she hasn't talked about him since." He puts the model down. "Sorry, Dad. I didn't mean to bring it up."

"It's okay, Jen." I wonder if he's just being polite, if I should continue. He picks up a tube of Krazy Glue, turns it in his fingers. "To be honest," he says, "I usually forget about him until somebody reminds me."

"Sorry."

"No, no." Dad reaches out, touches my arm briefly; it's okay, he's saying. "Honey, don't worry."

I wonder what Dad thinks when he looks at Elisabeth and me, if he first sees Mom in our faces, and then inspects more closely for the subtle differences. And I wonder if Dad looks for Montigue; does he walk down the street and look for men's faces that resemble his elder daughter?

"Dad," I say, "can I ask you something?"

"Sure."

"Would you ever know him if you saw him?"

He puts the tube back, picks up his completed model of a Japanese bomber plane, and holds it up, squints his eyes at it. "No," he says. "And I try not to think of the possibility. It's something I just can't let myself think about."

"How come?"

He looks at me. "Because your mother loved him."

"How could she love him?" My voice comes out scolding. "She didn't even know his last name."

"Jenna, she was just a child."

"Yeah, and everybody feels sorry for her." I can hear my anger, the subtle tremble of my voice, but I can't stop. "Everyone thinks it's sad, poignant somehow. One-night stands are never poignant until somebody gets pregnant."

Dad's face is still, his eyes sober. He wants to condemn my words, I can tell, but he doesn't say anything.

"Dad," I begin to apologize. "I'm—"

"Did you see the garden, Jenna?" he interrupts. "The bulbs? There are twice as many as last year."

Mom has made a perfect lattice-top cherry pie for dessert—mostly for Dad, she says, because he was too generous on her birthday. They're always doing things like this for each other; if one of them gives a little extra—a little more than the other—the other gives back. It goes on and on sometimes, making the air thick with obligation, and being around them ends up feeling like I'm underwater.

A thick steam fills the kitchen. I take a seat at the table across from the counter island with its built-in burners and grill, where there are several pots going, where Mom scurries about, opening and slamming cabinets and drawers.

Something sizzles in the metal saucepan on the stove—butter or oil—and Mom quickly throws in chopped celery and onion

from her heap on the breadboard. The liquid steam spatters her nose and forehead, but she doesn't flinch. She grinds pepper into the saucepan, her eyes fixed at the bottom. She must be tense, wondering what to say. With Seth gone, she doesn't seem to know what to say to me anymore. So I begin.

"I'm still thinking of moving away."

"Are you?" She moves back over to the cabinets and opens them, looking for something. "I think it might be good for you."

"Doesn't sound like you'll miss me too much," I say, then realize I'm jumping to conclusions. I should give her more of a chance.

"Don't be silly." Her voice is muffled by the oak cabinet doors and rows of canned goods. "I was just thinking you can buy that house you always wanted."

I wait for her to shut the cabinets and come back before I speak. "You used to always tell us to wait to buy a house...until we'd *really* settled down. Whatever that meant."

Mom tilts her head like a dog. "Did I say that?" she says, her eyes round and innocent looking. "I must have meant when you had kids. Sometimes you don't know where you want to live until you have them. There are lots of things you don't know until you have kids."

"You knew we weren't having any."

"I guess I forgot." She stops her pepper shaker in mid-grind, blinks away from the pot as if her eyes are stinging. "Did I tell you I'm doing child development in my class this year?"

Mom has her ways of making points. Her methods are subtle but stabbing, with just the right pauses or eye movements, with the perfect choice of hidden words, messages. I suspect what she really has been saying with her tipped head and illusory eyes: seven years without children—*how easy it must have been for you.*

"No, Mom. You didn't tell me."

She moves back to her cabinets, shuffles the bottled spices around. "Are you painting again?"

"I just can't right now."

"What are you going to do for money?"

"I've got money," I say, then hold back for a second, a bit hesitant to say what I want to. "Accidental Death and Dismemberment," I add.

"Oh..." Mom is back at the counter. I don't think I shocked her too much with my morbidity, or perhaps she wasn't really listening. Then, as if sensation has suddenly ignited, she looks me in the eyes. "How are you holding up, Jenna?" she says.

I'm amazed to get such a question from her.

Still the hot sweats and nightmares, I want to say. "Okay," I lie. I'm so used to answering this way at the studio, at the bank and the post office; sometimes it's easier just to say "okay," especially with Mom. The words have come out so many times—true and untrue; I can no longer distinguish what I mean by them or how I'm feeling at the moment.

But I'm tired of lying. "Actually, Mom," I say, "I'm not doing so well."

She pours her mixture from the saucepan into a large bowl. "Where do you think you'll be moving to?" She must not have heard.

"I don't know."

She reaches up to the hanging wooden file next to the stove. "Oh, Jenna," she says, pulling out some envelopes and handing them to me. "These came for you."

Northeast University, one says in the corner, *New England Artists* on another; I've been getting junk mail at this address for years. On the top one it's my maiden name MCGARRY in large letters in the center of the envelope, but Mom has crossed it out and written MORTON—not for the post office but for me, to remind me of my married name. Mom can't seem to remember, or doesn't want to remember, that I changed it back years ago— something Seth was not the least bit offended by, but Mom apparently was.

Then there's a letter from Paula in Maine, whom I haven't seen since Seth's funeral. Why she occasionally sends mail to Westbridge I don't understand. Paula does this from time to time; the Christmas card went to Cambridge, the last birthday card came here. It could be motherhood that has done this to Paula. Perhaps in a flurry of colic and diaper rash, she forgets things.

The television blasts from the living room. Dad's in there now, I can tell, as I hear the saw blade of a workshop show. I peek around the corner and see him—his lean figure slumped into the couch, the dark hair matted against the cushion, eyes blank on the television. I think of that first time I saw him when I was barely four, the shape that seemed so towering and protective, that new person in our lives who was so eager to move and laugh and love. The man named Bill, who suddenly appeared at the house and brought Mom back, who saved us.

He looks at me and lifts his arm in a lazy wave, then smiles gently, a reluctant smile. Perhaps he still is upset with me. Or maybe this is about Seth: it could be that gentle smile I get from people who know how sensitive I am still, who don't know what else to say to me.

"Why don't you go join him?" Mom asks from behind me.

I'm tired of Mom avoiding me, tired of obeying as usual. I move between the counters while she is turned away, so that suddenly I am standing right next to her. So that Mom cannot refuse.

"Mom?" I say, softly, so not to startle her. "Can't I help?"

Mom turns and sighs, rolls her eyes. "I've got it." She lifts her arms in front of her, her hands covered with blobs of wet bread crumbs, then wriggles her body around me—just enough to tell me I'm an obstruction, I'm in her way.

I step aside, see the rosebush on top of the microwave in the dark pantry. When I look back Mom is beginning to stuff the chicken, spooning her bread and celery mixture into the bird, then pushing it in with her fingers. She moves fluidly and with rhythm, as if sculpturing clay to music. How concentrated she is, I think, how good at tuning everything out. I imagine Mom teaching her class—explaining theories in human terms, listening to the students, actually responding to them. How odd it seems.

Mom scoops and stuffs, scoops and stuffs, cramming the stuffing in. The chicken will explode, I think, if she keeps going like this. Suddenly she stops and looks up. "What?" she sighs.

"What can I do?"

"Nothing."

"But I want—"

"Why don't you go see what Elisabeth's doing?"

"I think she's on the phone," I say.

"Again?" Mom looks up and frowns.

A reaction, I think. *An actual response to something I've said.* But as usual it has nothing to do with me.

I drift back toward the living room doorway. Dad doesn't seem to notice me this time. His eyes are looking forward; it's difficult to tell where to because his head is leaning back, neck stretched over the top of the couch, and his eyes are slits looking in the direction of the television. He must have changed channels, or perhaps his show has ended; there's a clatter of commercials, then the news. Another shooting, a man's voice says. A vengeful gunman, a terrible thing. He killed her in cold blood, witnesses say. *How could he shoot a woman in the back?* the people say, over and over.

Would this killing be different, I wonder, if the woman had seen her gunman? I think of another report I saw the other night, the murder of a "beautiful girl." The announcer said how beautiful she was—"How could anyone kill such a lovely girl?" As if *lovely* made this murder somehow more important, more poignant than others.

There were other deaths today, the television says—Somerville, the South End. "Such a tragedy," a reporter says. "He was a father of two...she was a mother of three." I think of the one-minute segment on the eleven o'clock news about Seth, the one that didn't have quite the sympathetic ring: *A man died tonight,* was what it said. When there are no children—when only a spouse is left behind, perhaps *spouse* is not worth mentioning.

I wonder how my prime-time epitaph would read: Widow of one, mother of none. Would anyone care?

I rest against the door frame, peel open the envelope from Maine, and peek inside it. I see a letter, a newspaper clipping from the *Maine Casco Herald,* on which Paula has scribbled CHECK IT OUT above a photograph at the top of the page. I recognize the picture right away: the old house in Cape Wood.

I have had dreams about the house for as long as I can remember: the yellow shingles, the vague backdrop of a front porch, the pastel gardens, the September orange and red of the Mountain Ash in the side yard. It all is clear in my vision, as if, in my dreams, I've always lived there.

"What's that?" Mom says, suddenly interested in what I am doing.

"Oh, it's nothing," I say, and stuff the picture back into the envelope as quickly as I can.

six

The tall man named Bill, whom I'd first seen at the edge of our yard, was coming by the house more and more. Soon he began to take us out—just Mom and me, leaving Aunt Adeline behind. I begged for Aunt Adeline to go with us, but Mom always insisted she didn't want to. One time I asked Aunt Adeline if this was true, and she only sighed loudly and said, "Your mom never bothered to ask."

I felt badly that I was going without her. She told me she understood, that she knew exactly why Mom never asked her. "Your mother wants it to be just the three of you," she said. "She wants to pretend you're a real family, that's all."

So it was always just the three of us taking drives in Bill's car, which was big and shiny and the color of a swimming pool, and which was always hot from sitting in the sunny driveway all morning. Mom sat up front and I sat in the back and hung my head out the window in the summer breeze. We'd go to the ice cream parlor or Tucker's Pizza or sometimes even to Harbor's Clams which was next to the ocean. Bill was the only one who could get Mom to go to the ocean.

Harbor's was my favorite because we'd sit outside at a big red picnic table on the rocks, and I could see colorful specks of boats and rafts and hear the gulls and the surf and horns out on the water. Mom let me walk down the grassy hill toward the sandy beach, where I'd watch tiny minnows in the pools of brown water that crept up my legs, and feel the cold spray as the tide crashed against the rocks. "Don't go too far," Mom would say with each step I took, and I'd have to look back at her face to see if my next step was a too-big one. She'd either smile or nod or push her eyebrows down and shake her head, and I didn't care either way, because it was just nice to get this much attention from Mom.

Mom was happier when Bill was around. Now she would get up early, and she smiled and laughed and let me do things I couldn't do before, like watch TV or have dessert after supper. When fall arrived we visited the animal farm up north and bought pumpkins, and in the winter we built castle walls of snow around the house or went sledding on the big hill around the bend. It was summer I loved best, though, and I couldn't wait for the next one—to sit in the back of Bill's car and feel the warm, soft wind against my face, to close my eyes and imagine that we were a family.

On my fifth birthday my dream came true. Mom told me Bill had a new job at the bank, that they would be marrying soon, and that I would soon call him Daddy. Can I call him Daddy now? I asked, and Mom told me no. "Not until we're married," she said, "when he really is your daddy."

I didn't understand why I couldn't just call him Daddy then.

When Aunt Adeline heard the news she seemed more sad than happy. She leaned over to hug me but started to cry. Her body suddenly grew heavy, and there was wet against my neck. Mom had to pull her off of me and help her stand up again, then tried to reassure her.

"Adeline," she said. "We're only moving a few miles down the road."

I was confused when I heard Mom's words. "Are we moving away?" I asked, and Mom nodded yes.

I had no idea that being part of a family meant that we had to move away from the house where I'd grown up. I wondered what would happen to Aunt Adeline, if she would be alone. She had no one.

Aunt Adeline put her hand on my head, tousled my hair. Her eyes looked bright green against her red, watery eyes. Ringlets of reddish curls had fallen into her face. "I don't want you to go, Jenna," she said, and as she looked at Mom her mouth grew angry-looking and twisted, then opened wide and let out a high-pitched yell. Her voice screeched high, like an injured bird—like nothing I'd ever heard; my chest felt hot inside. Then she dropped to her knees in front of me, took my hands in her own cold fingers, and lowered her head to my face. I tried to step back but her grip was tight on me. Her hair was right up against my nose, and I could smell flowers and faint sweat. "I can't let her go," I heard her whimper.

Mom's hand slammed hard on the kitchen table; my birthday cake trembled. "Jesus, Adeline!" she said, her voice sharp and frightening. "It's only a few miles!" She whipped around and stomped out of the room, and I could hear her voice coming from the kitchen. "You can't punish me forever."

I wondered how Mom could be so angry when Aunt Adeline was so upset.

When summer came Bill and Mom had a small ceremony at the chapel in town. We were a family now, and I was to call Bill Dad. It was okay if I forgot, he told me, but Mom corrected him.

"He is your father now," she said, "and you will address him that way."

It was difficult to remember at first, because I'd become so used to calling him Bill. But he told me not worry; it would stick eventually. It would become natural.

We moved into our new home, just a few miles down from the house that was Aunt Adeline's now. The apartment was clean and pretty, with two floors of wall-to-wall carpeting in every room except the kitchen and bath. I'd always wanted carpeting after living with wood floors that sometimes had splinters or old nails sticking up from them. I had my own bedroom, much bigger than the one at the old house, and with a huge walk-in closet. Outside were built-in window boxes for flowers and a mailbox next to our door. There even was a fenced-in swimming pool and tennis court across the complex. Still, everything seemed so dark and colorless compared to Aunt Adeline's place. The lawn out front was small, and the woods were weedy and full of mosquitoes. I already missed the yellow farmhouse with the plush green woods and peonies and the endless supply of butterflies. I missed Aunt Adeline.

seven

I am painting a *Dianella tasmanica*, a perennial also known as a Flax Lily, found wild in the heath and dry forests of Tasmania and southern Australia. At the center of the paper are the blue, star-shaped, drooping flowers, and I detail these with diluted watercolors, so the paint will bleed to a crisp edge. The wet color must not flow beyond the tip of the petal; it must stop at the precise moment. But this one has run over; the color has dripped past and ended in a blotch that's too stark, too random against the white background. My hand trembles over the ivory weave of paper; the brush totters in my fingers.

It's been like this for months, these sessions ending in defeat. I thought I'd try painting again when the Monet on the living room wall flashed color as I walked by, when the empty easel standing in the corner distracted me. But it's hopeless for me to attempt anything creative now. I'm too uptight, sentenced to this depleted, passionless life.

I begin to sift through Seth's things again, which I've been trying to do for weeks now—to sort, to clean, to get organized and move on. But I'm not accomplishing anything; I've only been sifting and letting new junk fall to the floor while I inspect the oddities, the unexpected.

I begin with the rocks. There are the amethysts and obsidians, the potassium feldspar crystals, a rare agate quartz. Many are valuable and should be preserved, perhaps taken back to the university. But for what? I wonder—to get mixed in with a bunch of samples for freshman to toss about, scrape across the black tables? They are just rocks, I assure myself. There are more like them outside, somewhere in the world, ready to be excavated.

But they are Seth's. He marveled at these very rocks, at their composition and creation. He touched them.

Until now, I didn't realize just how many of these things I have lining the windowsills, decorating every available corner of bureau or shelf. There are crustaceans on the end tables, fossils in front of the videos, even a large, distorted geode on the back of the toilet. This, too, will go in the box marked SETH.

The plant fossils are the closest Seth came to plants; I tried to get him to grow some, but he said he could not enjoy watching things grow in the confinement of a pot or greenhouse. I did manage to get him to take part in my fall-into-winter plant experiment back in October. Then after he died I forgot to water the seeds and just left them there; I neglected the pots for weeks. When I finally decided to give them water and nutrients, some of them grew, and today, almost six months later, one of the seeds Seth put into soil is peeking through the dirt.

I never did mark this plant, so I don't know what it is. Vegetable, herb, a perennial of some sort. This red plastic pot Seth used contains something anonymous. I've decided to take it with me—wherever I end up going, to plant it in his honor, to see what happens.

It's the least I can do for him.

In his closet there are photographs I've forgotten about, cards from myself, even—past birthdays and Christmases, the little notes. I left them everywhere I knew he'd be: in his tool chest or underwear drawer, in the box of Wheat Thins. "I love you," was all I ever wrote, I realize now. Why couldn't I have said something else once in a while?

Seth always had something original to say. Sometimes when I got into my car in the morning there would be a note scrawled with HEY BABE, taped to the steering wheel, EAT ME in my lunch bag. One time he put rocks in my plastic bag of carrot sticks—small pieces of mica he knew would flake and frustrate me perfectly.

On his metal hardware shelf there are books—not just the natural science books, but the mysteries and thrillers, the detective novels. Did he read all of these books? I wonder. On top of the shelf, amongst the university paperwork and spiral notebooks, is his mail—not mail he has looked at, but mail that still comes to our address. It's less and less over the past few months, but still it comes. I've opened some of it already, the stuff needing immediate attention—the personal, the financial. Others I've thrown into a shoe box that is filling up quickly. I'm always shutting my eyes at this mail, saying I'll look at it later. And everything takes longer these days; I'm in slow motion, falling more and more behind.

I look through some of my own mail, too: the bills from weeks ago that now are overdue simply from neglect, the renewals I haven't gotten around to, the newsletters from months ago. I spot Paula's letter Mom gave to me this afternoon. Something from a human being, I think, and open it right away.

Paula has drifted away since she married Gerard seven years ago. She was so delighted to have a man who loved her, I remember; she would have done anything for him, including move back to Maine. I should have kept in contact, too. I should have at least told her I was pregnant; perhaps we would have connected on something for a few months. But after losing the baby there would be nothing for us to talk about again. Funny how it ended up, after a year of "great friendship" at Northeast University, the only thing Paula and I had in common was art with a capital "A," namely foundation courses like perspective and four-color separation. Now I wonder if there had even been anything to talk about before all of it happened.

Paula has covered the manila envelope with stickers of animals—a zebra and giraffe, an elephant next to the return address. *This is me now,* Paula has written next to it, an arrow pointing to its rear end. Inside are Polaroids of baby Erica and seven year-old Josh, and a piece of Santa Fe-print stationery with a big HOW'Z IT GOIN'? written across in fat red marker. Below the writing is the Paula-chatter, which I skim through first for important news. She wouldn't have bothered to write unless there was important news.

We put up a new fence, it says, *Gerard got a raise...I'm the queen of Tupperware.* Then finally, and perhaps her true reason for writing, *Have you seen this?*

I pull out the clipping from the *Maine Casco Herald* newspaper, on which Paula has circled an article at the center of the page. It is titled "The Silent Crime," and within it is a photograph of what appears to be the old house in Maine, confirmed when I read the small text beneath the photo credit.

The former Winslow house at 124 Autumn Lane.

The picture is grainy, old-looking, but the house looks the same as it does in the picture—and the way I remember it: light-colored with a railed porch, the yard nestled by trees. There are other pictures within the clipping, all different titles and dates, different stories. One of them, titled "Sorrow Revealed," is the second one down on the page, and it is about Aunt Adeline.

Adeline Winslow's death in August of 1980 was another once labeled "puzzling," after witnesses at the nearby Wharfside Café saw her car plunge into the water near Mackerel Point. While the car at first seemed to be headed directly for the fence dividing the road from the water, it appeared Ms. Winslow had tried to regain control at the last minute. Witnesses were unable to rescue her in time, however, and when police pulled the car from the water, it was evident she had struggled to get out.

Tenants who recently departed Ms. Winslow's former house in Cape Wood discovered a small personal date book, hidden within a small alcove in the basement near the chimney. Apparently it had been untouched for twenty years. In the last pages of the book of personalized stationery, dated August 16, 1980, was what appeared to be a confessional. In the hand-written entry, Ms. Winslow stated that she would drive into the Maine waters that very next day. The sorrowful discovery of what may have been a suicide, contained within the date book, was immediately handed over to nearest surviving relatives.

Mom, I think.

The newspaper clipping feels like thin pastry in my fingers. My hand trembles, and I feel a rush of heat to my head, pressure behind my eyes.

I imagine the reporters when the book was found, running to phone booths like they do in movies, digging into files and family records like maggots. They may have even hounded Mom and Dad, wanted to interview our family or take pictures, *anyone who knew Adeline Winslow.* And meanwhile, I sat in my Cambridge apartment, in my own post-death stupor.

Suicide, I think. Why hasn't Mom told me?

I remember Aunt Adeline's face in the coffin: plumped and painted, surreal, like one of those rosy-cheeked queens from my fairy-tale book. But there was no sign of suicide—no tight-wrapped wrists or head wounds; this death had been neat and clean, an easy poison. And she was only twenty-seven years old.

There were many things I knew about death when I was seven. But there were things I didn't understand then: all this regret, all the stuff between Mom and her sister—the unsaid apologies, unspoken emotions. Aunt Adeline's death happened before I learned about guilt and regret, all those layers I would grow up and discover, layers that clouded and confused.

I always believed it was Aunt Adeline who was the stable sister, the responsible sister, the one who went to school and came back with a career, the one who didn't get pregnant. That it was Mom who got screwed up and knocked up at fifteen and a half, who didn't get her act together until long after her sister was dead. But maybe it had been Mom who was the smart, sound one—studying human psychology to better understand the instability her sister kept secret. To be better at keeping secrets herself.

Why didn't she tell me?

When I first found out Aunt Adeline had drowned in her car, I imagined her death: trying to get out, scrambling for a door, a window—any window; holding her breath. The image destroyed my sweet memories of her; it pained me to remember her laughing and being happy, not knowing how her life would be, a pathetic creature. Now it pains me even more to know that she chose this ending for herself—to picture her scrambling to get out of a car she drove into the water on purpose. How sad it is that she had planned this, and then decided at the very last minute to stay alive—that her last-minute attempt at a swerve was to rectify a stupid mistake. In this new vision I have she is more passionate, more desperate than before, as she changes her mind about the importance of life. *Why?* she must have thought just before going in, *Why am I doing this? What is so awful that I cannot live?*

What did that date book say?

I wonder what day it was that Mom found out about it, if it was one of those recent days when I visited, one of those gray, velvety days within the past few weeks, when Mom's normally marble face seemed more anguished somehow. On that day Mom must have relived what she had heard years before, that Aunt Adeline's car had driven steadily down the pass across the water toward Mackerel Point, that the car had swerved back and forth, witnesses said, trying to gain control, then slid off the road through the brittle wooden rail, and tumbled down the steep incline of rocks, finally turning over into the water.

Mom, too, must have relived the tragedy. And she must have this date book. I can picture it, all warped and dusty in a box in the attic.

———

I feel angry words building as I step up the front walk of Mom and Dad's, as Mom opens the front door. These aren't the same words I rehearsed the whole way over here—to make sure I'm gentle and rational and open to whatever excuse she might give me. These are different words, words from my gut ready to explode from my mouth.

"Have you seen this?" I say, throwing the newspaper down onto the armchair by the window.

"What is it?" Mom pulls her dust mop out from her armpit, begins to brush the mantelpiece. She turns, peeks over at it on the chair, doesn't bother to pick it up. "Why would I read the Maine newspaper?" She turns back to her mantel.

"The article, Mom. Look at the article."

"What?"

"Mom, look at it!"

She turns around, her face pale, timid, then looks down at the paper. She picks it up, and her eyes suddenly widen and fix. I wonder if this really is the first time she has seen the article. "My God, they didn't," she says.

"*They* who?"

"Damn reporters. Anything for a story." She throws the paper back down on the chair.

"Mom!" I move to stand in front of her. She tries to duck around me. "Mom, did you read it?"

"I saw enough."

"You know what it is, right? The *suicide*?"

Mom closes her eyes, forcefully. "Yes*ss*, Jenna."

"Why didn't you tell me?"

She opens her eyes again. "Look, I just found out, too. It was just a few weeks ago when they called me."

"Who—reporters?"

She chuckles, wipes her hair back from her forehead with her hand. "No, the police. I didn't even know any reporters knew about this."

"So you probably figured I would never know, too."

"I would have told you eventually," she says, her voice trembling. "I just didn't want to bring it up, with Seth and all."

I don't jump on her lame answer. I'll give Mom some latitude for at least not making up her usual textbook excuse, some psychoanalytical reason why a daughter of twenty-six should not know. I'll grant her a little sympathy for again having to deal with this horrible death, and for having to look at it in a new light.

"Sorry," I say. "Are you okay?"

"Am I *okay?*"

"Yes."

Mom turns away, begins dusting again. "Jenna, it happened so long ago."

"Yes, but—"

"Look," she interrupts, "I'm not as surprised as you may think. You didn't know her as well as I did."

"No," I say. "But I did know her." I can't believe how cold Mom sounds, how indifferent. Aunt Adeline deserves something more from her own sister, even after twenty years, even if there were bad feelings in the past. To mention this will be a mistake, though; I'm sure of it. "Anyway," I say. "Can I see it?"

"What?" Mom turns around.

"The date book."

She goes back to the wall, brushes the silky yellow mop over the brass candlesticks. "Oh, I had to throw it out," she says. "It was mildewy and rotten, full of dust mites and God knows what else."

I shudder.

Mom has done it again. She has displayed her apathy toward the meaningful, her concern and control of the absurd. I want to shake her, jiggle her brain so a nut will come loose and make her feel something. But a dispute will be pointless; Mom will win. The conversation will twist and deviate and finally slam into some unexpected barrier. And there will be some reason to let me know, once again, just how miserable I've made my mother's life just for being born.

part three
a more horrible death

{renee

eight

Renee sits on the floor of the attic den, smells the orange spice tea still brewing at her side, hears the almost-spring wind against the eaves. Bill is in his workshop in the basement, clanking around; Elisabeth is just below in her bedroom, thumping the floor to a disco beat. Jenna must be back at home now, angry with her mother, stomping back and forth across the floor the way she used to in her room. Jenna's stomping, her very movement before the pale bedroom wall, always reminded her of Adeline.

She can't blame Jenna for being angry. Not just for the date book, but for many things. She knows she was cruel twenty years ago when they moved here—plucking a seven-year-old from everything she knew, relocating her like an old couch. She knew Jenna would hate her for a while; perhaps Bill would, too. Better now than later, Renee told them, because as years passed, it would be more difficult to leave. Get it over with, she was thinking; the pain will be over soon enough.

Bill disagreed with her. *Why leave at all?* he would ask day after day, and Renee would just give him that look, the one that means she is serious. All she has to do is look at him and he will stop asking. She feels guilty sometimes, having this kind of power over him.

She opens the trunk beneath the dormer window, sees the green and white afghan, the hand-embroidered handkerchief. Adeline was good at everything—sewing, knitting, cooking, and gardening, of course. There had even been a time when she'd been good with the men, until there weren't any more. She must have one day decided to be alone the rest of her short life.

Inside the trunk are some of Jenna's things, too—a finger-painting from first grade—her last year in Maine: the old house in pale yellow, the lime-green lawn, dots of pale purple for lilac bushes, the name JENNA in bright red across the blue and white sky. There is another drawing from years later—junior high, Renee thinks, of the same yellow house—this time a tiny house—nestled, almost buried, within a forest of gigantic green leaves.

She remembers the Jenna from high school, always attempting different groups and activities, never sticking with one. The appearance didn't stick either; it was a new look every week. First, the brown hair shorn and dyed blonde, the triple piercing in the left ear; then the next year a head of permed curls in Bozo red, with renaissance clothes and heavy silver chains. The only thing that didn't change was the box of paints and sketch pad under her arm as she walked up the road to the school bus.

But when Jenna began college she cleaned up. She grew her hair to a natural, shoulder-length brown, and dressed in neutral slacks and sweaters. And suddenly she looked just like Renee.

Then she began to do all the things Renee wished she had done at age nineteen—to go out and frolic, to be free. It was not until Seth came along and Jenna got pregnant that Renee could relate, when suddenly there was this familiar shadow. How awkward it felt to suddenly feel connected, and want to make up for all those missing years.

Talking to Jenna is more difficult now. When Renee tries, it comes out all wrong. Perhaps she's speaking too much of her own suffering, of her unfinished teenage years. How does one prove how much they care, and show how much they've sacrificed, without sounding like a martyr?

Without telling every detail.

She thought that talking to a daughter would be easier. She thought they would have more in common, but instead they have separate experiences, different philosophies. Renee was insecure as a teenager—a follower, with no choice but to emulate Adeline, while Jenna is stronger than her mother somehow. And Renee knows how others see her: testy, heartless, incapable of emotion. She knows it especially when she hears people say *Poor Adeline* about her sister, poor Aunt Adeline.

It has always been this way.

How strange, to be thinking about her sister again. When the date book arrived it went away just as quickly; it was the best thing to do. Now she sees it again: the tiny sunflower logo, the name *Adeline Winslow* printed in red on every page. The handwritten words *drive into the ocean*. But that wasn't all it said. On that single page of writing there were words not meant for just anyone to see.

At the bottom of the trunk are some of Renee's own things—more things best kept hidden so she can forget, go on with her daily life. There are photographs—a young Renee and Adeline, dressed like twins in pea coats and fuzzy berets, each holding a brown paper lunch bag; then a young Bill with Jenna in his arms, sitting on a big rock in the yard; and finally Jeanette Winslow, the grandmother Jenna was too young to remember. In the background of each of the photos is the yellow house. Stacked along with the pictures are cards and letters, school concert programs, an invitation to Jenna's first art exhibit. And something else forgotten over the years.

It is the one letter she kept from him, the last words he wrote to her before he left for good. She opens it, fingers trembling, heart racing in her ears, sees the words that affected her most on that day when she first read it.

It can't ever happen again, not for a long time.

He never wrote again.

Renee thought she was safe from this memory, just like the memory of Adeline, of the old house. Why she kept this letter, she wonders; it must have been for some reason beyond her recollection. Some subconscious reason, she thinks now, the way she thinks about many other things. Recognizing the subconscious can give reason to so many things.

It may not help her this time.

She thought his memory was gone forever, ripped to shreds in her mind, incinerated with the rest of the garbage. Just like Adeline's words, which could be distinguished in such a way. But every now and then she sees a tiny scrap of paper on the floor and thinks Adeline's words have returned the way this has returned. These words may try to infect her, to sink in, and bring back all memories of that time.

jenna}

nine

It was eight o'clock in the morning when the phone call came in. "It's the police," Mom whispered to Dad, covering the receiver.

Mom's eyebrows came together, sharply and suddenly, and her mouth opened and let out a gasp. She flopped against the wall and began to shake, and the phone slid from her ear to her neck, then chest, until she finally let it go. Dad ran over as the phone crashed against the counter and to the floor. Mom collapsed into the doorway and began to pound the floor with her fist. "No, no!" she cried, over and over.

Dad reached out to me, pulling me close to him. "It's Aunt Adeline, honey. There was an accident...a car accident. Jenna...your aunt is dead."

My body began to tremble, then shake hard, like there was a machine inside me, making it do this. I couldn't stop shaking.

But I did not cry. I didn't even know what I felt; it was a strange feeling I had inside, more of bewilderment than sadness. Aunt Adeline was just talking to me the other day. She couldn't be dead.

Mom cried all night. I had never seen or heard her cry before, but on this night she wailed so loudly it came through my bedroom wall. I heard sobs and choking. It sounded so strange to me, so violent and uncontrollable, like something inside her was alive and trying to get out.

Still, I couldn't cry. I was numb; at least that was what others were saying. Aunt Adeline's neighbors came by and said it, and Dad's relatives. All of them said the same thing, that they were numb: they didn't know how to feel.

By the day of the funeral Mom was numb, too. She was quiet, perhaps so weak from crying that she couldn't speak. Or maybe she just felt terrible about how she had treated her big sister.

Mom and Dad let me go to the funeral. It was an open-coffin ceremony because, as I heard Dad say, Aunt Adeline didn't look too bad. He said an open coffin was a healthy way to deal with death. All I'd heard about death was that your body stopped working and you went somewhere else, to some place where it wasn't so painful.

When I first saw Aunt Adeline I trembled again. I was afraid. I expected her body to move or sit up as I approached. Still, I knelt before her, the way everyone else did. The coffin was shiny and brown and had white satin inside that was folded tight like ribbon candy; it looked like a big brown Cadillac convertible. Aunt Adeline lay inside, only the top half of her body showing. Her skin looked orangey and dry like putty, and her cheeks seemed fatter than usual. The tight-shut eyes appeared made up, unnatural. I leaned closer and saw stitches on her lids, black thread like her lashes, and thought of the Venus flytraps she had shown me in her greenhouse.

Suddenly I hated the open casket, the wake, because this tucked and painted body didn't seem like her. Maybe everyone was pretending she was alive so they could forget the way she really looked when she died, so they could stick her in the ground with good memories.

With Mom and Dad I sat on the first-row pew of the church, listening to one of Aunt Adeline's neighbors. "We remember her smile from just yesterday," she said, and I thought it odd that I had never seen this woman before, or many of the other people there. I felt like I didn't know who Aunt Adeline really was. The reverend delivering the sermon spoke loudly, and his voice echoed throughout the chapel. He said that Aunt Adeline had gone somewhere else, that she was in a safe, better place, in Heaven. I wondered if this was true. I looked at all the faces crying around me and wondered if they believed it. It didn't feel like anyone there really believed she was in Heaven even though they kept saying it, over and over.

I looked up at Mom's face and saw the tears just on the edge of her lower eyelids trying to come out. I remembered the last time Mom had spoken to her sister, how they'd had a terrible argument at the house. Mom had been so upset with Aunt Adeline that she didn't want me going to visit anymore.

I wondered if she was thinking of this now, and finally I felt like crying.

On the drive home from the graveyard I asked Mom and Dad about the accident. I wanted to know more because I didn't know what happened in a car accident.

"Those details," Mom said, "are not for seven-year-old ears."

I sighed and sat back into my seat. Dad looked at me in the rearview mirror. "It happened on the Mackerel Point," he said.

"Can we go there?" I asked.

Mom whipped her head around to me. "No!" She stared at me long and hard, then she shifted in her seat and looked out the window, upset, I could tell.

"Did her car go into the water?" I asked.

"That's enough!" Mom said. "How can you be such a morbid child?" Dad said nothing.

During the drive home neither of them said a word, and I began to feel a pain creeping up from my stomach, into my chest and into my head, behind my eyes. All of this silence was painful.

In October we cleaned out Aunt Adeline's house. There were personal items to go through, items that Mom and Dad had to decide whether or not to keep. It had to be done by the end of the month, Mom said, because the bank would be taking the house.

Each day that Mom went to clean the house she would come home angry. She would argue with Dad, and they'd go to bed quiet. This went on and on for weeks, until finally it was done and Mom came home in a good mood with something to tell me. We were going to move. We soon would be leaving Maine.

It had to happen, she said. Dad would get a better job, and Mom would go to college and one day back to work. And moving away to Massachusetts would accomplish all of this, like magic.

I begged them not to go. Dad didn't seem to want to go either. I heard them fighting about it after I went to bed. There were quiet evenings at the supper table, suppers so quiet I could hear only gulping and chewing, the clink of stainless against china. This went on for days, until one day Mom finally won.

Then there were strange meetings in the kitchen: men and women dressed in fine-tailored brown and navy, the shuffling of papers, the brass snap of briefcase latches. And suddenly we were moving out of our two-bedroom apartment in Cape Wood, Maine, and into a four-bedroom house more than a hundred miles away.

Before we left, Mom took me on one last drive to the ocean. She parked the car just off the road, near where Aunt Adeline had crashed, and we walked down the Mackerel Point jetty. As we stood on the rocks, the November wind was cold on my face, and the dark ocean billowed before us—small waves without foam, just endless curves of water. Mom was holding my hand, not tugging me or dragging me somewhere, but just standing there. It was odd to me because I couldn't remember ever just holding her hand. She whispered something into the wind, but it was lost in the roar of the sea.

Goodbye, I think she said.

ten

There was a time when I only painted dead plants: dried autumn leaves gathered from the yard, the curled petals of a wilted rose that once stood on my dresser. Even imprints of plants in their most extinct form, painted from fossil photographs or paleobotany lab samples. In a pile of old watercolors I find one of a Kauri Pine imprint, its once-green, fleshy needles now gray and flat as ferns, incorporated into 175-million-year-old Australian mudstone. The work clearly depicts the object as a fossil, with its vivid outline sloping to shadowy gouges. But embedded even in this rock there is that hint of life—rich minerals and molecules in a lustrous, sunlit metallic sheen.

Also amongst these paintings are some living plants—the fleshy leaves of a begonia, the seductive petals of an iris, both for Nature-Made seed packets. These are more my style, plants more alive, more wet and green; flowers more colorful. There is one in the pile that appeared on a June '92 calendar page, a bushy, magenta-colored Sweet William—the one Mom told me was too vivid in its contrast, too stark in its color.

"There's too much green," she said.

I'm still not sure why I did the dead-plant watercolors; I haven't done any like them again. They simply are remnants from that time—those strange months after I lost the baby, when death was a quiet preoccupation for me. When death was something vague enough, mysterious enough to call surreal. How easy it was during that painful time—to be surreal, to even add heaven and God to the mixture. For weeks I lay in my bedroom at home, praying to something, imagining the shadows on the wall were living beings that spoke to me, who told me that my baby had gone somewhere else.

Now death has a different impact: it no longer can be ambiguous, inexplicable. There can be no dreaming about the beyond. Now death is brightly lit, without shadows and angels, without God.

With the death of a loved one, there is a turning point when mourning ends and something else takes over. What once was relentless sorrow turns to bittersweet remembrance; what was weighty regret simply fades away. The pain grows soft over time, and the death becomes easier to reflect upon, the way a war is reflected upon long after it has ended. Aunt Adeline's two-decade-old death does not possess the pain of recency, but it does hold a shocking revelation, a new mystery. It is a death more curious than Seth's, perhaps more horrible. For the first time in months, though only for a few seconds, my thoughts have wandered away from Seth.

Perhaps this war is ending.

As I lift the pile of paintings up from the coffee table I see the top corner of the *Maine Casco Herald*, with MAINE, THE WAY LIFE SHOULD BE in bold advertising at the top of the page. Just below it is tiny black-and-white photograph of the Cape Wood house, empty now. Empty except for all that skin and dust from those who have lived there: Mom, Aunt Adeline, even me. A house which holds inside it my genes, and every now and then, pulls its invisible string of DNA.

I was only nineteen when I moved to this city of Cambridge, a place filled with music and theater and colorful restaurants, of glowing nights under sidewalk lamps. Where dinner is just around the corner, and shops and galleries line the streets. The vendors call out, and there is the smell of hot sausages and peppers, the hot brick and cold granite, the burning subway. And so close to the suburbs, with all things quaint and comfortable—my family just twenty miles away.

But living here used to mean something else. I cannot connect anymore to this city and all its distractions, to my family, to everything around me. The familiar now feels oppressive, like a weight. There no longer is the desire to explore the culture and colors of the city, the familiar faces in the suburbs. All this pavement, this perfect green grass, is dizzying.

I need some air.

I see Aunt Adeline's face, hear her soft, pained voice calling to me—back to my childhood, my old life far away from this apartment—this shell of a home where Seth still creeps in. My life here all these years now feels like a dream. It has been an experiment, I think, a vacation of some sort. Temporary, not like home.

Home is somewhere else, waiting for me.

———

At one o'clock in the afternoon Mr. Robinson from the Casco Bank in Portland returns my call. He speaks in a low voice that sounds like two packs a day, telling me the house still is for sale. "Lease is an option," he says. "With fifteen hundred down." He coughs in-between words. "You can work on the inside if you want, but nothing structural unless it really needs it."

"I lived there when I was very young," I say. "It was my aunt's house...Adeline Winslow was her name."

"I remember Adeline," he says.

"You do?" I hold my breath.

"Yes, I knew her."

I wonder how well he knew her, in what way he knew her. I never saw or heard of Aunt Adeline ever having a boyfriend, not even having good friends. I thought of her as alone, always alone.

"She was nice," he adds, his voice tentative, nervous sounding. "So sad about her accident."

"Yes," I say, and wonder if he has read the recent article about her.

"I met her when I was just starting out," he says, "when I used to sell insurance. I came by the house a few times, when your grandmother was still alive." He pauses. "So yes, I remember Adeline. And I remember your mother, of course."

"You remember my mother?" I ask, feeling a tinge of curiosity, excitement.

"Not so much as Adeline. But I did see her once in a while out in the yard."

In my memories it is always difficult to distinguish Mom from Adeline. When I think back to my earliest days, with both of them in the house, the snapshots in my mind are of some dark-haired woman, some mother. But I can picture Mom, a photograph I once saw of her standing by the apple tree in front of the old house. It is one of the few photographs of Mom and me at the old house, with me just a bundle of flesh and yarn in the baby carriage.

"The house is empty," Mr. Robinson adds, and I gather together my thoughts. "I can give you a key, let you roam around. Are you interested?"

"I can be there tomorrow," I say, and I think of the old photograph again, in which Mom is wide-eyed and startled, perhaps caught off-guard. She's a Mom that doesn't seem like Mom—with wild hair and bare feet in the grass, a flowing cotton nightgown. A ghost before the yellow farmhouse.

eleven

The fall after Aunt Adeline died we moved to Westbridge, Massachusetts, into our new beige colonial in a neighborhood of other new beige colonials. The town was thick with woods but amazingly bug-free, and the town center always smelled of pizza. Westbridge was clean and pretty, with green lawns and square lots and houses with fresh paint and new, smooth glass in the windows. But the town was boring in many ways. There were no fields of overgrown grass, no shallow ponds to wade in, no jagged hills or rock formations. And no ocean to be seen.

In my new school I had no friends. It was smack-in-the-middle of the second grade school year, and I was named "The Girl from Maine." I sat by myself during lunch while other kids dangled from seesaws and merry-go-rounds, or bombed each other with brick-colored balls. So I drew.

At first I did it right on the playground, drawing some of the plants and trees that were around me, and then I'd take my drawings home and continue them there. I'd sit at the kitchen table with my colored pencils and acrylics, just like I did when I stayed at Aunt Adeline's, creating my world of larger-than-life plants. In this world there were purple skies and bluish fields, children flying around. Mom referred to my pictures as "scary" and "unhealthy," but Dad said I was talented. After his work days at the bank he would watch me draw, while Mom took her evening classes. Before Mom left she told Dad to make sure I did my homework. "Don't let her dilly-dally with those drawings," she'd say, and Dad would give me a little smile after Mom shut the door, letting me know I was allowed to do a little bit of both.

I spent a lot of time in the backyard woods in Westbridge. It was not as lush and green as the woods in back of Aunt Adeline's old house; it was a bare, twisty wood where many trees were dead—fire-damaged, Dad said, from years before. But I liked the way the branches and vines twisted and grew around each other, the way the dead trees split and made way for living ones, how fallen limbs magically sprouted moss. The wood was the one and only thing I loved about our new town.

I especially missed the ocean, which, because of the skirted routes around Boston, was now a one-hour trip in any direction. Dad sometimes took me, driving us through the maze of traffic to the North Shore, where beaches were crowded and chaotic, sometimes littered. Or we'd take a more frenzied route to Cape Cod, and spend most of the trip sitting in the hot station wagon on high bridges, waiting for the traffic ahead of us to move. When we left the beach, the smell of the ocean dissipated quickly; the exhaust of cars and factories, of pavement and metal and brick quickly overcame it. And then we'd reach our neat little suburbs, where there was no salt water smell either, only grass and trees, and the confined feeling of inland.

———

The house in Westbridge has changed color four times since I left for college. Sometimes Dad just paints right over the old color before it has time to peel or chip. This year the house is white and red—his unfinished project from last summer. The red is on top, appearing to spill over the white, but I really can't remember which color is the newer one.

It's almost spring, time for Dad to work on the yard. Soon he'll be out there with his trowels and bug-killers and fifty-pound bags of mulch, transforming the lawn into a spotless, perfect green. Because Dad likes a lawn without chaos. But then he has his chaos in the basement—the half-finished cars and planes on the shelves and dangling like mobiles from the ceiling. These are things Mom never would allow upstairs, even though she has her own outlet with its potential for mess: the fabric paints she keeps in a tidy case and unloads upon the kitchen table every now and then. Like Dad, her messy hobbies are kept separate, buried beneath the everyday stuff. With Mom and Dad, there's a kind of Johnson Wax over everything.

Lately Dad has been working on the walkway. There's new gravel where last month it was muddy and concave, and where melted snow washed pebbles into the driveway. Still, there are sections he's missed; mud seeps out from under my thin-bottomed sneakers. I skip over these muddy sections—up to the front step, hoping he doesn't see.

Dad opens the door. "Hey, Jenna," he says, his dark, shiny hair flawlessly parted on the side, like Cary Grant's. Under his fuzzy wool pullover a white oxford shirt is buttoned to the top. He calls to Mom, and her holler back is tinny over the hiss of running water.

"Can't you see I'm busy?"

"Forget it, Dad," I whisper. "I'll go in and see her."

Mom is in the kitchen, her hair in a loose bun, and wearing a rust-colored blouse and brown skirt. I think of how there are mostly autumn colors in her wardrobe: no blacks, only ebony browns or the darkest of purples; no whites, only ivory. These colors of nature don't seem like Mom. Seth used to joke about it, saying she wore warm colors to make up for her coldness; but I corrected him, telling him how he was giving her too much credit, and that she recently had her "colors" done.

The smell of chicken and tarragon fills the room, and the windows are steam-covered. From behind the counter island Mom wraps a canvas apron around her waist, then uncovers the stainless steel pot on the stove. Dad takes my jacket and leaves us alone, seeming tense, as if he knows I am about to say something important.

"Mom," I begin, and then stop. Suddenly I can't say the words.

She wipes her brow and looks up through her steam, exhaustedly, like she's too busy to give me attention, as if any question will be insignificant. "What is it?" she asks with a sigh, and I wonder if she'll push me out of the kitchen—but then her eyes meet mine and she stops, seeming nervous, and quickly looks away again. "Is this about the date book?" she asks, timidly. "Are you still upset?"

"No," I say.

She reaches for her pepper grinder, grinds over the pot. Strands of hair slide from her bun and into her eyes, and she lifts her elbow to sweep them away with the back of her hand. Then she wipes her hands on her apron, her eyes scurrying around the room. "You have to understand," she says. "It's been so many years." She turns to the cupboard, begins to rummage through spice bottles.

"I know that," I say. "But really—it's not about the date book."

"I *am* sorry about that," she says, her voice soft amongst the clinking of plastic and glass within the cupboard. "It wasn't exactly a healthy thing to do—throwing it away." She turns her head and looks at me. "Something a shrink would never do, that's for sure." I chuckle and she gives a quick smile back, and before I can speak again there is the skip of feet down the stairs on the other side of the wall, followed by a thump at the bottom.

Elisabeth pops her head around the corner and skips into the kitchen, dressed in sneakers and sweats, her hair in a high Pebbles Flintstone ponytail. Despite the brief interlude between Mom and me, I'm relieved that my little sister has interrupted us. "How's school?" I ask. "Still doing gymnastics?"

"Yup." Elisabeth lifts her leg so her foot is against the wall above the wood molding. She hops closer to the wall, pushing her foot higher, then presses in, until her torso is flat against her leg. I clap my hands, impressed.

Elisabeth looks like me, auburn-haired and green-eyed, but more soft-faced and cheeky—most likely from Dad. Montigue must have had stronger facial bones, like Mom and me. Some have joked about the thirteen-year-old age difference between Elisabeth and me, as if she was one of those late-marriage accidents for Mom and Dad. They joke until they remember that I'm twenty-six and Mom forty-two, that it's me who is the enigma of the family.

I wonder if they also realize that Elisabeth was the fixture child, a true byproduct of Mom and Dad, to bond them like glue.

Today Elisabeth is hyper, excited about something. She flips her long ponytail forward, over her head and in front of her face, then jumps up and down. Her feet flex up, to tiptoes, then down; she bounces, as if on springs. I put a hand on her arm to slow her down, and Elisabeth stops, and leans against me to whisper something.

"There's a boy at school I like," she says. "Brian Norquist." Suddenly her eyes seem wider, a brighter green. *Boys*, I think.

"Elisabeth, did you finish your homework?" Mom interrupts. Elisabeth flashes Mom a dirty look, so quickly that Mom doesn't see, then whips around the corner and stomps up the stairs.

Mom still is behind the counter, a mound of green peppers on the breadboard next to her. A half-full glass of red wine stands on the counter in back of her, and I wonder if she had some of it already, if she is warmed up enough to take the news I'm about to blurt out.

"I'm thinking of moving back to Maine," I say.

"Huh?"

She must not have heard. She bends over and peeks into the stove to look at something—probably thinking about temperature, about how this oven doesn't preheat as fast as the old one. The oven door slams and she wipes her forehead with the back of her hand. "What did you say?" she says, and takes a sip of her wine.

"I'm moving back to Maine," I say. "Maybe...to the old house."

Mom continues to hold the wine goblet to her face, in mid-sip, perhaps, her eyes just above the rim, staring into the deep burgundy liquid. Her voice reverberates within the glass. "What old house?"

Just like her, I think, to play dumb; to pretend it doesn't exist. "Our old house." I take a breath, waiting for her reaction. "Aunt Adeline's old house."

Mom jerks forward, wine splashing her chin and neck, spattering her apron and blouse. "What?" She sets the glass down, looks down at her stained collar. I expect her to reach for a towel but she doesn't. "What did you say?"

"I didn't mean to upset you," I say, and wait for her to say something. She looks frightened, almost, her hands resting awkwardly on the counter and trembling slightly, her eyes darting about. A drop of wine drips from her chin. "It may be temporary," I add. I need to be gentle. "I may just rent for a while. Besides, it's only a two and a half hour drive to Westbridge. I'll come back and visit."

"That's not what upsets me," she says.

"Oh, thank you very much," I say, making sure my tone is sarcastic. "So what does upset you, then?"

"I just..." Mom stands tense for a moment, then suddenly shrugs her shoulders, as if she is loosening up. She shakes her head. "I just can't believe you want to go back there. You've really thought about this?"

"Yes."

"But Jenna, it's only been five months."

It takes me a second, then I realize. *Since his death*, she's telling me. "Seth would have wanted me to do this," I say.

Mom chuckles. "What was it that made you decide—the date book? That article? Is that what did it?"

"No," I lie.

She picks up the cutting knife. "So you're just going to leave everything behind?"

"Leave what behind?" I'd like to hear Mom say she's speaking for herself, about possibly missing me. I know she won't. "I don't have any good friends here anymore. And I can work anywhere."

"You'll be up there alone."

"There's Paula," I say. "Remember Paula?"

"You mean the Paula with a thousand boyfriends?" Mom grins, perhaps proud of her recollection and her embellishment of fact.

"She's married now," I say. "Gerard." I think of how different Paula and I are, how it's unlikely we'll be close again. But she's someone I can look up when I get there.

"I just can't believe you want to move away," Mom says.

"You didn't seem to care last week. Seemed like you wanted me to go."

"But why do you want to go *there*?" Mom holds the knife firm in her right hand, spreads the fingers of her left evenly, precisely on the pepper. "That house probably needs work." She stares down, looking for the perfect place to cut, but then stops and looks up. She folds the knife to the board, looks at me with intent, to hypnotize, it seems. Her eyes are ablaze in the sun from the window, almost topaz-looking. Above the bib of her red-spattered white apron, light reflects off her delicate gold cross. "Tell me," she says. "Are you looking for something?"

I wonder what she possibly thinks I'm looking for—a lost childhood? A lost aunt? Or lost blood—Montigue, perhaps. Does Mom think of these things? Is this what she's worried about? Maybe this isn't about me at all.

"Mom," I say, "I just need to get away."

Mom looks down to her pepper again, begins to cut. "So when are you talking about—when do you plan on going?"

"As soon as I can. I'd go tomorrow if I could."

"Just tell me," she says with a tremor in her voice, "why the old house?"

"Why not?" I say. "I should be asking *you* the opposite question—why *didn't* you want to live there?" I'm proud of myself for talking back to her. "You speak of the place as though it were full of rot and disease." Mom continues her cutting, ripping the knife through the green flesh, over and over, rhythmically, until there is nothing left but a sliver. The warped breadboard knocks against the countertop, making my head ache. "The truth is, I wish we never left." She stops cutting and clenches her mouth into a tight line. She shakes her head, her hair loosening, bangs astray in her eyes. "I do hope you come and visit me," I add. "You'd have a good time. It would be sort of...nostalgic."

"Nostalgic?" Mom scoops up the peppers and drops them into a bowl. She moves over to the cabinets, opens the cabinet doors and grabs something, then slams the doors shut. I have insulted her.

"What's the matter?"

Mom sighs, extra-loudly, moves back to the counter and glares into her bowl of green. Her eyebrows are raised—stuck up high, as if she is in a trance. "Nostalgic," she murmurs. Maybe to Mom *nostalgic* means Greta Garbo or something: soft focus, black-and-white perfection.

"I have to tell you something," I say, "and you may not like it." Mom's shoulders lift, and her chin hoists upward with her head so that she is looking way down at me. "Moving away from Maine was pretty traumatic for me when I was seven years old." Her shoulders relax again and she emits a loud breath, as if she was expecting me to say something much worse.

"Jenna," she says, "you would not have understood."

"I understood a lot then, Mom. A lot more than you think." Mom says nothing but looks bewildered, and her whole face seems to change color—from white to carnation pink, then to white again, in seconds.

Mom of a thousand faces.

part four
the rift

{renee

twelve

"This theory," Renee tells the class, "suggests that some memory traces become distorted over time, until they are unrecognizable."

Of the twenty students in her social science class, about a third are looking out the window, most likely because it is almost spring, because it is warm and sunny today, and because the bell will ring in less than five minutes. But first she must make them understand at least three areas of memory loss so they can write about it tonight. They seem to have made it through *decay* and *interference*, and have moved on to *reconstruction*. She needs to get their attention.

"Jay," she calls to the back of the room, to the dingy-haired, perpetual clown who seems to be half-listening. "Can you give me an example of this?"

He props up, suddenly, as if jerked by strings or caffeine, as though a quick response will get him out of the classroom and out into the sun of the courtyard. "Sure," he says, "it's like when a message gets passed around and around and ends up not being the same message." He was listening, after all.

"That's right," she says. "Good example." Jay smiles, fidgeting proudly in his seat. Nice to see a student proud, she thinks. "Can you tell me what causes the message to become distorted? Why does this happen?"

"I don't know." Jay shrugs his shoulders. "You tell someone something, and they tell someone, and the message changes each time."

"Yes, but why, do you suppose?"

"I guess 'cause we all have different ways of hearing or something. Maybe we hear what we want to hear."

Some of the students are listening again, perhaps because this cool classmate of theirs is speaking, and they can relate. Or maybe they simply are pretending to listen as the clock ticks toward two, as the day's end grows nearer. She looks out the window, sees green budding on the white birch in the courtyard, a young girl with brown hair like Jenna's sitting on the redwood bench, her face to the sun. She turns back to the class and sees them staring at her, and for a second, forgets how she is supposed to respond.

"Perceptions," Renee says, swallowing the lump in her throat. "You could say it has to do with perceptions. Or bias—what one already knows." The students are still watching her. "Depending on what an individual already believes, a story may change with each telling. When we retrieve information we tend to remember what is consistent with our *own* knowledge, with our *own* beliefs and morals. In fact, we store the *meaning* of events better than the details." The girl in the sun is smiling now, alone on the bench. Just looking up, smiling to the sun.

"So," Renee continues, "when we recall the story or event, it may contain details that are consistent with the meaning we have remembered. In effect, the forgetting—the omission of details— actually occurs during the process of retrieval."

She has lost them again. The students are fidgeting, shuffling papers, closing their books and sliding them into bags. They stand and head toward the front.

"Did the bell ring?" she asks Jay.

"Yes, Mrs. McGarry."

She hadn't heard it, hadn't realized that five minutes has passed. Twenty seconds, it seemed like. The students are scrambling toward the door like cattle, perhaps before an assignment can be given. "Before you leave—" she says, and hears the collective sigh amongst the foot and paper shuffling. "Pages 301 through 307. The Bartlett and Tuling theories, the experiments related to reconstruction. You'll be quizzed."

Another sigh.

They heard, at least. She has gotten them before they had the chance to make it out the door. They might have been exempt from homework if they had made it out the door while she was daydreaming. But she has caught them, and it feels good—not so much because she has caught them in time, but simply because she has caught them, and has the power to do that. Strange thing to be a teacher.

And a parent.

After class she corrects a paper while a student waits, a girl named Janice who has the same brown wisps of hair dangling over her peachy forehead that Jenna does. The eyes are bluer, though, not Jenna's sea foam green. She thinks of how Jenna's eyes no longer shine, how she has reverted to that defensive, directionless self she was in high school. Aimlessly wandering, hovering above decision.

Mrs. McGarry the teacher scratches red ball-point words at the bottom of Janice's paper. B plus, she gives it: the B because she missed on two points in essay number one, the plus added for passion. She doesn't have this kind of power over Jenna. The umbilical between mother and daughter was severed long ago, and has unraveled over the years. It was always Adeline's love that reigned like candy, and perhaps that is why Jenna is going back.

Or perhaps it is something else.

First it was the date book, those few simple words haunting Renee's sleep, making her stomach churn. And now it is the house, the key to that forgotten world, a house touched by so many—but not just Renee and Adeline and baby Jenna. Their memory is not the only one to seep into the smallest of crevices.

There were others.

jenna}

thirteen

During that final summer just before Aunt Adeline died, I spent almost every weekend at her house. She would let me roam free in the yard, sometimes while she worked in the garden nearby, other times as she washed dishes and watched me out the kitchen window. She said it was okay because she could always see me, but I knew this couldn't always be true because there were many times I was far off into the woods or behind the big rock in the yard. I wondered if maybe she only said she was watching me so I'd tell this to Mom.

Weekends were a perfect time to visit. Especially Saturday, because Mom had her classes and Dad worked at the bank until twelve. Sometimes I'd even stay overnight and the next day help Aunt Adeline plant things in the garden—or in wintertime, her greenhouse room. I'd play in the basement, in the secret alcove where the chimney stood, or in other nooks and crannies of the house. I'd take out my crayons and pencils and paints anytime I felt like it—something I couldn't always do at home, and Aunt Adeline would let me have the whole kitchen table to myself while she made me hot chocolate or pudding.

One day Aunt Adeline and I wallpapered the guest room, which she said I could still call my room. The paper had been tan and blue and yellow when I was a baby, but this new paper was deep green color with white flowers. Mom didn't like the new paper; she said it looked too dark and creepy. "Such a God-awful green," she said to Aunt Adeline one time she came to pick me up. "I can't believe you're putting that up in my old room," she added.

"Jenna's room," Aunt Adeline corrected her, and I liked the idea she had referred to it as that. I wasn't sure what Mom thought, though.

"Whatever," Mom said. "It will look like a cave."

Aunt Adeline put her hands on her hips. "I'll do whatever the hell I want with Jenna's room," she snapped, then turned to me. "Pardon Aunty's French," she said. I wasn't sure whether to laugh; she'd spoken so cruelly to Mom. I even felt a bit nervous, thinking Aunt Adeline could explode into anger any minute, maybe even at me.

"I'm just glad we don't have to live here anymore," Mom said.

But no matter what Mom thought about the wallpaper, I loved it because it reminded me of the woods in back of the house. When I was in bed at night I could look at the wall and pretend I still was out there playing in the woods full of pine and birch and blueberry bushes, and thick with hostas and ferns that sprouted like green fountains.

I wonder what color my old bedroom is now, or if it even exists anymore.

———

Twenty years ago the road into Cape Wood was narrow and bumpy, with maples and evergreens snug on both sides, and edges sloping to a sandy, pebbly trench. Now it is wide and neatly trimmed, bordered by a dark cement sidewalk and few trees. Most of the wood has been replaced by houses, many white, shutterless capes with high-pitched roofs, others cedar-shingled and green-shuttered, the L.L. Bean model. There are ranches in dull colors, most barely finished, the clapboard still showing, the lawn a mass of rock-filled soil. A neighborhood, raw and incomplete, waiting for some family to move in and save themselves, to make themselves whole.

Somewhere along this road used to be a path leading into woods. I would see it as I passed by in the car with Mom and Dad, and I would dream of riding my bicycle as soon as I was old enough. We left Maine before I had the chance, and there's no telling where the path may be now.

There's a chill of air as I roll down the window, but no salt water smell—only the mold of wet wood and leaves, the metallic scent of pavement. Small lumps of leftover snow spot the roadside; the snow is icy and hard-looking, speckled with dark matter, like it has melted and refrozen. And like some science experiment, it now is reformed, preserving inside those long-dead leaves and twigs from fall.

On my trips to Maine with Seth, we never took this route. We were close by, however—many times, on the major road that ran along the ocean and crossed over this road. On one drive up to Rockland, Seth suggested coming this way, just as we approached the exit to Cape Wood. Do you want to go see the house? he asked, and I said no. I was afraid he'd fall in love with it and want to buy it and move up here. I always thought Seth would love it, if not for the house itself, then to find out more about me, who I was long ago, before he came along—something I didn't talk about very often. Now I wonder why I didn't go. I drive up this road I missed all those times, this road that has changed so much over nineteen years. If I had gone I could have witnessed this transformation—seen it all change gradually; and now, two decades later, it might not seem different at all. I wouldn't know the difference.

I pass by a sign, JETTY BEACH, 3 MILES, and recognize road names: Summer, Juniper, and Crestview—a new road, then finally Autumn. I take the corner and pass over the hill, my heart thundering in my chest.

Aunt Adeline's house is smaller than I remember; not the looming house with pillars, but a moderate cape with a dormer roof and yellow shingles peeling to a pale, aqua blue. The house was yellow when I lived here—but a warmer, colonial gold-yellow, not this lemony shade. The twelve-pane window glass is wavy and pearlescent in places, where the late afternoon sun reflects. Colorful buckets are stacked at the end of the driveway, next to the porch, and rusted rakes stand against the side of the house. At the right side of the yard small birch trees line an elevation; they are broken and bent over, most likely from the ice storm in January. My eyes follow them to the backyard, to a large shed where Grandma and Grandpa Winslow once raised chickens.

I step out of the car and onto the pebble driveway, up to the porch with its thick white posts that are scratched raw in places. I open the screen door and fumble with the keys while the tight-spring frame bounces back against my shoulder. To my left is a tangled mass of bush in a rocky border alongside the porch. It's thorny and bare; a rosebush, I think. The door creaks open. I smell dust and musty wood, and see dark, knotty pine floors. The wallpaper in the front entrance is brownish-purple in the dim light, almost eggplant-colored. I flick on the light switch and see the staircase straight ahead—maroon enamel steps and banister, dingy white rungs. Around the corner through a wide doorway is the living room, where sunlight pours through the tall windows, a bright mist. The floor and fireplace are wood, but the walls are beige paisley paper on which picture hangers still protrude within ovals and squares that are unbleached by sun. I imagine what used to hang here—artwork, portraits, tintype photographs, faces staring out from the walls and mantel.

As my eyes move to the floor, I recognize a missing chunk of wood in the door frame of the dining room. The gouged section used to be boot-bruised and dirty, I remember; now it's painted over. But it's the same missing chunk, I can tell. I continue through the room and into the dining room, and see the column-like molding in the corner, then the tin ceiling, forged into petal shapes. It now is a pale blue, where it once was painted ivory.

I'm beginning to remember.

There is pock-marking in the dining room windowsill, a deep groove in the wainscoting in the hall. These all seem familiar, but no—it's been too long. So much must have happened in the house; it must have changed. But with each corner or wall I look at I begin to remember, and each new thing is familiar enough. This is too easy, I think, too familiar—so familiar that I don't trust my memory; am I truly remembering, or only recalling as I see? Like déjà vu, where I recognize and call it remembering, yet can never truly foretell. I must race with my body to predict what detail I will see next—what is around that corner, what is behind this door? I'm dazed, I can't keep up, so before I make the full circle to the kitchen I sit down on the stairs and rest my head on my knees.

With my eyes closed I imagine pictures—photographs from years ago: a collage of black and whites framed in the hallway, the oval sepias in the living room, then the bright Technicolor Polaroids in a photo album. It is a collage of faces, ones I may have seen once or twice as a child, but never looked at again. The faces are fuzzy, indistinguishable, but they move—overlapping like a deck of cards, and when I open my eyes they disappear. I close them again, and there is nothing.

I wait a minute before I stand, then walk past the small bathroom to the kitchen. It looks a lot like Mom's kitchen back home, with its long counter dividing it from the eating area, with the buff-colored refrigerator and stove, the clean oak cabinets. There used to be avocado-colored appliances in here, and a gold-speckled white Formica counter against which I would lean, my eyes barely clearing the top as I watched Aunt Adeline stir cookie batter. I would reach up for one of those stainless steel bowls, and tall, dark-haired Aunt Adeline would smile and gently pull it away, speaking with a soft, velvet voice—*Not yet.* But I can't remember Aunt Adeline's voice clearly, so the one in my head sounds a little like Mom's.

I go upstairs, past the water-stained, eggplant wallpaper, on steps that are short and steep, and that crack under my feet. The banister feels frail, wobbly, and is missing a post. Upstairs there are three rooms—two small ones to the right, and a large one across, which had been Grandma and Grandpa's, and later, Aunt Adeline's. The master bedroom used to have pink rosebud-on-trellis wallpaper and a shiny maple floor beneath the four-posted bed, and now the room is empty and plain, with white paint and a wall-to-wall beige carpet. The small room across, facing the rear of the house, was Aunt Adeline's when she was young, and later was converted to her greenhouse, with its dormer window converted to a large skylight, and grow lights installed along the inside walls. The greenhouse design has not changed; even the built-in black slab of a table remains in the center—it may have been too difficult to move. Or tenants might have found it useful, and the growing tradition lived on. As I leave the room I notice the remnants of dried, crisp leaves scattered to the corners of the floor.

Then there is my room. I always called it that, anyway, even though it was Mom's room growing up. But it was mine whenever I visited with Aunt Adeline, as it had been mine years before—when my bassinet, then crib, then small trundle bed, lay alongside Mom's. The ceiling has not changed—dull-sheen pine boards, like the floor, but the wallpaper is different, of course: a textured weave, lumpy and bubbling in places, a peach color, dappled with banana-yellow petal shapes like little butterflies. It was beige and blue paper in here when I had the room, until green was put over it—that green Aunt Adeline put up just weeks before she died. Mom hated the green wallpaper. She ridiculed Aunt Adeline for buying it, for having such terrible taste. But it wasn't the pattern or texture she didn't like; it simply was the green.

I once tried to remind Mom how the green she hates so much exists within many of her favorite autumn hues, how—without green, many of these colors hues would not be. Mom only sighed and rolled her eyes, and told me that she too knew her primary colors.

We even stood for ten minutes inspecting a six-dollar scatter rug at Sears, a rug in a gorgeous, deep teal, the color of the ocean at dusk. Mom asked if it was more blue than green simply because she needed to know. I couldn't decide which color was more dominant so I told her blue, and she promptly bought the rug. I realized then that, no matter how much Mom knew about human psychology, she was quite capable of fooling even herself.

The old green wallpaper is showing. It peeks out from behind the thick, textured peach in a peeling corner near the ceiling. It is a lovely sage green, faded and stormy-looking, with velvet-white flowers and lime-colored leaves. I have the strange urge to pull at the top peach color and see more of this older color, and all those layers beneath. Old paper, old paint. Family history.

Back downstairs I check the water in the kitchen and bath, give the toilet a flush. Across from the bathroom is the basement door, so I go down, pulling away at thick, gauzy cobwebs slung wall-to-wall across the stairs and over the railing. At the bottom of the stairs I pull a string to turn on the light, see fieldstone walls coated with gray dust, and two half-windows near the ceiling—also covered, opaque. The basement smells like wet rocks, pond water, and I feel dirty and dust-filled as I cross the hard dirt floor to the short doorway near the furnace, leading to the base of the chimney.

The place where the date book was found.

Mom and Dad must not have checked every nook of the house when they cleaned it out all those years ago. But then this doesn't seem like a spot one would check when cleaning out a house; it seems more like a place to hide something in confidence, for only one special person to find.

My old hiding place.

I duck below the opening and into the alcove. Slices of light enter from the gaps in the wood above; I see the jagged side of the chimney that rises to the second floor, then the thick, dark beams that lay at each floor level. I reach up and feel the top of the first beam, then slide my fingers across, through the dust and the bugs, searching, and there is something—an edge, a groove against my fingertip. Placing a foot on the wide base of the chimney I boost myself up, then step up again until my head is above the board. I can barely make out the top of it, but see the grooves in the wood. Letters. I read and I run my fingers along them to guide my eyes. It is large, childlike writing, straight lines crossing straight lines, the word JENNA carved deep into the board.

fourteen

It was the first day of spring in my tenth year, and the air had a wet dirt smell, with just a touch of spice, like a lime. Whenever I smelled this I thought of how summer was coming; I thought of cool blue water and colorful blankets on the sand, and how it wouldn't be long before school was out and Dad would take me to the beach. Dad said the beaches in Maine were the most beautiful, the most unspoiled. *Remember, honey?* he would say, but I couldn't remember that well because we never went back there. We'd go to our north shore or New Hampshire, maybe to Cape Cod, but never back to Maine. Why, I asked him, didn't we ever go to Maine?

Mom, he said.

I asked her about this on this fresh spring day, as she sat down next to me on the front steps. I figured I'd ask because she had come out to sit with me, and because she seemed extra nice today. She even was interested in the caterpillars in my plastic bucket. But when I asked why we never went to Maine, she quickly changed the subject.

"I have to talk to you about something," she said, so I asked her if I'd done something wrong. She said no, although it was hard to tell because her no always sounded unsure, like it was a question.

She had to talk to me because of my fifth grade science class, because I'd learned something new. "You're learning about reproduction," she began, her voice shaky, "in school." She nervously picked at the hem of her skirt, and I suddenly felt she didn't want to tell me whatever she was going to tell me. Or maybe this was just as strange for her as it was for me, this private conversation thing between us.

"Uh huh," I said, not really wanting to talk about reproduction—about s-e-x, my friends and I called it. It was embarrassing enough to talk about in the classroom; I didn't need to talk about it with my mother. But she continued.

"You know how men and women—" She stopped, looked across the yard, picked at her skirt again. I waited for her to continue, wanting to help her; I could tell she couldn't get the words out. Then suddenly she straightened up, composed herself, and turned back to me. "You know how the sperm fertilizes the egg?" she said plainly, and cleared her throat.

"Yes."

I knew all about the sperm thing. In Mr. Baraski's science class it had been explained, with pictures of the little buggers— like tadpoles swimming to the big sun of an egg. There were those words *fertilized* and *trimester* and *placenta,* and that short paragraph about the man and woman, "lying together and loving each other." There had been no pictures or detailed descriptions, of course, so I had to use my imagination. I pictured Mom and Dad lying together and loving each other, as the textbook described, their male and female body parts with a life of their own. It was a horrid sight, and it brought to mind the boys I liked. My crush on Rob Messing dissolved into nothing.

"Well," Mom said, and then suddenly blurted out the words. "Your father is not your biological father." It came out of her mouth very quickly, as if it were the only way to tell me.

"What?" I asked.

"You come from another man's sperm," she said.

I almost laughed when she said this, partly because I was embarrassed, partly because it didn't sound real. But then I remembered my confusion in school just a few days before. We had been learning about sperm and eggs, and suddenly I remembered Dad showing up at the edge of the yard, years before, drinking lemonade on the porch. It had been long after I was born, so I began to wonder how I had come to be.

But now it was coming together. "Okay," I said, telling Mom to continue.

"The other man," she said, looking down at the ground, rubbing her feet together. "We were together only once. We did not stay together. But I want you to know that a mother and father should stay together." She looked up, with a squinting, thoughtful look to her eyes. "But then...if this man and I had stayed together, then I wouldn't have married your father, now, would I?" She turned and smiled at me, her lips flat and tight against her teeth, a clown smile. It seemed like a forced expression, like there was sadness behind it.

"Where is my real father now?" I asked.

"*Biological* father," Mom said, looking away from me, across the lawn. "He's gone, Jenna."

"Where did he go?" I asked.

She was silent for a moment. "He's not coming back." Then suddenly her face began to light up—her eyes open and bright, the smile soft and real. "He wanted to be a sailor, you know—to join the Navy. Maybe that's where he went." Her smile quickly shrank back into sadness.

"Can't you find him?" I asked. "Isn't he in the phone book?"

Mom looked back at me with seriousness in her eyes. Her cheeks had grown flushed, and her forehead was sweating. "There's really no need to find him," she said, lifting her finger to my hair, wiping the bangs out of my eyes. She smiled her clown smile again.

"What was his name, Mom?" I felt like I shouldn't ask, but she answered.

"Montigue. I knew him only as Montigue."

"You mean like Monty?" I asked, because there was a Monty in my homeroom.

"I suppose."

"Did you call him Monty?"

Mom shook her head no. Maybe she never knew him well enough to call him Monty.

The news seemed like it should have felt important to me; I should have been happy or sad or excited about it. But Montigue seemed like just another male body part with a life of its own that once entered Mom. And in some ways, I felt I'd always known about it.

"Thanks for telling me, Mom," I said.

"No need to thank me," she said. "It's something you needed to know." But I could tell by the reddened, exhausted look on her face that telling me had been difficult for her.

I was a little embarrassed talking about sperm and eggs. I didn't know if I was embarrassed for Mom or for me—about the fact that I was a girl who would one day become a woman, that I would be doing these things. I didn't want to talk about it either.

So we never did again.

fifteen

At my farewell lunch Dad seems happy for me, even while there is a touch of bittersweet showing on his face—in the corners of his mouth, not turning up the way they usually do when he smiles. Mom's mood is unclear as she stares into her soup bowl, and studies her oyster crackers. Elisabeth is as energetic as always, excited about my move. I'm going on an adventure, she reminds me, and I suddenly wonder what she knows about Aunt Adeline's suicide. Come visit me anytime, I say, but Mom corrects me.

"On your next school vacation."

"Oh, Mom," Elisabeth whines. "That's a whole month from now."

"Don't talk with your mouth full."

"What's wrong with one weekend?" Dad says. "I can take her up on a Friday night or a Saturday morning."

Mom's spoon is in mid-flight when it stops. Her head rises before turning toward Dad so that her neck resembles a post in ground. She lowers her spoon back into the soup and wipes her mouth with her napkin. "Bill," she says, "let's give Jenna a chance to move in first."

"Elisabeth can come anytime," I say. "That would be fine with me."

Mom is adamant. "I said no."

"Renee—" Dad says.

"What?" Mom is cutting her grilled cheese sandwich into quarters. "Elisabeth needs to be serious about her schoolwork. She's going to start high school next year. Even now she needs to be serious—it will better prepare her for college."

I chuckle, cover my mouth. "College! Mom, you're *not* thinking about her going to college already?"

"Of course not. I just want to make sure she goes to college." She wipes her mouth with her napkin. "And finishes."

"You mean not drop out, like *I* did."

"I didn't say that."

Dad's face is pale, apprehensive. I wonder if he's pondering over which side to take when the conversation is over. Elisabeth's eyes waver to the wall, the window; she doesn't seem to be listening now. She probably is thinking about boys.

"Mom," I say. "You didn't go until you were in your twenties."

"That's because I was raising you."

Dad throws his napkin down, shakes his head. "Here we go," he says, and I'm surprised at his nerve.

"Quiet, Bill," Mom snaps and looks back to me. "It wasn't easy for me. It took me years just to get the high school thing done." She brushes crumbs from her skirt. "But I went back—all the way. I just think you had a better chance than I did. There was nothing holding you back."

"You mean no kids, right? And what—did I hold you back?"

"I didn't say that."

"Come on," Dad interrupts. "I thought we were talking about Elisabeth."

"What?" Elisabeth suddenly wakes up from her daydream.

Mom runs her fingers over the top of her head, flattening her hair, pulling tight at her scalp. She stands and steps back, her chair scraping against the wooden floor. "Let's just forget about it." She turns and walks away from the table, out of the dining room. I feel my sinuses filling, my eyes beginning to flood. I don't want to break down now, not when I'm so close to getting out of here, and not having to deal with this kind of confrontation anymore.

A quiet, awkward minute passes in which Dad and Elisabeth don't speak, in which I wonder if they're afraid to take a side because Mom could be listening. When she finally returns to the table she touches her hand to my wrist.

"Your father is right," she says, and I wait for something profound. "One weekend won't hurt." How clever Mom is at changing subjects, I think. "I'm sorry, Bill," she adds, taking Dad's hand.

What an awful feeling, whenever Mom apologizes to Dad. She must realize, must remember how it was Dad who always was there for me—for trips to the zoo, to the ball games at Fenway, the beaches. Just Dad and me it was, before Elisabeth came along. There was always some excuse why Mom couldn't go: *Too much to do; too tired,* she would say. Then there was her sad, suffering face as we pulled out of the driveway, her dusky figure like a ghost in the window. Sometimes when we arrived home she still would be sitting in that exact spot, that chair in the living room—just staring at some whirl of dust or granule of dirt on the windowsill. Later on as I was lying down to sleep, I would wonder if Mom had just been feeling sorry for herself or if she really did feel more than it seemed. Was there some universe I didn't know about in that speck of earth on the windowsill? Was Mom really feeling pain?

Mom's "down" times were less and less after Elisabeth came along, but still there is always pain in her. I can see it in her eyes, like turbid, icy ponds, and in the tight mouth that pulls hollows below her cheekbones to her temples—those narrow grooves that one day will be folds of yellowed skin. I just hope that this pain is not like Mom implies with her accusative eyes and slippery tongue—all caused by me.

After lunch Elisabeth and I sit Indian-style in her very pink bedroom, on her new extra-firm mattress from Sears. She doesn't like squishy mattresses any more, she tells me, as if this is some sign of maturity, some symbol of womanhood.

"I hope you can come up soon," I say.

"We'll manage it." Elisabeth sounds grown up. "Did I tell you—" she says, lying back on the bed and lifting her pointed toes toward the ceiling, "that I kissed a boy?"

"No," I say, and a tinge of heat shoots up my spine. "When?" I take a breath, try to calm down so I don't seem too maternal or too curious. "How did this happen?"

"It was just last week," she says. "Monday. We were running through that field in the back of the Carney's house—you know, that field? Well, I tripped, and we were just rolling around and stuff." Her breath is skippity, exhausted, and her eyes crinkle and glisten at the corners. "Then we stopped rolling, and Brian was lying next to me—almost on top of me—and he kissed me."

"Be careful," I say.

"Oh, geez, you sound like Mom." Elisabeth drops her legs to the floor and stands. "I'm not stupid, you know." She moves in front of the mirror on her dresser and pulls on her cloth pony-tail-holder until it glides out of her long hair. It looks almost painful but she keeps pulling, then twists her hair and plops it on top of her head into a bun, one hand holding it, the other on her hip, posing.

"Mom probably thought the same thing," I say.

"No. Mom *was* stupid."

"That's not a nice thing to say." But inside I agree and realize how the years have made me a better liar than Elisabeth.

"Yeah, but it's true." Tendrils of curls fall from her hand and drop to her neck. She twists the hair around her finger and then glides her finger to her collarbone, strokes her skin. "No offense to you, of course. I'm glad she had you."

I wonder how much Elisabeth understands about my story. Mom did explain most of it to her just after it happened, that I lost a baby before I married. I wonder what my little sister understood then about human biology—about human nature—when she looked up at me with her six-year-old eyes, ripe with knowledge and said, "But then he married you anyway. That's so sweet."

Sweet.

"How's this?" Elisabeth asks, turning gracefully, her silky-white arms in the air, hands on her head, her bare neck garnished with wisps of mahogany curls.

"Pretty," I say.

"Really?"

"You're very pretty, Elisabeth. And I bet Brian Norquist thinks so, too."

"Whatever. Maybe he does, maybe he doesn't."

I chuckle. "I thought you liked him."

"I guess. But it's not like...the way you and Seth were."

And how was that? I think. How many ways are there to love a person?

I wonder what Elisabeth feels. I hope she feels something—anything, at least an innocent, soulful crush, something I might have felt if the boys had liked me when I was thirteen. It would be disappointing to find that it's all a game for her, just a source of attention. Or worse, that she simply craves the kiss.

———

The afternoon turns muted and shadowy, and we gather on the front step for good-byes. "We'll be in touch," Mom says, and I wonder if it's true. I'd like to hug her—just a quick hug, but she has one arm wrapped tightly around her waist like a belt, and the other holds the door frame.

"Good," I say, and reach up to her hand on the door. When I touch her she twitches in surprise, then lets go of the door and takes my hand. "I hope so," I add. She smiles a quick smile, her lips tight and bashful. Her eyes are glossy, and for a moment, looking right at me.

Elisabeth jumps between us to hug me. Dad clenches my shoulder with firm fingers but does not hug; perhaps he does not want to upstage Mom. "Take care," he says. No one speaks a word about the house. It's as if I'm going nowhere, or to some secret cloud whose name can't exist in our language right now. Terms like *old house* and *Aunt Adeline* are forbidden right now, like profanity.

As I begin to pull the car away Elisabeth runs up, perhaps to say something else, something private. "Jenna," she whispers. "Are you going to Maine to find Montigue?"

"Of course not." I check to make sure Mom didn't hear. "Did Mom say that?"

"No way," she says. "Mom would never talk about *him*. I was just wondering."

"Well, that's just silly. Besides, I wouldn't even know how." I reach out my hand and she takes it.

"I'll be up soon," she says. "I'll sneak up if I have to."

"Mom said you could come up, didn't she?"

"Oh, come on, Jenna." Elisabeth suddenly sounds like an adult. "You know Mom." She leans over and hugs me, her body warm and delicate next to the cold, hard metal of the car door. "I'll miss you."

I give another wave to Mom and Dad and back out of the driveway. As I drive away I look into the rearview mirror and see Elisabeth running to the mailbox. Mom disappears from the doorway, melts back into the darkness, but Dad still is there, waving a sad, mechanical wave, a wave that seems it will continue even after I can't see him anymore, forever perhaps. I imagine my car from his eyes: just a speck on the charcoal road, getting smaller, smaller, headed back to the place from where I came. Just before I pass over the hill I see Mom's face in the living room window, muted and dusky, afraid to be seen.

As I cut through the maze of streets leading out from the suburbs to the highway, there is a tightness in my stomach and back, as if I am a long, winding tree whose roots are planted far away, stretching and tugging. I'm not sure if it's Seth I'm feeling, or the supple yet resistant umbilical of Mom.

I think of Seth's face—a face he often had during our New England road trips: his eyes focused as he drove—frozen on something far ahead, perhaps the mountains in the distance. A face that suddenly perked up when I spoke, as if awakened from a sleep—responding, laughing, happy, always there for me. Dad seems so different with Mom; his desire seems propelled somehow, burdened by a hopelessness, a weariness. And there is a blindness in his stare, a defeat behind his eyes, as if he has stopped trying, as if part of him has died. I think about Elisabeth, wonder what it is that she craves, where her destiny lies. I think about Dad and his obligatory warmth, Mom and her coldness, and then me—the lost, widowed soul who no longer knows what she feels.

The sky has turned a dark purply gray, and the yellow highway lines ahead glow like neon. I pass between patchy hillside and late-winter skeletons of trees, through towering, rust-colored granite on both sides of the highway—solid rock that has been conveniently sliced and divided for my passage and for all people like myself, flocking to happy havens and hiding places.

part five
the color of water

{renee

sixteen

She tries to imagine what it looks like now, if the colors are the same, if the shutters have fallen off. There were chances to look at it, those visits to Portland, Acadia. *But why?* she said each time Bill asked, knowing the house, the town would only bring bad sentiments. And wondering, any time she stopped into a country store or fish market, if anyone would recognize her.

"Adeline's younger sister," they probably would say, because Adeline was the one who was noticed, even before she died.

Renee was four years younger, four inches smaller. Skinny and spunky and average, with hazel eyes and hair the darkest shade of brown. Then there was Adeline, with her sand-colored bag and broad-rimmed hat, her frame six feet in chunky beach sandals. A statue of ivory skin and emerald eyes, with deep mahogany hair, bones long and strong. Adeline the goddess.

Renee followed her big sister wherever she would take her—to the parks, the shopping centers, on walks through the woods, secret paths only Adeline knew about. They explored nearby Portland, with its glorious gourmet foods and the creations of artists. They basked in the sun on the Cape Wood Park lawn, amongst the flurry of children and Frisbees and all the bright colors, occasionally dropping their sunglasses to check out the boys. And looking just like those advertisements they saw in *Glamour* and *Seventeen* magazine.

Cape Wood became a beach town in the summer. The transformation was like magic, especially in the town's center, which was separated from the coast by miles of road and patches of pine forest. The sidewalks were decorated with street vendors and art displays for the tourists who flocked in with their cameras and Caribbean shirts. On the weekends music was heard throughout the area, usually coming from the youth center or the radios on the green, which one had to pass through to get to the main beach.

At the coast the salt air would permeate all clothing and wood; it filled nostrils and mouths, and coated lips and teeth with the faintest layer of the grainy sea. But the hot summer was nourishing in its stickiness, as a crisp breeze came with it. At the shore the sand was sharp and pebbly, and dark with the blue-black shells of mussels. Along the grassy beachside hills the trees leaned out and then upward, as if reaching back for the land, afraid they would be sucked into the water.

The jetty near the beach was a quarter-mile of intricately stacked gray and salmon-colored granite that extruded into Casco Bay. In the summer, many of the teenagers fished and sunbathed there, or simply sat on top of the rocks with their binoculars and cameras. They awed at the speedboats whizzing by, cutting through the green-black water and stirring up foam. They observed the islands, on which trees and large boulders looked like moss and pebbles from a distance.

Mother didn't like Renee hanging down at the jetty unless it was daytime. She had heard the rumors of rowdiness, of the older kids jumping into the night waters. But Adeline could go. She was nineteen—an adult, already in college. So Adeline would tell Renee about her nights down at the jetty and at the nearby youth center where she could dance and get refreshments. She told her how her crowd was calm and well-behaved and more interested in reflecting on life and love than splashing into the ocean with the younger kids. Mother doesn't understand, Adeline said. "She's wrong about the rowdiness."

But perhaps it wasn't rowdiness that Mother feared. Perhaps it was the boys.

There was Mark Fisher, who was twenty and worked for the Marine Patrol, blond and blue-eyed and always tan, even in the winter; then Bobby Thompson, who was sporty and rambunctious, who whistled at all the girls but was boyfriend to no one; Rob Wetherbee, who was shy and skinny, but who came alive on stage during the drama festivals in the summer. And there was Bill, of course—Renee's Bill. He always was there, following the older boys around the way Renee followed her big sister.

Then there was the new guy who showed up one night—a dark, deep-voiced young man who wanted to be a sailor. The one no one could get, perhaps not even Adeline.

jenna}

seventeen

Whenever I try to imagine Aunt Adeline, I think of the tall silhouette at the end of my childhood bed, a glow of light from behind her. But it's a memory that has always confused me, as I once thought this vague image of a tall brunette figure was Mom.

I sometimes thought it was Mom tucking me in and cuddling with me, walking me around the yard to show me plants and flowers, all those living things she no longer loves. There was the silky hand I would touch, to lead me around the yard, the voice like liquid in the wind. I would follow at her feet—watching the smock dress brushing, the little hairs that grew on her ankles where her razor didn't reach. I remember the smell of lavender floating in the warm air surrounding her, and flowers, petals floating everywhere, dropped by a pale, smooth hand onto my shoulders and into my hair.

These sights, these sounds, I never will know for sure.

There was the warmth of chocolate baking in the oven on my birthday—butter and cocoa and a touch of nutmeg in my nostrils, the plastic bowl I would slide off the countertop to scrape frosting with my palm. Sugar and shortening, the heaven of childhood, then a mother's gentle shadow, soft hands taking the bowl away, never scolding. The mother would float away, white apron and flip-flops, hair in a ponytail. Mom, a hundred feet tall.

It's been too many years, so memory is vague, skewed. Was it Mom who watered the cactus and African violet on my windowsill, and checked the closet for goblins before bedtime? Or who, on a seeping, humid summer night, washed the white sheets and crisped them with an iron to get rid of the "fuzzies," then folded and placed them in the refrigerator before putting them on the bed? Thoughtful, innovative, this mother was; she always had the solution. So on the stickiest of nights, when the varnished wood chairs sweated and moths panted against my window screen, I would crawl into my smooth white bed of ice cream. And I would see that face, the gentile hovering, a mother silhouette staring down at me in the dark.

Aunt Adeline.

―――

The garden possibilities are enormous here at the new house: three lawns, two weedless plots on both sides of the porch and another at the edge of the yard. I imagine patches of flowers: Shasta daisies and poppies, purple coneflower, bushes of catmint. Perhaps I can grow vegetables—something besides herbs and a patio tomato plant. There is a good spot directly in the middle of the small side lawn, what is left of a garden—a rectangle of dark, well-fed soil, like a grave in the center of the fresh, sprouting green.

Seth's grave is more than a hundred miles away now. But it is just a grave, I remind myself. He would not want me to miss his body, his shell.

Furniture is scattered throughout the house. I asked the movers to leave it so I could rearrange it myself, but first there are floors that need scrubbing, rooms to be painted, wallpapered, perhaps. There is dust and dirt in the corners of rooms, and in the backs of closets and kitchen drawers. Fixtures are slimy with grit, and mildew grows in the bathroom corners and beneath the kitchen sink. I shouldn't think about this dirt, though, or about doing any kind of work today. This evening I only want to explore my new surroundings and to do so without other responsibilities. Then I will unroll my fat, red-plaid sleeping bag and camp out in my old bedroom.

It's beginning to get dark; there's a luminous pink glow on the horizon beyond the house and barn across the road. The air blowing from the east smells of sea water, and there is a raw, pungent breath in my lungs as I inhale. I look to the other houses leading up the hill to the right, I try to remember which ones were here before, wonder if anyone who lives here could possibly remember Aunt Adeline, Mom, or even me. A boy named Hunter Jones used to live up the street, just over that hill. I wonder if the big red house is still there, if he or his family still come to Maine in the summer.

Hunter and I spent a good portion of my last summer in Maine together, but it was a short-lived friendship, taken away from me. Eventually everything was taken away, if not by some God-like force, then by Mom. Or at least that's how it felt sometimes.

I walk around the yard with my trowel, sifting through the crumbly soil on the left side of the house, careful not to disturb perennials that may be there. There are speckles of bright green just below the surface, the faint smell of thyme. The last tenant may have grown herbs here; Aunt Adeline grew tarragon and thyme here long ago. She also grew all those flowers by the front porch: the columbine, the strawflowers and catmint, then the peony bushes against the white fence that divided the yards. The peonies may not be here anymore, although there is a row of tall bushes alongside the gray wood fence—I'm not sure what they are. Bare crabapple trees surround the lawn, and a budding forsythia stands in the middle. The grass is patchy in places, and there are patches of bugleweed, which soon will spread like a carpet and then erupt into purple spikes of flowers. Aunt Adeline once said how her mother hated the bugleweed. Grandma would do all she could to keep it from coming up, poisoning the lawn with sprays and pellets of weed-killer. But Aunt Adeline loved the weed; she was happy whenever any of it survived, because if it lived it would thrive and invade the patches of dirt with its purple chaos. Grandma usually found it and ripped it out every morning. Like everything else, it eventually came back.

I can't remember Grandma; she died of a heart attack when I was six months old, just a year after Grandpa died of cancer. But I can picture her, the way Aunt Adeline described her wiry hair and freckled skin, the thick middle that neither my aunt nor my mother ever had. I could tell that Grandma was strong, the way she endured the death of Grandpa, and how she raised two teenage daughters by herself and managed to get everything settled before dying herself.

It had been Grandma who'd decided she needed Aunt Adeline to help take care of me. Adeline came home and transferred her studies to Portland, and after Grandma died it was just up to Aunt Adeline and Mom.

I look out beyond the edge of the lawn and see movement, beyond the row of small, bare trees that separate me from my neighbor. There is color amongst the gray, dead wood: red, then green, moving. Someone looking at me.

The figure stops moving, and I can make out the flesh color—a face below a dab of red, the green of a shirt or jacket. A man. He appears to be fortyish, maybe fifty, and with a pudgy build and plain, rounded face. He is looking toward the house, just staring. After a moment he turns, a straight, stiff-necked rotation, and begins to walk away. He saunters up the road with his back hunched, his legs dragging like heavy logs, and moves up the street and over the hill until he disappears from my sight.

This is a person who doesn't know my past, who won't try to console me. It could be a relief to have a strange neighbor, someone different from what I'm used to—those phony smiles living downstairs who pretended to care. I am not afraid.

In my old bedroom, which used to be Mom's, the bubbly wallpaper needs to come off. The room is dim now, and in the tawny leftover light of day from the small east window the peach color appears a strange, pinky-lavender color. I can see irregularities now, the shallow gouges behind the paper, a faded area where a desk or dresser used to be. I notice another corner that has started to peel, and can see the faded sage green behind it. Squatting down, I pull at the paper and it lifts as if it were glued just minutes before; moisture must have seeped in over the years and separated it. I hold it tight and pull back, and the peach lifts several inches before tearing off in my hand. I think of what Mom would say about my method—about doing such a thing without tools, without a plan. She would scold me about it, something cutting, like, "You could have taken the plaster with it."

So what, I think. It feels good to be destructive.

And it is fascinating to see this green paper behind. This is the color I stared at as a seven-year-old when I came to visit Aunt Adeline that final summer, as I lay in the bed she had prepared just for me. It is the same paper she put over the old beige-and-blue. Strange that she wallpapered just two months before she took her own life.

During those final visits I would awake to the sun on the wall and the smell of pancakes downstairs. "Jenna," Aunt Adeline's gentle voice would call from beyond the closed door, "time to get up." It was such a pleasant feeling—the smell of buttery break-fast, my aunt's velvety tone. And that wall: a subdued yet earthy green—a green that, with the correct lighting, was a forest I could explore when I wasn't outside playing in the real one.

In one of the corners at the far right of the wall, the edge behind the peach curls outward to reveal a thin slice of another layer behind—a heavy, plastic-like paper in a drab beige. This must be the old color, the color that was in here when I was a baby. Funny how those who lived in this house after we did never bothered to remove the paper first. "Such a lazy way of doing it," Mom would probably say.

I pull at the green edge; it is crisp and dry, and it flakes like piecrust as I touch it, then falls off. I try again, manage to grasp it with my fingernail, and pull.

The green is coming off.

The more it lifts, the more resilient and pliable it is. I peel toward the center of the wall, both layers at once, and peeking out between the two layers I see an edge of white, a corner. As I look closely at the tiny section of white paper I see something on it: the curve of letters in pencil or faded ink. Words.

It could be old scrap paper to make up for uneven sheet rock and lumpy plaster, to smooth out gouges and cracks, to cover imperfections below. I pick at the white paper, but it's wet from the glue-backed paper above it; thin and pulpy, ready to dissolve. It will only come off in shreds if I continue to do it this way. Mom would be correct for scolding me; I'll have to wait until I have the proper tools.

I open the bottle of wine I put in the refrigerator, a chardonnay Seth reserved for a special occasion. I pour myself a glass and take the drink upstairs, where I unroll my sleeping bag on the wooden floor, sit down, and drink. The wine is crisp and buttery in my mouth, and brings a warm, buzzing feeling to my head. I lie back and stare at the knots of pine in the ceiling in the dim glow of the nightlight until I am getting tired and the knots are starting to blend together. As I wait for sleep to take over, I wonder if I will have that dream again, the one in which I have children.

In the dream the children are perfect—sweet and obedient, with cherub-like hands and twinkling voices that fade in and out like a ballerina music box, opening, closing. Boy and girl, I think, but it's hard to tell because their faces are blank, no matter which angle I see them from: blank milky cataracts below dark mops of Seth hair that, as I reach out to it, slips right through my fingers.

But I don't dream this dream. Instead I dream about this house. It is present day, and Mom, Dad, and Elisabeth are with me, along with those who have died—Seth, Aunt Adeline, even Grandma, whose image I've conjured up from old photographs. The dead are more indistinct and less animated than the living; they stand like blurry mannequins around the house, speaking without moving their mouths, their voices muffled and cottony-sounding. Aunt Adeline is the blurriest of all, her face like a blob of putty, her voice gurgly, like a warped tape. Mom is upset, frantic because Montigue is coming over, because it's going to rain and the furniture will get wet. As I look up I see how there is no ceiling on the house, how there is an upstairs and downstairs and a roof, yet every room is somehow open to the sky. There is a knock at the door and Mom rushes to open it, and there stands the silhouette of a man, a tall man with a broad upper body, dark hair, it seems. This man could be anyone, I'm thinking, perhaps not Montigue at all, as I try to make out the face within the shadows. The sky beyond him blinds me as it is beginning to brighten and swirl, even change color. So I wait for the voice, to distinguish this man from any other in my life; but he does not speak and he never moves his darkened face from the light. And suddenly the sky beyond looks like one of my book cover drawings: swirling and stormy, and an odd shade of green.

eighteen

In my eighth grade art class I painted Thumbelina. I was in awe of her leafy environment, of the fleshy vines and fuzzy lily pads, at the fact she was so small, almost invisible. I loved all characters whose worlds were colossal and green—Alice with her oversized, cartoon-like Wonderland, Dorothy with her vivid Oz colors. I created them all in my exaggerated way while other kids in my class chuckled and painted landscapes and boring bowls of fruit.

My painting of tulips won first prize. This surprised me because none of the kids in my class liked the painting. They said my tulips didn't look real because they had purple stems and faces in the blossoms. I wasn't trying to make them look real, I told them, but they only snickered and gave me dirty looks.

The teachers liked my painting. They used words like "surreal" and "symbolic" as they stood in the hall and admired it while I watched from the water fountain across the hall. Some of the teachers spoke quietly; Mr. Roberts leaned over to Mrs. Darzio, his mouth close to her ear, but I could hear him.

"It looks like the tulips are mating."

I took the painting home to show Mom and Dad, who were entertaining Dad's parents and his sister Myrna, all up from Florida that week. It was a busy house so I had to speak faster, show them things more quickly than I normally would. Mom was in a hurry, as always—exhausted, as always. She was especially worn out with her growing belly, sometimes letting out a moan or two when the kicks and pains came, even leaning on me for support.

"Show us, Jenna," she said, but I could tell by her voice that there was little time.

When I held up the painting Dad smiled and Mom made an overtly confused face. "Are those tulips?" she asked.

Dad nudged her. "Of course they're tulips, Renee," he said. "And they're almost...sexual." It was something he wouldn't normally say, something that seemed like it should feel forbidden. But it didn't feel forbidden, for once. It felt normal.

Mom sighed. "Don't be putting ideas into our thirteen-year-old daughter's head." *Ideas?* I wondered. Mom had no idea how much I understood already.

———

On an afternoon during the relatives' visit I went downstairs for snacks and could hear the chatter in the dining room next door. Aunt Myrna spoke in a high, shrill tone that seemed to rattled the glass knickknacks against the windows, while every now and then Gramps' voice billowed and Grammy chimed in with a squeal. Mom was quiet, but Dad was a chatterbox as he began to talk about a funeral.

Aunt Adeline, I heard, and I closed the refrigerator, moved closer to the doorway—something about car doors, how they don't open easily underwater. I was confused and listened closely. "You should hear," he said, "what an undertaker has to do..."

I pushed through the wooden half-doors without even thinking, without considering that I was interrupting this adult party, and revealed myself around the dining room doorway.

"Aunt Adeline drowned?" I asked. They all seemed surprised to see me, all open mouths and tentative smiles, except for Mom, who was glaring at Dad.

"Yes, honey," Dad said.

I thought it had been a simple accident in which she died on impact. But I'd always wondered, ever since I'd asked on the day of the funeral and had gotten no answer. Mom continued to stare at Dad as if he had said something wrong again, as if he should have lied to me instead. And it would be a lie, I could tell by all these tentative smiles; Aunt Adeline's car had gone into the water.

"Why didn't you tell me?" I asked.

Suddenly Mom's shoulder's drooped a bit and her head lowered, as if in defeat. When she looked up again there were tears in her eyes. She slowly stood and walked over to me, took hold of my shoulders. Her hands felt thin and hard, as if there was no flesh on them. Her face was pale, a yellowy-gray. Perhaps she wasn't prepared to talk, to think about her dead sister again.

"We would have told you eventually," she said.

I wondered if this was true. But I couldn't be angry; I wasn't allowed to get mad at Mom or Dad for not telling me. Mom was six months pregnant, perpetually miserable with her aching back and hot sweats, her abdomen like a Hippity-Hop. And Dad had to be there for Mom, always supporting, always agreeing. A Dad walking on eggshells who would do anything for his wife as he waited for their first biological child to be born.

So I didn't get mad. "Do you think she suffered?" I asked.

Mom didn't answer, but her grip on me tightened and her body leaned, as if suddenly she was unstable, unable to stand and needed me to support her. I then knew that each time Mom would touch me in the future, I would think of her cold, bony hands on my thirteen-year-old skin, this moment of truth.

When I went to bed that night I saw Aunt Adeline's face. Not her living face, but the one I'd seen in the coffin six years before. I could see through all her orangey makeup to her skin, all veiny and green-blue, all breathless from crying out. I could see her eyeballs moving beneath her lids, and then suddenly her spidery lashes began to twitch. The stitches ripped apart and her eyes opened.

But she was not scary. She was looking right at me, her big sad eyes confirming this story I hadn't known all these years. She had died underwater where others could not get to her, where it was too dark for them to even see her. How would they ever know when she really died?

———

That January Mom had the baby, a girl. It was strange to have this new living thing in the house, strange to have to be quiet and cautious all the time. But Mom and Dad seemed happier when Elisabeth came along. They hadn't used to seem so happy.

Their attention toward me teetered off, especially Dad's. He gave this newest and natural child the expected amount of attention, and more. It made me realize how, for all those years before, he had tried so extra hard to be my "real" dad. Maybe it really was better to have a child that wasn't part of some stranger. Maybe the blood connection had gotten to him after all.

So I thought about Montigue. I wondered if Mom thought about him, too, and if one day I'd have the guts to ask her. How could she not think of him? Sex was such a wonderful, powerful thing a person didn't forget. It was two people giving part of themselves, two people blending, becoming one; it was something that made you different forever.

Or so I was told.

———

While Mom and Dad were busy with Elisabeth, I spent a good deal of time exploring the nooks and crannies of the house in ways I'd never cared to before. I would sneak into the attic chest and look at Aunt Adeline's old things. There were dried flowers pressed in plastic, leaves matted and sealed with shellac. And there was Aunt Adeline's will.

I was shocked when I read it, when I discovered that Aunt Adeline had left the house in Maine to Mom. I had known only what Mom had told me: that we *had* to leave Maine all those years before, that the bank had taken the house. The truth was that Mom must have quickly sold the house her sister had left to her so that she could move us more than a hundred miles away. What was supposed to happen didn't; we were supposed to move back into the yellow farmhouse I loved, to live there forever.

It was not the first time Mom and Dad had concealed something concerning Aunt Adeline's death. I had to confront them, even though I knew I'd get in trouble for sneaking into the attic chest; it was worth it.

"Tell her, Renee," Dad said when I asked, and immediately I knew it had been Mom's choice to keep the truth from me. Mom's reply was as lame as all the others.

"If we had told you then," she said, "you would have hated us for leaving."

What Mom didn't realize was that I hated her for lying about it all those years. The feeling made me want to do bad things, to make her angry. So I tried hard to do the one thing Mom wouldn't want me to do.

To think of Montigue.

nineteen

On my first Monday morning in the house, Dad calls just to say hello. "Does the town look the same?" he asks. "Can you smell the ocean from the house?" Because he can't remember, he says.

Sometimes when I talk to Dad on the phone—when I hear the rich, low-toned words but cannot see his face—I imagine Montigue. It is only for a second, but when it happens, this faceless, missing father is a glint before my eyes—a single flash—and I feel a strange swirling in my stomach. For this reason, I do not like to talk to Dad on the phone.

But I do love his deep movie star voice, and picture him with his Cary Grant hair and cardigan sweater, like a 1950s TV dad. I wonder if he looked this way when Mom met him, or if marriage and fatherhood did it to him. Mom told me that Dad had been ready for, even desiring, such a life. He was a nineteen-year-old man who loved babies and who was more than willing to love a woman who already had one. Dad must have been eager to impress Mom, and Mom must have been impressed.

Having a child at such a young age nearly destroyed Mom, from what Aunt Adeline told me. But as soon as Dad came along, she magically transformed. She came back to life, as if the presence of a man had mended a deep, wide hole in her soul.

Over the phone I ask Dad how Mom is doing, and he is quick

with his reply. "Fine, she's fine," he says. "She's thinking about you, too." I wonder if he's telling me the truth.

———

There's little traffic noise here compared to Cambridge—an occasional passing car, the mail truck, a delivery van. I can actually hear the wind against the side of the house. I change into my jeans, a T-shirt, and sweater, make some fresh-ground coffee, and from the kitchen window watch the chickadees feed out back where I've splattered seeds.

The morning is unseasonably warm for late March—the window thermometer says seventy. Soon the grass will come up and the mud will dry and the sun will melt all the gray away. As I step onto the front step a wall of warmth hits my face and neck, a cloud of oncoming spring. I can smell something spicy next to the porch; the lavender bush, I think. The buds on the tiny bare rosebush suddenly seem plumper and have turned to a rosier brown with a hint of green. There is green emerging from the earth in the small plot along the side fence and next to the front porch. The air smells clean. I inhale deeply, removing the last traces of old city smells, of my old life.

With my trowel I push aside dried weeds next to the porch, and with my shears, trim down what appears to be dead spearmint and thyme from last year. The pulling and sifting is invigorating, and I can feel sweat beneath my T-shirt and sweater. I move over to the large garden at the center of the lawn and trowel the edge of the plot, turning the soil just enough to drop Seth's tiny seedling in. This plant is unidentified, premature, most likely. I just want to see if it survives.

I head up the street for a walk through the neighborhood, recognize the house just over the hill a few houses down—the red colonial nestled within the spruce and mountain ash trees. Hunter Jones's old summer house.

The old-fashioned sign still hangs out front: STONYBROOK FARM. A gravel driveway splits into two, one side curving around the back of the house, turning muddy as it bends, continuing out through the field in back, appearing to end at a dilapidated gray barn. Next to the house is a smaller house about the size of a garage—a carriage house, perhaps. It also is red, but it seems newer with its more modern door and large, double-paned window. A shovel rests against the house next to a dark pile of freshly dug soil at the base of the blade. A sign of life.

Hunter was seven, like me, when we first met. His family came to Maine most summers, but the summer we played together was his first summer in Maine following a long stretch when his family stayed in Maryland. On weekends when I stayed over at Aunt Adeline's we would ride our banana-seat bikes down the hill between the houses to a wide stream at the base. A gunpowder mill once stood there, Hunter told me, but it had been blown to bits more than a hundred years before. "Lots of people died," he said.

Hunter spoke about death a lot. He talked about how the gunpowder accidents killed dozens of people and about what the newspapers said about the victims' remains—how bodies were dismantled and scattered over the landscape. He took me down by the river to show me the remains of wheels and stone, the metal strappings of casks and boxes. Amongst the ruins we found newer items, too: the shell of a burned-out car, the bottles, the beer cans. Some items we needed to dig at to get them out of the dirt: larger pieces of rotting wood, chains, horseshoes. Hunter even found something he thought was bone and cleaned it off in the stream. A squirrel or bird carcass, he said, but to me it just looked like a piece of plastic.

I wonder if Hunter could be here now after all these years. And I wonder if he knew what happened to Aunt Adeline later that summer. I never had a chance to tell him. It might be nice to see him again, to see someone who knew me before adulthood, before all the damage.

Main Street runs through the Cape Wood town center, past historic graveyards and a tall brick fire station, through rows of white colonials renovated into offices. It's difficult to tell one building from the next, unless I look closely at the engraved bronze plate on the door reading *Law Office* or *Historical Society*. There used to be a drug store on the corner, and across from it an ice cream shop, but many of the other buildings were inhabited by families back then. The pizza parlor remains—Tucker's, with the big red cursive sign out front.

At the town hall I collect leaflets about car registration, pick up recycling permits. Across from the town hall is the year-round farmer's market, where I find fruits and vegetables and plants imported from local greenhouses. There are tomatoes and peppers, things I can't buy fresh until the end of the summer. There are seeds, too: lettuce and cucumbers, zucchini, more vegetables than I can eat; then French tarragon and dill plants, some flower seed packets—someone else's illustrations. These I'll plant along with my vegetable experiment, Seth's sad little plant. Growing things will be good therapy.

Just down the street is the Cape Wood Public Library, another building that looks like it's just a house, so I almost drive past. As I pull into the driveway I see only one car parked out front. I imagine some elderly librarian behind the desk, alone and waiting for someone to come in, occasionally retreating to her upstairs living quarters to check on something cooking.

Inside the building the air is calm and musty. An ancient-looking radiator hisses in the front hall. The walls are book-filled shelves that tower behind revolving racks of paperback novels. A red oriental carpet runs parallel to a staircase, along which a sign posted to the banister reads CHILDREN'S UPSTAIRS.

The room to the left is carpeted a dull lint gray and decorated with leather-covered chairs and round coffee tables spread with magazines and newspapers. The main desk is a massive, laminated structure that doesn't belong, that curves around the far corner of the room. Behind it is a closed fireplace, its former hearth now painted black, the mantel topped with an odd collection of statuettes in carnival colors. A young blonde-haired woman moves in the shadows behind the yellow-toned wood desk and lifts her face out from behind a hardcover copy of *Pippi Longstocking*.

"I love that book," I say. I'm surprised at the ease of words flowing out of my mouth and think back to Cambridge, where I was so afraid of being recognized, scrutinized. *I knew your husband*, many would say, as if DEAD HUSBAND was written on my forehead. And deep inside I would feel that knot of discomfort and want to run away.

The woman behind the desk gives a quick, almost embarrassed-looking smile as she closes the book in her lap. "I've only read it about *seven times*," she jokes. "Can I help you with something?"

"I'd like to see your archives," I say. "Newspapers, if you have them."

I follow her into an alcove off the large room, through a doorway above which the sign ARCHIVES is posted. The small room is dark, shaded by depressing brown curtains on the tall windows. Nestled in the corner, beyond shelves filled with small labeled boxes, are four cubicles with computers and microfilm machines.

"This is our mainframe," she says, a blue wad of gum flying around in her mouth. "Do you need help?"

"No, thank you," I say. "I'll be all right," I say. The young woman seems relieved and heads back to the front desk.

On the computer I search under NAMES, and type in ADELINE WINSLOW. Three reference numbers appear—three articles, all from the *Maine Casco Herald*. I find the microfilm slide and move over to the other machine.

One of these articles I already have seen—the one Paula sent to me recently.

Adeline Winslow's death in August of 1980 was another once labeled "puzzling,"...

The next two articles are from August 18, 1980.

CAPE WOOD—One person is dead after an automobile accident that occurred at approximately 11:20 P.M.. last night on the pass leading to Mackerel Point, along Casco Bay in Cape Wood. The victim, Adeline Winslow, 27, of Autumn Lane in Cape Wood, was pulled from the car and declared dead on the scene.

Witnesses from the nearby Stone Wharf Tavern saw the car swerve and break through the wooden side rail, skidding off the road and overturning into the water. The cause of death has been listed as drowning, as there was no sign of internal or other injuries. "There appeared to be a struggle to get out," said Sgt. Robert Henderson of the Maine State Police.

Ms. Winslow's accident is just one of many tragedies to occur within the area. It is reported that 37 deaths, including various drowning incidents, have occurred within the small bay within the past ten years.

Police are further investigating to determine if alcohol or some other element was a factor in the accident.

I move ahead to the obituary page.

ADELINE ROSE WINSLOW, of Cape Wood, accidentally, on August 17. She leaves behind a sister, Renee McGarry, also of Cape Wood, and a niece, Jenna Ann McGarry.

A longtime lover of plants and flowers, Ms. Winslow co-managed the Victoria Gardens in Yarmouth while she worked as a botanist for the Maine Department of Inland Fisheries and Wildlife. She also volunteered at the surrounding schools, heading field trips to local parks and museums.

Visiting hours will be held from 11 A.M. to 1 P.M. on Thursday, August 19, at Watkins Funeral Home on Pine Street in Cape Wood.

Funeral services will follow, at 1:30, at the United Methodist Church on Selby Road in Cape Wood. The sermon will be delivered by Rev. Alden Knott, resident pastor. Burial will be at the nearby Lawrence Kaplan memorial cemetery.

As I drive away from the library I think of how odd it is to see the words in print about someone I knew, someone I loved. It seems more like reading about a stranger, a celebrity, the same way reading about Seth was.

Except with Seth, there would be no follow-up articles two decades later, nothing left behind. There may have been if there had been some mystery to his life, if it later was discovered that he meant to crash his car that day. People might even have cared more if something so shocking had come up; it would have filled the television, the papers. I had expected *something*, at least—as the police followed up with me on the crash investigation. I expected an update, some new blurb on the news—some "Last week's accident..." But to anyone but me, his was just another car crash on the evening report like the ones I had seen almost every day of my life.

For weeks after it happened, I visited the crash scene. I wanted to stand in the very spot where Seth took his last breath, to see the same road he saw before he died. When the route was not busy with cars I would park in the breakdown lane to inspect the skid marks and follow them with my eyes—*his* eyes, I imagined. The dark, blue-black streaks faded, though. With each passing day they faded more, until one day they were coated with snow.

Still, I looked for them.

Sometimes I'd examine the dirt alongside the two-lane highway, the grass beyond the guardrail. I searched for glass, metal, any piece of the car that could have been missed by the cleanup crew, so that I could be the only one to find it. Just to be involved.

These were things that didn't cross my mind when Aunt Adeline died. Even years after the accident, when I learned that her car had gone into the water, I never thought about visiting such a ghastly scene. And even if I had thought about it then, there would be no sense—at age seven, at age thirteen—in looking for relics, souvenirs of death.

How morbid one becomes with age.

———

As I look out at the ocean from the jetty, the salt air stings my eyes, fills my nostrils. The granite feels sharp beneath my thin-bottomed sneakers, and the wind is cold. I can see the docks several hundred yards across the water and the boatyard behind it. Clusters of buildings line the inlet—fish markets and bait shops, a restaurant/bar, then a large barn-shaped structure with the sign FLEA MARKET SUNDAY 9-3 where the old youth center was.

The Mackerel Pass road, from which the jetty extrudes, has the same steep embankment of rocks the jetty has. Aunt Adeline's car drove down this road, through the feeble wooden fence that now is a metal guardrail, tumbling down these rocks and turning upside down before it hit the water.

I wonder where, exactly.

The wind is rough and wet as I step back onto the road. I follow the outside of the guardrail atop the steep embankment of rocks that angles down into the ocean. I can't see any sand or rocky bottom where the rocks fade in, only the blackish-green water. A sign is posted along the embankment, NO SWIMMING ALLOWED.

I suppose I'll never know what lies at the bottom, just ten to fifteen feet below the surface; perhaps tiny pieces of scrap metal left behind after they towed Aunt Adeline's car out. Anything could still be down there—a piece of fender, a tailpipe, perhaps her watch. How would anyone even know if she had been wearing a watch?

The water looks dark and cold, the waves sharp. And it truly is green, as Mom once said—as opposed to the blue seen in postcards and in *National Geographic*. It's not at all like those sunny, happy pictures, where the ocean is a clear, Caribbean blue, and the foam is spotless, like meringue against a crystalline beach.

There are two oceans, Mom used to tell me. There is one that is blue—a clean, bright Disney World blue, which simply is the mirror of a clear sky above. But look at the ocean on a cloudy day, she would say, and here lies the green ocean—the true ocean, full of algae and kelp and slimy creatures, evil lurking in the shadows.

part six
the thaw

{renee

twenty

Adeline could have almost anyone she wanted. She knew it and often rubbed it in Renee's face with some bragging detail about the night before—the whistles or hollers made by handsome men on the street, the proposals she'd received at the youth center. When Renee dared to ask if this might happen to her one day, Adeline was venomous in her reply.

"Don't count on it."

Renee wonders if Adeline felt badly about making such comments, years later, perhaps, just before she died. The words on the sunflower stationery never seemed to suggest this; there was nothing there about guilt or apologies. But then maybe the note wasn't for Renee at all.

Adeline hadn't always been so cruel to Renee. They had been best friends as young girls, sharing bikes and Barbies, fighting only over doll clothes and coloring books. Years later, when Adeline entered junior high, she sprouted breasts, her skin became rosy, she garnished herself with jewels, and still she shared secrets with young Renee. Even in high school when Adeline began to date boys she sometimes would take Renee along to the movies or the arcade. It wasn't until Adeline went off to college that she changed. Father had passed away the summer before, leaving Mother distraught and Renee lonely, but it was time for Adeline to go.

Mother and Renee did not hear from her too often, and when she came home she often was distracted. She spent much of her time on the phone with boys from college and no longer cared to hang out with her little sister. Soon it was evident that Adeline would even knock little Renee out of the way just to get attention from the boys.

Renee tried to get their attention, too, but she wasn't comfortable painting her face or wearing push-up bras like Adeline. Even when she wore a simple skirt there was that feeling of eyes on her—eyes she'd once thought she wanted on her that now gave her a dirty, sticky feeling. She tried to dress and act the part anyway, but when Adeline came home her attempts were criticized.

The summer after her first year of college, Adeline was worse than ever. She would watch Renee giving herself one final look-over in the mirror, and just stare, making Renee crazy with her head-shaking and her little sideways comments. "Some people got it and some people don't," she would say.

Renee gave up on the dresses and rouge, but then found she could make friends with boys at the youth center anyway. It must have been in a tomboy sort of way, she figured. *Just one of the guys,* Adeline would remind her.

Renee knew it was true; she was one of the boys. But she hoped the boys would one day see through her blue jeans and ponytail and see her as a woman. More and more each day she grew hungry for this kind of recognition. And the more Adeline told her how plain or boyish she was, the hungrier Renee grew.

Until finally it happened.

jenna}

twenty-one

Northeast University was a world away from home even though it was only ten miles. There was the constant sound of automobiles, the squeal of buses and trains. The smell was of pavement and oil and newspaper ink, with an occasional whiff of salt air if the breeze pulled in from the coast. It was autumn, and the burnt, oily leaves curled into sidewalk corners and gutters, gathered and stuck in street drains. They swept before me along the hard gray steps of the art building, crisp, bright leaves against cold, gray granite.

Each day I took the bus from Westbridge center to the Green Line station just a few miles away. I saved money this way, not having to own a car, not having to endure the parking hassles at the University. And I needed to save money; I had only my small scholarship, my savings from my framing job, and a little from Mom and Dad—of which Mom made sure to remind me, as she wasn't happy with my choice of direction.

"If you want to teach art, that's fine," she said, "but what else can you do with it?"

I could do lots of things, I told her, but she didn't understand. I said I'd take my chances like many artists did, and perhaps end up poor but passionate, knowing that the choice was mine.

Maybe Mom just wanted me to end up teaching because that's what she did. I should have asked her why she didn't take her psychology education all the way to a private practice, ask her why she didn't try to make lots of money. But I didn't ask because I couldn't imagine Mom being a shrink. I thought she should stick to terminology, classification. Textbook psychology.

I took psychology at Northeast University and found it intriguing, all this human mind stuff about why we did things, how human actions had consequences on the brain. The more I learned about it the more I couldn't believe Mom filled her days with the subject.

But it was art that I really loved.

My paintings of plants and flowers were bright and extra-colorful, with unexpected outlining and shadows, things one might not see with the naked eye. It was these exaggerations of living things that got my work noticed, and I began to partici-pate in local art shows, painting with my abstract flair. I soon got my first commissioned job, providing the cover illustration for a children's coloring book. Three book illustrations followed, and one day I had my own show in which my work was described as "daring, vivid, on the verge of surreal." A lily pad drawing was described by one reviewer as being plump and dewy, shimmer-ing, "exuding innocent sensuality."

Mom didn't like my paintings. She said they were too sugges-tive: the succulent green of rockfoil and stonecrop, the floppy petals of a spiderwort, all those half-opened buds. "They're too wet-looking," she said, too plump. "Like they're ready to explode."

"Do you mean sexual?" I teased, but she corrected me.

"I mean like they're alive."

Mom would have liked my required graphic design course in which there were straight lines to draw and cut, where there was perpendicularity. We studied color and contrast, layout methods. I found this study too restrictive, too confined, and when I arrived home each day I felt the need to bring out my canvas and go wild with the brush. I wasn't doing well in class, and the professor knew it. But if I could just swing a C I'd be happy and then go back to my painting.

Paula was another freshman in my class, and she also wanted to swing a C. But Paula was a graphic design *major* and wasn't doing well—and not because she found it artisically restrictive, but because it restricted her from partying.

Paula and I didn't have much in common except for the fact that we both were from Maine. She was a sports junkie and bar-hopper, while I preferred movies and going home at night. But hanging out with her was exciting; fun seemed to follow her around. Or maybe I'd just been neglecting to look for fun on my own.

Paula had many boyfriends, a different one every week, it seemed. She often took them back to her dorm and had sex, and each time told me she was in love. The sad thing to me was that it really seemed she was in love, and none of them ever stuck around for very long.

She tried to hook me up once with a sophomore name Derek. He shouted and belched and leered at each woman within his sight, even while sitting with me. After a few drinks he leaned close to me with his foul breath and told me he wanted to take me home.

After that night I realized just how different Paula and I were when it came to men, and I told her never to hook me up again.

———

Paula calls just as I've prepared my chisel and Unglue Magic mixture from the hardware store. Her voice has that tinge of rep-rimand that I remember well. *You were going to call me, remember?*

"Yes," I say, "after I'd gotten settled in."

She tells me how she's trapped in her house, how she doesn't see anybody. "It's so hard when you have children," she reminds me, and I back down to her, shrinking with the presence of my old friend's voice the way I always used to.

"Sure, I'll come over."

It's a thirty-minute drive to Paula's house in Easton, just outside Lewiston. I drive down the stretch of Land's End Drive, another Maine neighborhood where houses have replaced timber, where the road is straight, smooth, and bordered by nothing. The house plots are square, grid-like, the lawns perfectly manicured. I imagine the grass soon to be a bright and blinding green, without a blemish of rock or twig, without a single dandelion in the summer. Lime and fertilizer—some special concoction. Some poison.

The houses in this neighborhood are clustered into semicircles, deliberately facing each other as if to promote a front-door greeting, some social preservation. I picture the area from the air: my car cutting down the long, narrow line through the snap-in-place homes, then turning ninety degrees to the same congregation around the corner—like a giant Monopoly board.

I look for Paula's road within the neighborhood of tree names—ironic, as there are few trees: the Oak, the Chestnut, the Maple. Finally there is Walnut, a gathering of smaller, less expensive-looking models—all ranches, all identical except for the shade of pastel and the shape of black mailbox. Well-blended, homogenized.

I wonder how Paula and I will be—she with her homemaker life, me with my damaged, empty one. There were few similarities in the past; our gatherings were always accessorized by wine or dinner, something to take the edge off. We never got together without something there to distract us. I wonder if we will clash in our sober adulthood and have made sure to bring a bottle of wine.

When I pull up Paula's driveway I check the street number twice; this house does not seem like her, with its pinky tone and garish lawn ornaments. Standing amongst the daffodils by the front door is a life-size silhouette of a man cut from black metal or wood. The dark figure is vivid against the pale house, like the shadow of a killer creeping across the flower beds. It looks so bizarre to me, this faceless, two-dimensional man amongst the yellow and green of Paula's garden. It reminds me of my dream, of Montigue.

I get out of the car and head up the paved walkway, then step up and ring the doorbell. I feel silly, like a stranger standing on her front step with a bottle of wine and the wedge of smoked Gouda tight against my chest. A cardboard cutout of eggs and Easter bunnies stares out at me from the glassed-in outside door, all baby blue and sickly sweet pinks. Suddenly the door opens and there is Paula behind the glass, with her expansive, thin-lipped smile and her wide, overeager brown eyes.

"Hi," I say.

"Jenna!" Paula opens the door and we hug—a stiff, antici-pated hug. "How are you?" She looks heavier than the last time I saw her, or maybe it's just the outfit—the baggy canvas pants and thick embroidered sweatshirt. Her dishwater blonde hair is ragged-looking, trying to escape from her ponytail. I'm surprised she didn't get dressed up to impress me—to compete the way she used to, and I'm glad I wore jeans and a sweatshirt.

"I'm fine," I say. "How are you doing?"

"No, I mean, really." Her face bows down, her eyes still look-ing up at me. "Are you okay?"

Perhaps Paula wants to clear the air of Seth, get him out of the way so we can talk and be normal. Or so that she can have license to talk about men in general, which she inevitably will do.

"Really," I say. "I'm okay."

"Come in," she says.

I step up and into Paula's front entrance, see striped wallpaper walls decorated with religion and art: a sad-faced Jesus on a jewel-encrusted cross, a frosted gold, recessed Virgin Mary, like a glittery Jell-O mold. Down the hallway there is framed art: a metallic-looking world map, a Norman Rockwell, and right next to me, a large wood-framed print of a farmhouse by the sea. This one is an original, with vivid detail in the tufts of grass that sprout from white sand.

"This is nice," I say. "Egg tempura, isn't it?"

"God, I don't know," Paula chuckles. "And don't ask me who painted it, either. Some dude named C.K."

Back in art school Paula didn't pay much attention to paintings. She preferred colorful graphics, the bold letters of advertising, and chose the precision of layout work to the meditation of drawing and painting. When it came to paintings I'd seen her match them to couch fabric or a patterned rug; I'd even heard her comment on the blue sky in a landscape, how it must match the nearest stick of air freshener. The muted, teal green of the ocean in the farmhouse painting does indeed match the furniture I can see just around the corner in the living room. Alongside it are four silhouette portraits of each Smith family member, a green-marble background with black inset. Black and featureless, like the silhouette in her yard.

"That figurine in your yard," I say. "What is that?"

"You mean the Shadowman," Paula says, motioning me to follow her to the kitchen. "Everyone's got one."

I picture more of them in the neighborhood—perhaps I just didn't notice, imagine them scattered on the lawns like militiamen. Like the man with the red hat next to my own lawn. "I've got a live one in my yard," I joke, but Paula doesn't ask me what I'm talking about.

I follow her around the corner and through the living room, which reminds me of the waiting room at the doctor's office back in Massachusetts, with its dull mauves and teal blues, all that brass and glass. We enter a bright white kitchen, where little Josh sits at the table with crayons and a coloring book, and baby Erica sits covered in pea-green mush in her high chair, slapping her fat, dimply arms on an oatmeal-scattered tray.

Both of the children have small, marble-like eyes—more like Gerard's, and low, pouchy cheeks. Erica smiles at me, but Josh looks up in a guarded stare, his crayon stopping on the coloring book page. I have no idea what to say as I bend down to Erica.

"Well, hello there," I say, my voice coming out lighter, higher pitched than usual, sounding silly. Erica's face puckers, her mouth and nose caving in as if she just ate a pickle, her forehead and temples turning pink, then red at the edges. I wait for the cry but it doesn't come. Paula breathes out a sigh of relief. "I hope I didn't scare her," I say.

"She's fine."

Josh still is staring, his fat crayon stuck on the page. His eyes are pried open, watchful of me, as if I am some kind of intruder, some adult monster. Or maybe he's aware that I am uncomfortable around small humans like him.

"Hello, Josh," I try.

"My sister only likes Daddy," he says and slides off his chair, picking up his book and crayons and carrying them into the next room.

"That's not a nice thing to say," Paula calls after him, but she is apathetic in her tone; she lets it go. "Kids are difficult sometimes."

She doesn't seem like the same Paula from college: Paula the Party Animal, the one always wilder than me. But she is the same person—here with children, a full house, the delicate cross like Mom's around her neck.

There are no religious pictures in the kitchen, only four fruit prints that hang in a square arrangement above the stove. White canisters stand in rank along the fake white marble countertop, and matching creamer, sugar, and salt-and-pepper shakers gather beneath the cupboards. I imagine matching white handles on the silverware within the white drawers, and white Rubbermaid racks holding alphabetized goods behind the white cabinets.

White.

There is some color in here, though. A glass stands on the windowsill holding bright, open flowers—a marigold, two tiger lilies. It's early for these; I walk over and inspect them more closely, see no water in the glass. They are indoor flowers—fake plants, like Mom's. Until I was this close, I couldn't tell the difference.

"We gonna open the wine?" Paula asks.

"Sure."

I wasn't even sure if wine would be a good idea; so much has changed since our college days, our late-night talks over cheap white and red. I hand Paula the bottle and she opens it. I unwrap the cheese and slice off delicate bites of it, like I used to do when we first discovered such glamorous food.

"So," Paula says, "you were saying something about a man in your yard."

She was listening after all. Why didn't she at least respond when I first said it, and put me on hold for a minute? I wonder. But that's just like Paula, to assume others will wait for her. Something that hasn't changed. "Yes," I say, "there's this guy I saw at the edge of the yard. He was just standing there, staring. He seems harmless enough."

"How do you know he's harmless?" Paula chuckles, any chance to laugh at me. Her mouth is full of cheese, and she is refilling her glass already, so I gulp mine down and refill. I feel the tingle of alcohol in my head and neck.

"I guess I don't."

"How many times have you seen him?"

"Just once." I should probably downplay it; Paula will go on and on this way if I don't change the subject soon. "Like I said, it's probably nothing."

"Is he good-looking?"

"Oh, please."

"Oh, please yourself," she snaps.

"So," I say, deciding to change the subject, "you pretty much know how my life's been over the past few months. What have you been up to?"

"I might be pregnant," Paula says.

I think of the same words coming from her mouth years ago. "You're kidding," I say.

And I remember what followed—how she decided to go through with it, how she couldn't see it any other way. But then when she finally got married and had the baby, she seemed to change. It was like she succumbed to something mysterious, something I couldn't put my finger on. I never told Paula I was pregnant. By the time I thought about telling her it was too late and there no longer was any need to tell.

"Hey," Paula says. "Don't get too excited for me or anything."

"No, that's great," I say. "Congratulations." I want to be happy for her. I want to believe she's happy. But there's something weary behind her eyes; these babies that make her so happy are wearing her out. But then I could have ended up like this too—if my own baby was alive now and seven years old.

"I'm not positive," she says. "I need to take a test. But I missed my period two weeks ago, so I'm pretty sure."

"You'll have to let me know," I say and point to the wine glass in her hand. "But should you be drinking that?"

Paula lifts her glass in a salute. "Hey, like I said—there's no proof yet."

I watch Paula drink, watch as her eyes move to the window in thoughtfulness—hope, despair, whatever. What is behind those eyes? My brain floods with images—an egg, a seed growing inside, a tiny mouth and fingers forming, a twisted chord. Peachy skin and tiny, wrinkled eyes, crocheted booties and blankets, white cotton balls, white sheets. A bright light overhead.

Blood.

And suddenly I want to escape and go back to the house without babies where I can be close to Aunt Adeline—someone like me, who never had any.

twenty-two

The floor in my old bedroom is littered with newspaper flooring and rags, and the acidic smell of wallpaper remover permeates what little air there is, making the room seem smaller somehow. I feel claustrophobic, the way I sometimes felt as a child in this room, when I was sad or lonely or confused, or whenever my stomach got that tight, twisting feeling. I would lie on the small twin bed and stare up at the ceiling, thinking of how the room also had been Mom's—how Mom had awaken to the same pine ceiling with the knots. For a few minutes, I would actually feel close to her.

I open the shade and window, and the bright April Fool's sun pours onto the wood floor. As I look outside I see the flicker of a shadow just beyond the tall hedge of budding lilacs and crabapples. There is a speckle of red, the flash of pale roundness—a face perhaps. It may be the strange little man in the yard, either him and his bright red blob of a cap, or the cardinal I hear each morning but never see. When I look out the window to the front yard, nothing is there.

Under the thick skin of dust, the wallpaper is a brighter peach than I originally thought—an apricot, almost. The green beneath it is crustier, almost breakable, but with my chisel and Unglue Magic it peels off more easily. Still, I am careful, tearing from the bottom corner up.

It's coming off in strips and scraps. The pieces are sticky from the twenty-year-old glue, damp from the humidity that has seeped in between the bubbles and cracks. There are those odd square pieces of white beneath the green paper; I pry the chisel beneath one and pull at its corner. It comes right out—I must have torn it, but when I pull back the green and peach I see there is no more to this tiny white slip of paper. This paper was torn before it was put on the wall.

I look closely, see how the paper is bluish at the edges, and with pale striations—perhaps ruled lines that have faded, blended with the white. Notebook paper, college ruled, with blurred ink that seeps through to both sides; it's difficult to see on which side the ink is written. The letters are a smear of black ink, washed to a blur. But cursive letters, I can tell, seeing the curve of an S, a U, an M.

summer, it says.

I peel another piece of peach and the green stuck to it. There are more of these white pieces, the corners here and there, behind where the top layer is lumpy next to the warped seams. The wallpaper is coming off more easily now; the top layer is softening, loosening, and the green seems to come with it. One piece tears as I pull, leaving hair-like tendons at the edges, but I manage to not destroy the next one. A white sheet dangles from the wallpaper in my hand, begging me to remove it.

The hint of blue lines across the page are more evident on this one: lined paper, for sure, perhaps stationery. The writing is wet and bloated, fat cursive, but it is clearer than the last. I hold it up to the light.

miss you

A note to someone, a letter of some sort. I search for more words, find two pieces that seem to belong together, each with a brighter, bluer pen than the last—two pieces with saw-blade edges like teeth, cut to match. They do go together—they do, because the letters are large and frantic and line up at the same angle, dragging the word parallel to a straight edge of page.

Dear Renee

My heart stops and sinks into my belly. Heat rushes to my forehead as I lean close to the floor to look at the words.

Dear Renee

This could be Aunt Adeline's cursive, which I used to inspect on old notes, years after she died—the Christmas cards, the postcard from Hawaii. I always found her handwriting on them to be ragged, erratic, like this. If I were to look at those same notes now—knowing suicide would be her fate, I would examine them more closely. I would scrutinize the curve of each letter—the sweep of the "y," the hard, frustrated crossing of the "t"— searching for some key to Adeline's pain.

She may have written letters to Mom, then regretted it. I wonder why they ended up here, under the wallpaper she put up just weeks before she died. Is this how her madness manifested itself? Is this another one of those things she left behind for all of us to see?

Or perhaps not all of us. Perhaps in her secret insanity she bought the green wallpaper just to leave these notes, knowing Mom would live here one day and tear it down.

There are many other white pieces to pull off—some in tiny shreds, some two-ply that I may not be able to pull apart without tearing. Many of the pieces I manage to pull off are so blurred with writing that I cannot read them. They might not be illegible if they weren't so wet; perhaps if they were dry I would not see clear through them. I will try drying the pieces I've removed, lay them out in the afternoon sun of the floor. Then maybe later I'll be able to read them, all of them, piece them together like a puzzle.

If Seth were here he'd say these scraps were nothing but random pieces of paper. Old letters, yes; old notes, perhaps—but random notes merely here to fill cracks or to smooth out the plaster beneath. Maybe they're Adeline's, he would add, so as not to destroy all of my theories. Then he would smile and comment on my vivid imagination and how desperate I am for family history, for some kind of connection.

———

I drive down to the arts and crafts store for more tools, eye the paints and chalks and pencils instead, the wonderful blank papers and canvases. These creative tools make me hungry to do my art again, but I know I'm not ready. I'm like someone on a diet eyeing the bakery goods, knowing it would be silly to buy them; the paints would go unused, dry up in the hallway closet. Or if I did use them, the paper would be dribbled upon, spilled upon—then perhaps stabbed. The paints would be thrown across the room. How I envy the other artists who are in here now, thriving on their ingredients, knowing they still can do it.

I imagine myself dressed in a smock before a deep-angled easle, standing on the bare wood floor in the north light of the living room window, my hands conducting before ivory paper that is textured like a cobblestone street. The brush sweeps lightly, the paint flowing from my brush like a stream—absorbed into the weave where the water hovers, swept away where it moves. I see leaves and flowers, the perfect points of petals and stamen, the reflective edge of a summer wave.

Suddenly a young man is leaning over me, his breath like old coffee, his face pale and pimply, the hair dyed black. "Can I help you?" he asks.

"Just looking," I say, embarrassed, wondering how long I've been standing here, wanting to escape.

———

At the farmer's market I look at wildflower seed packets, notice they're using photographs on most of them now, not like the old Burpee collections, the antique ones I have framed. There also are large bags of wildflower seeds—a variety pack, with healthy dirt thrown in. On the front of the bag is a photograph of the perfect garden, a wildflower Eden. But this batch of dirt and seeds came from a bigger batch of dirt and seeds, most likely. There could be anything in here; could all these flowers really exist in this bag?

As I read the label I hear a voice and a name, coming from a young man standing a few feet behind me.

Hunter Jones, he says.

Behind a pyramid of metallic-red tomatoes stands an older woman with stormy-colored hair that is molded into a mound of waves. "He's one of our boys, yes," she says to a dark-haired man standing next to her, an Italian-sounding accent. "He's working at the farm today."

"Will he be coming in?" The man is wind-burned and sporty-looking. "I'm a friend of his. We worked together last summer."

"They'll be making a delivery today, yes."

As he walks away I approach the tomato stand. The woman is short and plump, with olive skin that is wrinkled but has a supple, mediterranean sheen. "Excuse me," I say. "Did he say Hunter Jones?"

"Yes." The woman smiles, her lips full and rubbery, her ivory-blue teeth glossy in the overhead fluorescent lighting. "He and the other boys bring us the produce."

"Does he work with you?" I feel silly asking questions about a person whom I haven't seen in twenty years, who might still live three doors down from me.

"He works at Stonybrook," the woman says, and I think of the sign at the end of the Jones' driveway. "In summer we get our supplies from there." She blinks her long black lashes. "Are you his friend?"

"Oh, he wouldn't remember me."

"Do you want me to give him a message for you?"

"Well..." Silly of me, I think, to leave a message here instead of knocking on his door or looking him up in the phonebook. But perhaps I'd rather he come and find me. "Can you just tell him Jenna Morton says hello?"

"Jenna Morton," she repeats. She nods her head, her Aqua-net hair not stirring.

"I mean Jenna *McGarry*. I keep forgetting I changed it."

"Is it McGarry?"

"McGarry."

"Ah." The woman squints as she smiles. "It's difficult to lose your *real* name."

Real name, I think. I've heard maiden name, old name, family name. *Real* I don't hear too often. "Yes," I say, even though she's got it backwards, no fault of hers. Seth's *Morton* was fine when I married, but I decided I missed McGarry and changed it back. But it's too complicated to explain to strangers, so I won't go into it with this stranger now.

The woman sounds out the name. "JEN-NA MC-GAR-RY."

She may not remember it. "How about this," I say. "Just tell him that Jenna says hello—Jenna from Cape Wood."

"All right."

Jenna from Cape Wood. I like the way it sounds, without the surname—with just that touch of ambiguity. Like something out of a bygone era, with only my birthplace to distinguish me.

———

My last few weeks with Hunter were spent in the backyard woods at Aunt Adeline's digging up pieces of the past. It had become so fascinating to us that we decided it might be fun to bury things, too, so that we could come back one day and dig them up again.

We did bury things, starting with a small, smooth rock on which we have carved our initials and little smiley faces with Hunter's pocket knife to distinguish it from other rocks that might be underground. I picked out a special rock to bury, one with painted seagulls and a lobster which I'd bought at a restaurant gift shop with Aunt Adeline. We left marbles and dice, gumball-machine treasures, even rhinestones from my beading kit. The more items we buried, the more unique they became.

Some items we couldn't wait to dig up; we waited only a couple of weeks. But Hunter said they weren't really treasures if we did this. He suggested we leave them for months, maybe even longer—to not touch them and hope that someone else could come along and find them. Only Hunter and I would know where our treasures were buried. Someone would be sure to come across them one day while digging for things, of course.

"Years from now," he said, "when we're dead."

I hadn't thought of that. Death didn't seem likely for us, not ever. "My brother is dead," he suddenly added, and I felt electricity all over my body.

He told me his brother Angus had died in a swimming accident. Hunter never even knew him; it happened before he was born. But it didn't seem to matter that he didn't know his brother; he missed him still.

I had only lost caterpillars, I thought—things kept in a jar. Suddenly Hunter was different to me; he was like no one else. I wanted to know what it really was like—to lose someone through death.

———

In the dark, private computer room at the library, I think of the last day I saw Hunter, just two days before Aunt Adeline died. He'd given me a special rock to bury, engraved with both of our initials and wrapped in a soft, camel-colored suede bag with leather twine. It was Angus's, he'd said, with a tear in his eye. We placed the suede bag inside a small tin box, and beside it Hunter placed a picture of his brother. Angus was a willowy young man with dark hair and shadowy eyes, a haunting pale face. I wondered how Hunter could feel so much for someone he never knew. Maybe it was because they were brothers, or simply because Angus died such a horrible death.

As I type in the name ANGUS JONES, I can still see his face and the glint of metal as we shoveled dirt over the box.

July 18, 1972

CAPE WOOD—*One person is presumed dead after a swimming accident that occurred at approximately 9 P.M. on Saturday in
Casco Bay, near the Mackerel Pass jetty in Cape Wood. The victim,
Angus M. Jones, 19, of Rockport, Maryland, whose family was vacationing here in Maine, had presumably fallen into the waters in the
vicinity of the jetty, and while attempting to swim toward the nearby
docks was pulled out by a strong undertow. Several persons witnessed
his struggle, and one man was said to have jumped in after him.*

*An overnight search by the coast guard was performed, but to no
avail. No word has been given as to when the search will shift from
a rescue to recovery operation.*

July 25, 1972

CAPE WOOD—*The search continues for a man who witnesses
said was pulled out to sea on July 17, near the Mackerel Pass jetty in
Cape Wood.*

*Nineteen year-old Angus Jones of Rockport, Maryland, fell into
the waters of Casco Bay, and while attempting to swim toward shore
was pulled out by a strong undertow. After a one-week search by the
Coast Guard, his body still has not been recovered. "This is a terrible tragedy," said Kyle Jones, Angus's father. "Our lives will never be
the same."*

August 12, 1972

CAPE WOOD—*An ongoing search for a 19-year-old man has
resulted in defeat for the Maine Coast Guard.*

*Angus Jones, whose swimming efforts were overcome by the strong
undertow in Casco Bay, was presumed dead on the evening of July
17 earlier this summer. After a thorough search by the Coast Guard,
his body still has not been recovered.*

*Mr. Jones, of Rockport, Maryland, whose family owns the
Stonybrook Farm in Cape Wood, had been vacationing and working with his family. "Maine will never be the same for us," said*

Terese Jones, Angus's mother. "We're not sure if we can come back here again."

July 18, 1973
CAPE WOOD—On the one-year anniversary of a young man's death, a small town remembers.

Angus Jones was only nineteen when he was pulled out by the fierce undertow of Casco Bay on July 17, 1972, and like many victims taken by the sea, his body never was found. After an extensive search by the Maine Coast Guard, he was declared dead nearly one month later. A candlelight vigil was held at the foot of the jetty for each night the search continued.

Mr. Jones lived in Rockport, Maryland, but spent summers in Maine with his family, living and working on the Stonybrook Farm in Cape Wood. "He was a good worker," said Paul Hawthorne, who managed the farm and acted as caretaker for the house in the winter. "And a sweet boy. He will be missed."

Last night a gathering of people met at the foot of the jetty, carrying lanterns and candles. "We're waiting for Angus," said a friend.

The Jones family was not present at the vigil, as this is the first summer they have not returned to Maine. "We may not return," said Mrs. Jones just after her son's death last summer. "Not for a long time."

There is no obituary for Angus Jones, at least not here. There must have been one in his home town, or perhaps somewhere else. But when did they decide he was officially dead? Without a body, without a trace, how do they ever know?

part seven
awakening

{renee

twenty-three

Renee had picked out the rolls of wallpaper that lay in the corner of the room: a beige with blue flowers, with just that trickle of white. Adeline had wanted the green with yellow flowers— "a nice transition from the yellow in the hall"—but Renee had said no. There could be no green.

It was Renee's favorite as a child, the color of her bicycle and her favorite blanket. Two of her favorite dresses were a bright, tropical aqua, almost the color of the Florida ocean she'd seen in postcards—the one with the white sand beach where dolphins come to shore. But now she knows the ocean really isn't that color. The more she looks at it the more green it is, and just thinking about what colors could possibly lie beneath its surface make it even more so.

This reminds her of what Jenna has told her about colors and painting—about the base colors one uses when creating the human face. Skin is not peach or ivory; it is green and yellow and blue. Once these foundations are learned they are not forgotten; an artist will forever see these base colors when looking at skin.

The wallpaper in Jenna's old bedroom will be coming down, Bill tells her. He spoke to Jenna just the other day on the telephone, and says she will be peeling it, layer by layer, starting with a yellow-speckled peach that is on top. Renee wonders how many layers are under there, who bothered to peel and who simply painted over. Maybe Jenna will reach that layer of beige and blue that Renee put up herself, or perhaps even that green Adeline put up just before she died, that green paper Renee saw on the front porch still wrapped in plastic. Why did she put up that God-awful green?

But years before it had been beige and blue, which Renee had picked out herself. She still can see the rolls, see herself in the bedroom on the warm wood floor, curled up in flannel. Her arms wrapping her legs, knees bunched to her chest—difficult at this time, with her growing abdomen. She sees the paper unrolling as she tries to put it up—springing back into her face, unraveling, like her life.

She remembers waiting, waiting forever it seemed, curled up on this warm wooden floor, papering this room for a baby that was coming. Then things started to happen to her mind, her body. First it was the forgetting—forgetting everything, it seemed—then the body out of control. Shaking limbs and numb fingers, the dizziness. Doctors couldn't pinpoint the source of her illness. Stress, they said. Weakened immune system.

You're having a baby.

She did irrational things, they told her, like put shoes in the refrigerator and cheese in the bathroom closet. She cut the leaves off the plants—her own plants and Mother's plants, and, God for-bid, Adeline's experiments for school. After Jenna was born she walked down the street in her pajamas, leaving the baby behind. It was strange letting her body do such things, while her mind hov-ered outside somewhere, just on the outside of her skull. Strange for things to be fuzzy, always out of reach, whether doorknobs or flowers or her own baby. She was no longer intact or in control.

Then one day she looked for bones. Something told her they were there—some voice, some echo from the past. She wanted so much to believe it, to find evidence; she needed to know there was some truth to this memory.

She didn't dig far; she only skimmed the surface of the lawn, looking for irregularities, little white specks. Mother would stop her from wiggling her body through the grass and dirt, saying, "What are you doing?" and with a terrified look on her face that spoke something else to her, something Renee always will remember because she didn't have the strength to answer.

Have you lost your mind?

When Mother decided she would ask Adeline to come home from college and help, Renee begged her mother not to. She tried to convince her she could do it alone; she could get better. Anything. She could not bear to see Adeline, not after what had happened—after what she had taken from her.

jenna}

twenty-four

I first saw Seth in the back row of Physical Geology. He was all disheveled hair and papers, with deep, soulful eyes that moved curiously over the room. A quiet type, he seemed, with wrinkled clothes and untied laces, a restless manner. I managed to peek back at the clock—and at him—several times during the class, hoping he didn't notice. Our eyes met, but did not stay.

In my second semester we shared another class, Psych 102, and again he was quiet and mysterious, at the back of the class. He wriggled nervously in his seat until the third day of a class on memory, when the professor mentioned the word *genes*.

"Isn't there a theory," Seth spoke up in a low, earthy voice, "about inheriting memory?"

The entire class turned to look at him.

"Race Memory is a theory," Professor Mulkey replied, "that we will not be discussing within this curriculum." Seth nodded, scratched at the back of his head, shifted in his chair. For the remainder of class he twitched his shoulders and tapped his fingers on his desk.

I thought about him when I went home, about how agitated and confined he had seemed, how his dark eyebrows moved up and down in fierce curiosity. I wished the professor had given him some encouragement; it was disappointing to think that a student might just let a thought go—that a spark of interest could be extinguished so quickly and easily. Perhaps this was how people lost passion for things.

The next day in class, Seth spoke again. "Maybe it's true," he said after memory segued into genes again. "Maybe we can inherit a past generation's memory the way we inherit other genes."

Again the professor decided to drop the subject, and Seth didn't pursue it. He ran his fingers vigorously through his thick, dark hair, as if releasing an energy, a frustration of some sort. And for such a little thing, I thought. How odd; how passionate. I wondered if he noticed me turning around, bouncing my goofy eyes back to the clock, to his territory. When the bell rang, he stopped me outside the door.

"What do you think, Jenna?"

As we stood in the classroom doorway, I admired his dark hair and deep-pool eyes, the shoulders and back of an athlete. There was an awkwardness about him that was also attractive—the way his tall body hunched and his large hands waved about, expressing as he spoke. He motioned his head toward the stairs, requesting me to walk with him, and I didn't refuse.

His stride was slow and rhythmic, rocking slightly—his body angled forward and toward me as he spoke, ignoring the outside world, gracefully avoiding other students who whizzed past and parted around him. I was entranced by the rhythm of his words and his walk, and as I spoke to him I detected a flirtatious curve to my own voice, even sense my eyebrows lift in a teasing manner. It felt strange, like it wasn't my voice and face reacting to him. I was flirting seriously for the first time, and when he smiled back and stared down at me with his chocolate-brown eyes, I knew I couldn't stop. Suddenly I was electrified, terrified, realizing that I would one day sleep with this man.

I had never been with anyone—only two kisses: David Marcus, in tenth grade, and Ben Freidkin in eleventh. I didn't recall much sensation from either, only a sense of achievement, a romantic success. The feeling I had now was euphoric. And it was mutual, I could tell—by our voices, our eyes, and in our disguising metaphors, brought forth in our hallway discussion about human genes.

These were seductive words.

His room was dark and earthy, a secluded attic above an elderly couple's garage, miles from the dormitories, far more private than my bedroom at home in Westbridge. It was here that I smelled his pine incense and sipped a rich, dry burgundy that was like velvet to my lips. And then, by his deep eyes and massive hands, I was seduced.

———

Wherever Seth and I went, he would teach me about geology—about the earth and where all things came from, whether it was the orange cliffs in Vermont where we camped, or the tall granite buildings of Boston. He helped me to understand the origins of things—all things, so that even the most pre-fabricated seemed extraordinary. I knew that Seth would soon be teaching others, too. I just hoped that when he did, he would continue to teach me.

The more I saw of Seth, the less I saw of Paula. I felt bad about it, and offered many times for the three of us to go out together. We did manage one session at the comedy club, complete with beer and nachos and many laughs, but I got the feeling that Paula was bored, hoping for a wilder and crazier time.

She had a new boyfriend named Gerard, an accountant from Lewiston, Maine. A month was a long time for Paula to be dating someone, considering most of her boyfriends had come and gone like spring daffodils. But I couldn't help seeing him as a sleazy man. Paula even admitted to me that Gerard was not a man full of humor or passion, nor was he blessed with any particular beauty or charm. When I asked if she loved him she simply told me he'd make a good father, that he was sure to produce sperm. "I know because he's had kids before," she said, as if talking about renting a U-Haul, "with his first wife." This was all strange to me, because having a child had always been the last thing on Paula's mind.

Then she told me she was pregnant. She had known for a month, so I wondered if the earlier comments she made about Gerard and sperm were to give herself control over the whole situation. Perhaps she needed to desire something because she didn't have a choice. They would be getting married, she added, so I didn't bother to ask her the *love* question again.

I was scared for Paula because Gerard seemed to me to be nothing more than a male chauvinist couch potato with a bachelor's degree. He was a master at calculus, but would never hold a spatula or take a kitchen sponge in his hand. His idea of a turn-on, according to Paula, was the local Naked Jamboree. I didn't know him very well, though. The closest I'd gotten to him was one evening I visited them, and on his way back to the refrigerator he burped beer and enchiladas in my face. Be careful of what you want, I thought at that moment.

In April Paula married Gerard and quit school, then moved back to Maine, and suddenly her wild and promiscuous college days were over. Perhaps this would be good for her; perhaps it was inevitable and she had no choice. I didn't know what to think.

I did admire the way she'd been able to transform overnight, an instant mother-to-be. Or maybe I was just trying to convince myself there was something well and good about this because my own period was three days late.

twenty-five

I'll always remember that first time I spoke to Seth, in the door-way of Psych 102, down the hallway past the blur of students and teachers. He told me that day how one needed to be open to new theories, to be more open-minded. "People are too scientific," he said, "always trying to tag things, to pinpoint origins." But soon after this Seth became that kind of person; he returned to his geology studies and transformed into Seth the Scientist, a man who needed to classify, to justify. And all the while I poked fun at his search for truth, at his need to find layers beneath the layers.

If only he could see me now.

In my half-green, half-peach bedroom, small white papers are scattered on the floor. The pieces are brutally wrinkled and brit-tle, and seem to have been folded or crushed at one point. There are sharp darts, and creases that are worn and fuzzy. Others have smooth surfaces but are crisp and curled, like the bill I once found in the rain and dried on a sun-soaked windowsill. The ten dollars I was able to save, an unexpected treasure. I hope to find something, make some sense out of these notes. They don't belong here and need to come up, like some shipwreck.

I can read only some of the words on these papers: words like *want* and *see*, then the longer words that trail off into smudged ink and are indistinguishable. A few of the words are paired to make a phrase; but there are only the obvious, general ones like *come home* and *work for*, words anyone could have written to Mom.

But as I peel and peel, and the layers of wallpaper come down, the pieces become bigger. More words, more phrases, part of a sentence even.

> *you another letter*
> *opposite—I want to make*
> *wanted to respond*

As I peel back a thick chunk of wall paper, a C-shaped piece of white curls back against my hand—a complete square of paper with a single bite missing. I am careful as I pull it off, and as I do, see the corner of another. I slide my chisel beneath the papers and gently pull back, expose another, then another almost-full page. I lift them off the wall, one by one, the second one tearing into pieces. I am careful as I lay a portion of paper on the floor next to another, onto my tarp. I see an earlier piece I pulled off— the half-moon of words. It fits together, two fragmented paragraphs, with chunks missing here and there.

> *I suppose you've had a busy week and haven't been able to write. But I couldn't wait so I sent you...wasn't trying to push you away...things too fast and ruin...maybe you wanted to respond but I forgot to include the address on my last letter. I've included it again, just in case I...The crew I'm working with...guy named Pete...Portsmouth and will be going to college...than that there's not much to do...Warm beer is good when you're looking at dirt and potatoes all day! I can't wait to come back and see the coast...miss you...our night...wish I could call...to know that everything's okay, that you're not upset...*

A large section of the page is missing, but just above the address *Hillwilde Farm, Carbur, ME* is a single letter written as a signature, a big cursive letter.

—*M*

My stomach swirls, a dizzy, twisted feeling. Is this Montigue?

Supposedly she never saw him again. But was there some other man with whom Mom had a relationship? She never had another, according to Dad. There could not have been time between Montigue and Dad.

It doesn't make sense, just like it doesn't make sense for letters to be buried beneath the wallpaper. The deep green wallpaper that Aunt Adeline put up just weeks before she died.

I wonder if Mom left these behind when we moved out and into the apartment at the other end of town—if she hid them and forgot about them, and Aunt Adeline found them later. But why put them here? Why would Aunt Adeline do such a thing?

I had thought Adeline was the strong one, the sane one. The one who gave everything up to help Mom, to take care of me. How does one act when on the verge of suicide? It must be a lonely time, an isolated world.

I look down to the other half-complete pages I've pulled off the wall. They are wet and blurred with the same curve of writing. One of them is mostly illegible; I can make out only a few phrases—and again, the letter M at the bottom.

July 14
Renee,
Here it is, only Monday and I'm writing again. Every day I feel like...only assume...letters, and maybe...want to make sure you're not...for us to still be together. I want to take it slow, that's all...be a while before anyone can know...happened between us shouldn't...hope you're reading this...wrong with the mail because I

haven't heard from you...I won't talk about potatoes this time. If you
get a chance...Just a few words will do.
—M

July 20
Dear Renee,
I'm starting to get worried. It's been ten days and I haven't heard
from...haven't received my letters...asked Mr. Murphy...called your
house around 7 o'clock and someone picked up...sounded like
Adeline, so I hung up...phone was busy...know I'm not supposed to
call there...don't understand
—M

Could this be the man who never came back? And who
deserted whom? Maybe Mom was the one to leave him without
answers or explanations. Maybe he still floats around Northern
Maine, wondering what happened to his teenaged love.

If this is true, I should be furious with Mom. But instead I
want to tell her, to give her back something she lost, something
Aunt Adeline found in her final days and plastered onto the wall.
Perhaps, in a rush of delirium, this was Aunt Adeline's last connection with her loved ones, with the sister she fought with just
two days before she died. But would Mom even want to know?

Maybe I want to tell Mom just for myself—to hear the words
from her mouth, to find out once and for all if my blood father
was *not* just a one-time deal, that he was someone who really cared
about her. Who might have cared for me if given the knowledge.

Maybe I want to make Mom confess to another lie.

Or perhaps it's true that Mom barely knew him, and
Montigue simply wanted more; he wrote and wrote and tried to
tell her. But in these letters he seemed to expect a response; at
some point, Mom must have been in contact with him.

We were together only once, she told me. What did she really
mean?

I walk across the hall and into my bedroom, pick up the phone without contemplating or rehearsing; it will only make me worse. It is only two rings before Elisabeth picks up. She sounds excited to hear from me. "Can I come up this weekend?" she squeals.

My stomach churns as I wonder what I'll say to Mom once she gets on the phone. "Did you ask Mom?"

"She said it would be okay."

"Really?" My response to Elisabeth is only half-attentive; my mind is somewhere else. "That's great."

"She said Dad would take me."

I'm paying attention again. Of course Dad will take her, I think. Of course Mom won't make it up to Maine. "This weekend is fine with me," I say, and take a breath. "Is Mom there now?"

"She's out," Elisabeth says, and I'm relieved. I want to hang up quickly, before Mom can get home. I think of all the other times I've confronted her about things, how this time it's different. I don't know how to do this at all.

twenty-six

Eleven to twelve weeks, the doctor told me, and I felt sick hearing the words. I knew Dr. Bashi could tell I wasn't happy by the way she was explaining—with that apprehensive half-smile on her face—how some women did get pregnant on the pill. She must have thought I was an idiot after I'd admitted I hadn't taken pills for several days in a row. She must also have found me selfish for not being happy about such a wonderful thing. "Your husband won't be happy?" she asked.

"Boyfriend."

"Your boyfriend won't be happy?"

I told her I was a sophomore at Northeast University, hoping it would be enough to make her understand. Dr. Bashi didn't answer; she only nodded.

Please say something, I thought. Suggest something. *What,* I didn't know. I just wanted some magic right now, to make time reverse itself, to make this baby go away. But there was no magic, so instead I took a breath of stale, doctor's office air and endured, trying to be like everyone else, all those who *could* be happy about such a thing.

There were many who would have loved to be in my place—who had tried for years and years to fight nature with technology just to have a child, and failed. What would they think of me? I thought of how wonderful Seth was, how pleased I should be about his genes blending with my own, but my thoughts quickly shifted to the things I would never experience, how I would be transformed into a mother overnight.

Into Mom.

I took another breath and endured, and snaked my thoughts through the maze of obstacles to come, all the way to the end of the puzzle. I could get through this, I thought. I could make this wonderful. *I could do this.*

When I told Seth I was pregnant, his face lit up. *A father,* he must have been thinking, or perhaps he was looking at me in a new light. I felt static, as if I wasn't a person but just a photograph before him. I wondered about my body—was it strong enough?—and then my mind—were my doubts anything to be afraid of? Because this was the thing Mom had feared most; it was the thing Mom had let happen with a simple surrender to lust or mere curiosity, or perhaps something else beyond explanation.

Mom's first reaction to the news seemed to be fear—not fear for me but for the family. "What am I supposed to tell people?" she said, slapping her hand down on the dining room table.

"What did you tell people when *you* got pregnant?" I quickly replied.

"Don't start—" Mom didn't finish her reply. Perhaps it was easier not to talk about it at all.

"I'm sorry," I said, wondering how all of this had happened. How did I suddenly end up a mother-to-be?

"Just know—" Mom said, a warning in her voice, "A baby will change your life." What was she really telling me to do?

I did love children—their sweet and innocent minds that were not yet invaded by adult rules and moralizing, by politics or religion. Ask a child about God, I once told Seth, and he wouldn't ponder *which* or *how* or *why;* he only wanted to know if there was one. If only I, too, could have thought this way—

without doubt, with my imagination intact. But instead I thought of how I lacked that desire for a child and that stable, permanent feeling I was supposed to have with my true love—Seth. Having a child would make that love more permanent, it would mean complete devotion, it would be dividing myself in two. As far as I was concerned, there wasn't enough of Jenna McGarry to do that.

And there was something else. I knew this child would perhaps mirror its parent, and I didn't want a mirror of me. I'd seen too many people attempting to clone themselves—a better prototype, a fresh model. I'd seen those who'd had children to carry on a name. What's in a name? I wondered. I couldn't afford to care about names, about carrying on the blood. I didn't have a choice, not with that family fork-in-the-road, the McGarry bloodline that strayed at *Jenna*—those mysterious genes of Bio-Dad. Unlike Paula's line, where blood and undeviating names were crucial. Names and titles and carrying-things-on; they were like jewelry to her, a family hope chest. Carry on, carry on the DNA.

Of course Seth didn't know all these things going on in my head. I didn't have the heart to tell him. And then suddenly I was getting married.

I wasn't sure how it happened; Seth and I hardly discussed marriage, but it simply was to be. My first feeling about this was relief—that Seth didn't have to think twice about it, that it was not just out of responsibility but out of love. But then I really thought about it: I was getting married, having a baby. Life was about to change.

Mom unexpectedly changed her opinion about the baby and suddenly was happy for me. She kept saying over and over that Seth and I would be married and would soon have a child; we would be a family, a complete picture, just like her and Dad. She sparkled when she said this, as if some light of realization had gone off in her brain. Funny, this sudden turnaround by Mom, who had treated me so badly just weeks before. She'd never liked Seth and me together so much until he planted this seed in me, and we'd decided to stay together forever.

Once again Montigue has crept into my dreams, as the figure in the doorway, the faceless man who came back to see Mom. Only this time the strange sky outside had changed, shifted its shadows, and the man's face emerged into the light. The face I finally saw was a familiar one, though—eyes dark and deep, cheekbones sharp, a gentle mouth. In my dream, Montigue was Seth.

One wall remains to be peeled, and it is coming down slowly. I have been careful to not ruin what I might find in the process, but I have yet to discover anything on this wall. This one seems to be the product of simple wallpapering; there is no evidence of a mental unbalance.

I have arranged all the irregular pieces of letters in one corner of the bedroom, pieces I'd hoped to fit together like a puzzle, a mosaic. But they don't fit together as easily as I thought they would; too many of them are sharp and curled, and they crumble like crisp phyllo dough when I touch them. Others have angry lacerations, edges impossible to fit. So the words will have to wait for the obvious match, or to end up in my pile of scraps and edges.

Then there are pieces that were too wet and blurry, still too illegible to read. Others, which I can read, are only half a word or part of a letter, or are commonly spoken words like *need* and *love*, which, by themselves, don't tell me anything.

I come to the final corner of the wall, the last section of green in the room, and see a corner of white. Pulling off the remainder of wallpaper, I see an almost complete sheet of paper beneath, and remove it carefully.

I wonder why this one lies alone on the wall. Did Aunt Adeline change her mind at the last minute and decide to include it? I hold it into the light of the window.

July 21

Renee,

just wrote to you yesterday but I needed to…called and your sister Adeline answered…difficult to call, and when I do it's never you that answers so I hang up…I need to know why you haven't written back. Maybe you really just don't want to talk to…important that we…need to tell you in person. I'll be back on Friday, and I'll call you then.

I love you, Renee

—M

Mom must not have received these letters, at least not in due time. Perhaps she never ended up seeing them at all. Is it possible that Mom never knew about this love? I would like to show her, to give them back to her. But will this only encourage more bitterness toward Aunt Adeline for something else she did wrong?

Stuck to the back of the final wallpaper section I see a smaller, perfectly rectangular piece of white. It is thick when I pull it off, like cardboard, and it does not tear. Beneath a film of paper residue on the piece I can see letters—printed in blue—part of something, another half-sentence, half-word perhaps; it's difficult to tell. I peel at the paper residue and reveal the printed word on the untorn card: *Kodak* in blue, diagonally across.

A photograph.

As I peel more I see the letters scribbled across the printed Kodak, in the darker blue of a pen, in the familiar handwriting.

—Your M

I hold my breath as I turn the picture over, see a black-and-white studio-style portrait behind speckles of wallpaper. I chip away at the surface with my fingernail, tenderly, patiently, until finally I see the face. It is a young man with dark hair and brows, pale eyes against vivid lashes, features strong, his face thin-looking and shadowy, almost gaunt. The studio light is bright on his forehead, and he smiles a tentative smile, his eyes staring up and to the left of the camera, perhaps looking away when he wasn't supposed to.

But even looking away, the eyes speak to the camera, penetrating dimension and time, speaking to me. There is a sensation in me I've only read about, only heard others proclaim as a cliché. *I can feel it in my bones.*

The air in the room suddenly feels cold and thick, like a fog that has crept up the into the house, through the tiniest crevices in the structure. The face in the photo knows I have freed him from this giant scrapbook of a wall; his presence is as vivid as the wood and paper and plaster of this room. I feel connected to this face—as a savior, as blood.

Is this my father?

The thought dissipates as I remember what Mom told me about Montigue—about never knowing me, about one-night stands. The Montigue she told me about wouldn't have given her photos or sent letters. It can't be true.

But there is something here, a flicker of familiarity, of warmth in my heart. Montigue is here in the room with me.

I have always believed Mom when she said he never knew about me. I believe it even more now, as it feels like we are meeting for the very first time.

twenty-seven

Elisabeth has finally made it up to Cape Wood, just for the day. While Dad does his once-a-year visit to L.L. Bean's four-hour expo of lectures and demos and gadgetry, he will be leaving her here with me. Of course Mom didn't make it for the trip up.

When they arrive I give them a quick tour of the house. Elisabeth seems only mildly interested in its history; her eyes bounce about the rooms and out the windows as I point out details on walls and doorways. But Dad is fascinated by the nostalgia of it all as he turns each corner. The colors and patterns are familiar, he says, and the kitchen is exactly the same as it was, except for the linoleum and appliances. "I remember this," he says, opening a tiny door to a cubbyhole closet at the top of the stairs. "You used to put your dolls in here."

"You did?" Elisabeth perks up, peeking into the hole.

"Yes," I say, imagining my ragged Raggedy Ann doll tucked within Mom's blankets and towels.

"Looks like you've been working hard," Dad says, and I turn to see him poking at the half-opened door to the right.

The letters, I think. It was the one room I hadn't bothered to clean before they arrived. I had intended to hide the evidence. But that was before I got carried away with tidying the rest of the house, doing my last-minute supermarket run. They'd arrived just as I was putting the groceries away.

I think of how I can distract from the letters, not let them see. I'd rather Mom know about them before Dad so she doesn't have to hear about them secondhand.

As we enter the room, I see the scraps scattered across the wooden floor, the pile of larger pieces in the corner. The photograph is in there somewhere, sheltered beneath a layer or two. As Elisabeth moves toward the window, a corner flutters in her movement, and I see it: the tiny portrait, the young man with striking eyes. I need to conceal the pile quickly, to protect Mom.

But Dad sees it first. "What's all this stuff?" he asks.

"Oh, the papers—" I begin. I can't lie. "I found them under the wallpaper."

"Really," Dad says, interested. "What are they?"

I take a breath, feel a lump creep up from my stomach—fear about getting it wrong, about telling him before Mom. "I'm not sure." I squat down to the pile, make sure the photo is safely buried. I pick up a piece with the most illegible writing I can find. "Letters or something. I can barely see the words."

"Letters." He takes it from my hand, tilts it into the light of the window. "Hillwilde Farm," he reads, his voice rising in recognition. "I know that." He squints his eyes in thought. "What is that?" he asks himself out loud. My heart begins to flutter, as I wonder what else is on the piece of paper—if this is half of a letter, if *Renee* is on it anywhere, clear and bold. Perhaps I should just go ahead and tell him; he'll know soon enough. The facts may satisfy him in a way he's never been, and complete the circle, the mystery. There may be things he's always wondered, sat up late at night in bed and contemplated. I've always wondered just what Dad knows, what he does or does not want to remember.

And how could this mystery affect Dad and me? Would it change our relationship? How would Dad feel if he knew I was pondering over this other father of mine?

"I'm not sure what Hillwilde is," I say, buying time. I see his eyes widen again, his face begins to settle. He is remembering.

"Oh my..." His words trail off, do not finish. *Oh my God*, it seems he was going to say. "What it is—" he continues, his voice reverting to a more light one that simply recognized something, as if he's trying to make it less than it is. "It's a potato farm." He clears his throat. "Up north."

I wait for more. "Yeah?"

"I remember the name." Dad wants to say more, I think. He seems stunned, off somewhere else. "That's all." He looks away to Elisabeth, who is picking at a scrap of paper that dangles from the wall. He hesitates, then motions to the pile in the corner. "What else is there?"

There are so many things I want to show him, so many questions I want to ask. But I'm afraid of bringing out pain in him, afraid of betraying Mom. "Not much," I lie. "Most of it's all just paper." He moves toward the pile, and I wonder what he can see. "Or blobs of ink. I'll be sure to let you know if I find anything as I keep going."

He turns to me, his gaze serious. "And your mother."

"Oh, yes." I'm relieved when he moves away from the corner, over to the window.

"Look at the sky," he says, and I look out and see steel gray clouds at one edge of the horizon. "I think there's a storm coming."

———

After Dad leaves I take Elisabeth to the town park, a ten-acre plot of bike riding paths amongst gardens in progress, all short dips and turns for bicycles. At its end is Carbur's Pizza, where we order big fat calzones and take a seat in a booth of red vinyl.

It's been a while since Elisabeth and I have done anything together outside of the house, months since sharing a public place. I've forgotten how quickly she's grown, that soon she will no longer be a child. It takes the turning heads of boys, even some men, for me to realize this.

She's dressed plainly, a loose sweatshirt and jeans, and her hair—while not secured in its usual ponytail—is unkempt, sporty and youthful. There's no makeup, perhaps a smidgen of her fruity lip gloss. Still, there is a freshness, a vitality just on the verge of sexy that shows through. I've seen boys notice her before, but today is different, as she seems to notice back. Her eyes seem bright and hungry, sometimes following them down the aisle or out the door. Her tiny mouth is turned up at the corners, dying to smile, perhaps hoping to get noticed.

"Elisabeth," I say, and give her what feels like a devilish smile, "how's your boyfriend?"

"Boyfriend?" She clicks her mouth in disapproval at me, gives a quick sigh. "We were never *going out*." I feel her foot give me a swift kick under the table. "You know Mom would never let me."

"You know what I mean," I say. "Brian…is that his name?"

Elisabeth is distracted as a busboy passes down the aisle next to us. As he walks by, his head whips around quickly, this time looking at me. "He wants you," she says, proud of her humor.

"Doubtful," I say. "He only saw the back of my head and had to check out the front."

Elisabeth giggles. "Don't you hate when they do that?"

When they do that. Something one of my old female coworkers might say, something Paula would say. Odd to hear it coming from my little sister. Does she experience such a thing often enough to joke about it?

"So anyway—Brian," I say, and lean into the table to let her know I'll welcome any tidbit she wants to give me. Although inside I'm dreading it; there's something very uncomfortable about her talking about boys.

"Oh, he's old news," she says, waving her hand in the air. "He was a jerk." She sips from her soda, her eyes on the table, a saddened look. She stops sipping and goes right back into joking mode. "But there is this guy named Tommy…" She raises her eyebrows as if proud, like she's telling me she won a prize. I don't say

anything; I'm still taking it in. She takes a large bite of her calzone, then proceeds to talk with her mouth full. "Are you gonna
tell me to be careful again?"

"No."

Of course I want to, but this time it doesn't feel like caution
for Elisabeth that I feel. There's something else, a tinge of jeal-
ousy, perhaps. And not because Seth is gone and I'm alone; this
time I'm going back ten, twelve years, wondering why I wasn't
more like her, why I didn't act on all impulses I may have felt. I
had always imagined there were no impulses to act on, that there
were never any boys who liked me; now I'm thinking there were
many opportunities.

"How are you doing now, Jenna?" Elisabeth suddenly asks,
her eyes more relaxed, sincere. "I've been wondering. I wonder if
you feel different...better...being up here, away from home."

"It is better." I want to be honest with her, but wonder what
I even feel. "It feels more calm now, and quiet. Unusually quiet,
like I can hear more and think more clearly."

She plays with a chunk of green pepper left on her plate, rolls
it around in her fingers. "So do you feel more—I mean, sadder?"

"No." I think of how strange it is that the solitude doesn't
make me sadder. "I almost feel...less? I don't know."

"You mean like it's not real?" she asks.

"It's real all right. I'm connected to this place. I remember this
place so well. It's like it was yesterday that I was here." Elisabeth
is listening, her eyes on me, not the boys, her lips parted, not
pursed and posed. "But at the same time I'm such a different person now, so—"

"So maybe," she interrupts, "only the *old* you is here."

I chuckle at her insight, the way she speaks like an adult.
"Maybe," I say. "Maybe I haven't connected the new me—I
should say, the new model, the burnt out, decrepit, terrorized
me, with this place. I guess you could say in that way it's not
real."

"Like you're hiding." Elisabeth says this with such non-chalance, as if unaware that she's just made a psychological assessment about my state of mind.

"Have you been reading Mom's textbooks?" I joke. "Maybe you should be a shrink."

She sips from her soda, gulps hard. "I never want to be like Mom. I love Mom, but—"

"I wasn't saying Mom is a shrink," I correct.

"Oh, but she is!" Elisabeth blurts. "Isn't she?" She slurps the bottom of her soda loudly, then tilts the glass and pours an ice cube into her mouth. "Hey, aren't you going to eat?" I look down and see that I've only taken bites of my calzone. I pick it up and begin to nibble at it again, but my stomach isn't liking it. "So, Jenna," she continues, "can I ask you something?" Of course *something* meaning something personal, I realize, and nod yes. "While you're up here...are you sure you're not looking for your father?"

I almost choke. "No," I say. "At least I don't plan on it. No." She doesn't say anything, seems to be waiting for more of an answer. "What gave you that idea? Did Mom say something?"

"No!" she gasps. "I just—" She hesitates, then tells me. "If I were you, I'd definitely want to find him."

"I can't say I've never thought of it," I say. "But I think of Mom, too, how she might feel. Or Dad."

"Yeah, Dad," Elisabeth says. "By the way, did you see him before he left for Bean's? He seemed all weirded out for some reason."

I thought she hadn't noticed.

———

After lunch we head out to Jetty Beach, over the pass to Mackerel Point. I show Elisabeth where Aunt Adeline's car went off the road and into the water, wonder how much she knows about Aunt Adeline's death, the suicide. I can't imagine that it would possibly intrigue her as much as it does me; Elisabeth never knew her aunt.

We take the road Mom and Dad used to take me down—a winding path of scrub pines and rose hip bushes, en route to the beach. At the end of it is Mack's Point boat yard, where dinghies and larger boats cluster within the cove amongst several docks that stretch into the water. Just parallel is the long rock jetty, the last place Mom took me to before we left Maine, I tell Elisabeth.

"Mom came *here?*" she asks.

I agree, it does seem odd now.

We walk along the pebbly beach and collect rocks and mussel shells. Elisabeth is fascinated by all the tiny dead crabs, their crusty, hollowed-out bodies scattered over the glistening sand. She picks them up as we walk along, puts them in her canvas tote bag. She seems taller than the last time I saw her, but of course it's only been a few weeks. Her arms and legs are long, a hint that she may have a few inches left to grow, may end up taller than me. The rest of her has also developed quite fast; her figure has a trim voluptuousness about it, round edges to a delicate frame. While she seems aware of this new womanly body, she does not possess that inhibited poise that others her age do, that I did. She appears completely conscious of herself, yet confident in her movement and composure. I watch as she takes off her sneakers and steps toward the water, where the tide is moving in.

"It must be freezing," I warn her.

"It is," she says, not flinching as the water seeps over her toes, her ankles. Her eyes are closed as a lump of seaweed moves across her foot. Slimy, I think; it would make me jump. She calmly looks down. "Look at this," she says.

She squats and picks up something, a bone of some sort. As I move closer I see what it is, a complete jaw, teeth intact.

"A shark," I say, recognizing the shape. "Seth probably would have known what kind."

Elisabeth is staring at me, as if knowing something before I do, as if seeing something in my face I don't recognize yet. And then I realize the power of his name, his memory, right here on this beach. Talking about him hasn't been too bad, especially not in the past few weeks, whether to strangers or loved ones. I have become adept at controlling my reactions, those instantaneous responses to any mention of him—something I had no choice but to get used to, or to at least make numb in my mind. I've become good at this self-medication; even while alone I've been able to restrain the most moving memories into static, emotionless images.

But not now.

Around me is this clean, breathable air, the living ocean, and the endless view of crystalline sand, with miles on which to walk and jump and delight in. And there is Elisabeth, the once tiny flower girl at my wedding, now a young woman in front of me, so vibrant and real. She still grows and lives while this beach and water and mortal world waits for her, and meanwhile Seth is gone—as dead as the limp, twisted mass of seaweed at her feet.

The sound of the tide rushes into my head, louder and louder until it's nothing but a blast of white noise. The ground beneath my feet melts away, first softening like quicksand, then just gone, and I cave into it.

Elisabeth grabs my arm as I fall, but she can't hold me. I hunch to the earth, my palms flat against the sand. The water moves up and over my hands, then my knees and shins, saturating my jeans. I know it is cold, so cold, but I cannot feel it, as if my extremities have become separate from the nucleus of my body. I am somewhere else, in a tiny hole or speck of glistening sand that I hover over.

"Jenna?" I hear Elisabeth say, her voice a quick breath of panic. "Jenna, are you okay?" She puts an arm around my back, tries to help me stand, but still I can't move. I feel unattached to my own body, although I can feel my lips and mouth, numb. Can I speak? I wonder. "It's okay," Elisabeth says. "We can stay right here for a second." She rubs her hand on my back, a circular motion. Slowly I begin to feel the cold of the water, the wind on my face. A rush of heat moves to my cheeks. My body, the world is coming back to me.

"I'm sorry," I say, out of breath.

"Sorry? Why are you sorry?" Elisabeth's voice is comforting, like a mother's. "Don't be sorry. I can't imagine what it's like to go through what you've gone through. I would never want to be you, Jenna."

twenty-eight

As life grew inside of me, I began to change. I became in touch with feelings I'd never had before, as if the seed growing inside had tapped into a new brain function somehow, or perhaps had blocked another function off. This newfound consciousness opened alternate doors, doors that should have been closed and sealed, and suddenly there were other men, other destinies, another life altogether. I felt confined, as if my nineteen-year-old life was over.

This seed inside me was permanent.

Not that Seth couldn't have been the permanent one. He was love, friendship, the carnal. He was the ideal husband-to-be. But he was not all those other men, those men I hadn't yet been with. I hated feeling this way, and wondered if I always would have these regrets—regrets I'd never had before. Was there really such a thing as getting something out of one's system?

Suddenly there was someone who liked me. Not one of those high school boys who dared to like me all those years before, but a professor—a dark, thick-lensed ancient history man called Professor Banes, who had an obsession for art and ancient artifacts. And for me.

Professor Banes caressed the air as he described a vase or bowl displayed on a slide, with long, almost dainty fingers that painted in the darkness. These fingers parted and closed so smoothly, like the time lapse of a waking flower, I thought, so naturally—like exhaling. He walked toward me in his beige khakis and suspenders, his fingers opening before my face, then turned away. It felt like teasing. Each time he looked back again our eyes met, and his gentle fingers closed and released, closed and released. I wondered if I was imagining it, and looked around the room at the other students who didn't seem to care.

After class Professor Banes and I spoke in academic language—about assignments, about formalities—but then one day he said something else, his black, Indian eyes digging into me.

"I would love to teach you more."

I shuddered at what I was thinking, felt a tingle through my collar bones and into my chest and stomach. And for a minute there was no Seth, only the flesh of this man before me. I imagined a strange lump in my belly—not my twelve-week-old fetus but something else growing next to it. This new lump rose and fell, trying to come out, trying to make it back up to my heart and head. But it fell again, down next to the baby, like another heart pumping, another baby growing.

A soul, sinking.

Nothing ever happened between Professor Banes and me, except for the realization that there were other men in the world, men who—like Seth—could want me, maybe even love me. I feared the word *permanence*, and the life growing in my abdomen now was nothing more than a seed. I was beginning to despise the seed growing next to my sinking soul: baby Jenna, baby Seth.

A baby that would not be.

———

I give a quick call to the house to make sure Dad and Elisabeth have made it home safely. It's Mom who answers, a soft and self-assuring *yes*, as if happy their trip is over and done with. She also seems happier than usual to speak with me, perhaps because I'm more than a hundred miles away. Because we're safe this way.

I think of the letters, so much to tell her, not sure where to start. Instead I tell her about my afternoon out with Elisabeth, our trip to the park and the beach.

"Elisabeth's worried about you," Mom says. "You had a little spell?" The compassion in her voice is a little overwhelming for me; I'm not used to it. Of course she's my mother, so it's natural that she'll be concerned. But for a moment I hope it is more than that.

"I'm okay, Mom," I say. "I just—" I try to think of how to describe what happened to me, and can't. "I guess it all came to me or something. Reality."

"Seth," she says, her voice sympathetic.

"Yes." This feels new, this discourse. There have been other conversations—about being alone, about missing him. There have been hugs of sympathy, many hugs. But until now all of it has about my getting better, my going back to life as usual. Never has there been any sanction of my pain, about letting me just feel it. Perhaps no one—especially Mom—thinks I am capable of breaking, and the idea that I've come close is troubling her. Maybe she's been there herself.

"What about your aunt?" Mom suddenly says, but more deliberately, her usual trained self. "Is that painful?" Still, odd for her to ask. I think about Aunt Adeline, how her passing seems more curious than painful.

"I think about her a lot," I say. "But it's been so long, I can hardly feel anything."

There is a pause on the end of the phone line. "Time heals," she finally says, but I'm not convinced she believes it herself.

———

The man with the red hat is standing behind the lilac bushes again. He's just outside the fence, a large pair of garden shears in his hand. He steps forward, moving beneath the apple tree on the outside corner of the lawn, and rocks his head back and forth a few times, then stops and turns to the side, away from me. He is like a statue among the trees, pale and blank and mellow-featured—a stiff figure in his plaid jacket and thick-leg pants, his red hat like a cardinal amongst the branches. I watch him until he steps back from the tree and into the road.

I step out the front door, see nothing, and sit down on the front porch step. I look across the street and up and down the road, scanning. Two blue jays land directly in front of me and begin to dig at the grass, and a chickadee sets down on the porch railing. Strange how they don't fly away, I think, and then I hear a voice.

"They like you."

I look up and see my strange man standing in the walkway, his red cap in his hands. His pale scalp is visible and is surrounded by unruly brown-and-gray hair.

"Hello," I say.

"Hello—" His voice is high and feeble, and his lips continue to move after his greeting, as if beginning to form another word, but then close tight, pinching to dimples at the corners. He steps closer, his head oddly leaning to his right as he approaches, as if his left ear is listening to something above him, up in the sky. I stand and reach out my hand.

"I'm Jenna."

He stares at my hand while wiping his own against his jacket, then reaches forward and shakes—a light, impotent shake. He pulls his hand back again quickly and puts it in his pocket, and turns his body slightly away from me. "I know Jenna," he mumbles. He seems a bit childlike, slow.

"You know me?" I ask. "I did live here once. Do you live around here?"

"There." He points up the hill, then looks shyly down at his shoes. "I like your house. It's fifty years old." He takes a step back, as if he'll be leaving, then looks up again and points to the picket fence at the side of the yard. "There are peonies along the fence."

"I thought those were peonies," I say, then ask gently, "How do you know me?"

"Your mother. You look like your mother."

He didn't say aunt; he didn't say Adeline. It's usually Aunt Adeline they remember. "You knew my mother?"

"I remember her." He appears nervous, as if he can't look into my eyes. "That's all. It was nice to meet you." He nods his head down once, low, as if bowing, then turns back to the street.

"Wait," I say. "What's your name?"

He turns around again and smiles, pleased that I have asked. "Rick Holmes," he says.

He walks back up the road in a soldier-like gait, legs straight as crutches, arms swaying with them in rhythm. A stiff, almost crippled-looking walk. I wonder how well he remembers Mom and me, and why he's so interested in the house and yard.

I run inside and grab a key to lock the door, then follow him up the road, staying far enough behind so he can't see me. He moves at a fast clip in the sand along the street, while I stick to the grass, close to the trees. I stay far enough behind so that I can dodge and dip behind a tree or telephone pole if he should turn around. I pass over the crest of the hill and can see Hunter's house, and now Rick, as he turns his mechanical body into the driveway. I stop at the far right border of the yard, behind a pole. I feel silly as a car drives by, look at my watch so I'm not looking at Rick, to seem inconspicuous.

Rick hobbles up the cobblestone walkway to the house, knocks on the door. A minute or so passes and he knocks again, waits. Finally he steps across the lawn to the smaller, garage-sized house next to the big one, and with a key, goes inside.

Just as I am about to turn around and go back, he emerges again with a large knapsack over his shoulder. He locks the door and ambles down the driveway that leads out back, toward the barn. Following him now would be trespassing; he may just turn and see me, and he would have good reason to ask why I am there. There would be no excuse. But now I even wonder if I'll bother to duck into the woods or behind a tree if he should turn around. I follow him down the gravel drive toward the barn, which he passes and continues onto a path into thick evergreen woods. As we enter the woods, I hear the buzz and hum of machinery—tractors or lawn mowers—and smell fresh cut grass, the pungent scent of dirt. The smell is raw and clean, invigorating as it blends with the crushed pine needles beneath my feet. The path through the trees is short, and there is light ahead, an opening. Rick exits to a field of grass and rows of tilled soil within, stretching for a mile, it seems. I don't follow him through the opening; instead, I duck within the bushes at the edge of the wood and lie down in the leaves to hide.

There is another barn in the distance, and two tractors between it and the woods, a man on each of them. One of the men stands up on his tractor and calls out, waving his arms until the other man sees him and turns his machine around. They converge, come to a stop, and wait as Rick approaches them. The man who called to his friend steps down and slaps Rick on the back. He is young looking, with sandy blond hair and tawny skin, a long, sinewy body. Could it be Hunter?

The man from the other tractor is darker and a bit shorter. He joins the taller man, and as they turn in my direction I imagine my big white face behind the bushes. I duck my head into the wet, mildewy leaves. The ground cover is slimy on my skin, and I wonder what lies within it: bugs, beetles, slugs maybe. I lift my head again, see them sauntering away. None of them seem to notice me.

I keep my body flat for a moment and stare out at the field of soil, the border of reeds in the foreground. The grass is tall and leaning, matted in places—dried grass and milkweed from last summer. It is wheat-colored, straw-like, but as the wind blows fierce it leans and parts, and there is green visible—short grass that is trying to come up. Soon the old grass will be hacked away to reveal this new growth, or perhaps it will dry up and give way all by itself. I watch as the grass leans and parts, leans and parts, its rhythm hypnotic.

I close my eyes and imagine how thick and cushiony it would feel beneath my back, lying within the tall reeds and tuffets, and suddenly I am there in my mind, except that in my head the overgrown grass is green and silky, the way it must have been in July or August. It streams and curls in the wind, over my body and then away again, brushing against me like a lover, silk parting before my face—green parting to blue, blue sky, blue eyes, and suddenly, there is pain.

This is how it happened.

I open my eyes to the wet soggy leaves, the flowing grass that is several feet away. There is a pain in me—a pressure in my abdomen, but this time only a light pain, a trivial one. The pressure spreads to a cramp—my period, I think as I turn onto my side; it is that time—it is that familiar ache in my pelvis, that suction within. I have felt this before, many times, some worse than others. But then there was that time when I looked up at the blue sky and the pain became much worse, a hundred times worse, it seemed.

I never did see my baby's body. At three months, what exactly was there to see?

part eight
the calm

{renee

twenty-nine

It was last year, when Bill turned forty-one, that Renee first noticed the section of thinning hair. It was high on his head and not seen by all those people who stood several inches shorter. She sees it today as his head lies in her lap, as she strokes his hair like she would a kitten's, so that he can feel her warm, slender fingers glide over his crown.

"What's this?" she jokes. "A bald patch in the forest."

If only Jenna could see her mother's sense of humor, her warmth.

Jenna may have seen it only a few times in her life. And Seth—he probably never saw it, even on those pseudo-happy occasions like Thanksgiving dinner or Christmas Eve. Too bad Seth got the visitor's treatment, the one Renee couldn't help, the one where she coated herself in an icy layer and didn't thaw out until everyone left. She wanted to connect with Seth, but sometimes the mere sight of him was hard to keep her eyes on. He reminded her of too much.

It's no secret that Renee seems rigid and cold. The girls have even joked about her low temperature problem. "Chill out," they'll say to their mother, followed with a giggle. And Renee usually answers back with something on the serious side, something about pain.

"This is what it does to people."

She can't help it, though. The words, the reactions just come out of her as natural as breathing. She wishes they could see this light, charming side that Bill sees a little of every day, which she perhaps puts aside and saves just for him. "You're so good to me," he'll say, and look at her with all-knowing eyes, as if he's saying something else.

Forgive yourself, Renee.

This doesn't make her forgive herself, or forget. It only reminds her, and makes her once again wonder if she married him just to get out of that house.

It was that Cape Wood Bicentennial parade when she first saw him again—the first time in three years, across the street behind the red and the blue, amongst the brass and the cotton candy and the smell of barbecue. Bill was fuller-bodied, stronger in the jaw, and straight out of his Associate in Business program from Orono. He was just right.

They had first met at the youth center, a place where most kids in town gathered; a place intended for teenage outcasts, but over that time developed into a meeting place for both the shy and the popular. And while there were legitimate activities going on such as Ping-Pong, pool, and arcade games, there was little supervision, and the center became the place where one could swear, buy drugs, and meet lovers. To grow up.

There was one day when Renee could finally follow Adeline there—her big sister, who was mature and sophisticated, adored by everyone. Adeline would glide into the pool table area with her long-legged elegance and her effervescent smile, sifting through the vinyl pants and stiff-fur sweaters, as if she were silk brushing against bark. And everyone noticed.

But it was not Adeline Bill noticed, Renee would find out later. It was Renee—a pretty, plain fifteen in those days, with freckled ivory skin and hazely eyes, her limp hair always secured in a barrette. She was a tomboy in the summer games at the park, where her trim body had a fawn-like gallop, and then at the youth center, where she could deal seven-card stud as well as her father had. Still, Bill noticed she was a girl.

He never seemed to belong there, amongst the boys who weren't as shy—boys who whooped and hollered to girls wandering in. Some of the girls seemed to enjoy these catcalls, especially the older ones. They played their eyes and bodies to it, waltzing by at exactly the same time each night, their tight skirts and shorts clinging to fertile hips, their mouths curving slightly when they heard the male sounds. Meanwhile, quiet, awkward Bill only watched.

He still has a little of that shyness he had back then, that hang-back posture and tentative manner. He even stops in mid-sentence whenever Renee looks as if she is about to speak. "You go ahead," he will say.

Today he tells her that Jenna seems to be doing well. He talks about how Cape Wood has changed quite a bit, how the house has not changed much at all. Jenna's working on the garden, he says, painting the trim on the windows, tearing down the wallpaper. The pine-knot ceiling in the bedroom remains, still unpainted. Renee thinks of the wood, how it looked from her bed or from the floor, how the knots spoke to her sometimes, convincing her to forget. How accomplished she became at it, this forgetting thing.

But she does remember how one night young Bill McGarry walked right up to her—right in front of his boys, how he smiled and said hello. She smiled back, but must have been too scared— or perhaps too distracted—because she knows she didn't answer. She only stared into the far corner of the hall where Adeline was surrounded by elegant friends and the sharply dressed, most handsome boys.

And although Renee didn't know it then, Bill would not attempt to talk to her again until years later, when she was the mother of a young toddler, when they just happened to look across the street and see each other through the brass and red and blue parade. It is sad to know this, that years before she didn't answer, and he just watched. He must have noticed her distracted eyes, her mind and body drifting elsewhere. It would take enormous pain and need for her to love him back. How sad it is that he loved her even then, and that he watched her mature and transform from afar. She sometimes wonders how he still could love her today.

"Oh, and the wallpaper," he suddenly says. "Jenna found something under there...some letters or something."

"Letters?" All she can think of are the ones she never received, ones that may have proved love was true.

"Yes," Bill says. "Right under the wallpaper. Remember that green wallpaper? Looks like the same stuff. Guess somebody papered right over it."

Could it be the same green? she thinks.

What kind of letters? she asks him, but Bill doesn't know. She wonders if he really does know, or if he's guessed what they could be but would rather not think about it. She imagines the pine ceiling in the bedroom, the knots in the wood making her spin. How she longed to know why he hadn't written as she lay on the floor and watched the ceiling spin.

Bill never asks about those times, those sad times she spent before he came along. It must have been sad for him, as he'd watched her from afar all those years. He must have seen her with that older boy—a man, really—the dark, quiet one who worked farm fields in the summer, who wanted to go into the Navy and fight for his country. To die at sea, if necessary.

jenna}

thirty

I awaken to heavy rain and think about my dream in which I was standing next to Hunter Jones in a farm field. Up close his hair was rippled with coppery highlights and his eyes were a bright, cerulean blue, and as he hovered over me I could see dew over his upper lip. I had the strong urge to pull myself against him and wipe my lips against his, to swim against the sweat on his collarbone and neck. When I awoke I felt disgusted and dirty, and remembered how, years ago while life grew inside me, I suddenly wanted other men.

And then I thought about the last day I ever saw him, the day we buried Angus's picture in the ground. How we hugged afterwards, our innocent, seven-year-old bodies warm but indifferent, not aware we were boy and girl.

I never did tell Paula about the crush on my ancient history professor, but I do tell her about my dream, about how uncomfortable it made me feel. "Like I'm cheating," I say.

"Uh...huh." Paula is in her own world, barely listening. She spoons jarred apricot dessert resembling shampoo into Erica's mouth while the baby's arms flop and slap the tray. Paula's hair is decorated with specks of peachy goop.

"Maybe acceptance is the key," I add. "I need to accept the

fact that it's okay to have these dreams, that they don't mean any-thing. You know what I mean?"

"Oh...I'm not sure. What?"

Paula isn't with me. Perhaps she has something on her mind. Being pregnant, perhaps. "Did you get your period?" I ask.

"No. And I didn't take a test yet."

"How will you feel if you are?"

Paula nibbles at her fingernail. "I don't even want to think about it." She seems afraid of being pregnant again. I wonder how that feels after having two children, as opposed to being pregnant for the first time. "What were you saying before?" she says. "Your dream?"

"Oh...men," I say. "That it bothers me, having these feelings."

"What part bothers you?" Paula's voice has a slight condescend-ing tone, like I'm crazy and making a big deal out of nothing. She scrapes the plastic-looking food from Erica's chin and from the edges of her open, twisted mouth, and with enough food on the spoon, shoves it back in. It falls out again, and Paula pushes it back. *All the way in*, I think. *Stay in there so your mother can listen to me.*

"The physical aspect of it," I say. "It was very...physical."

Paula laughs. "Jenna, it was just a dream."

"So?"

I think of how ridiculous I sound and wonder if it really does bother me as much as I'm saying, or if I'm just talking to get my mind off of things. There are so many things I couldn't possibly explain to Paula, who doesn't know that I've lost a child, who doesn't know my origins are so ambiguous. For some reason, I prefer it that way.

Paula leans over toward me, puts a hand on my knee. "Jenna, I know this is probably not my place to say this—and maybe it's too soon to say this or whatever—but Seth would want you to, you know, be happy. But that's not even what we're talking about anyway. We were talking about a little fantasy—not even your real-life fantasy, either. Your *dream*. It was a *dream*."

I remember this tone from years ago, how it made me self-conscious and frustrated, how it made me want to stop talking to her. I wonder how I used to listen to it, and why I bothered to come here today and listen to it again. "Whatever," I say, but I won't let her talk me down. "Let's say it wasn't a dream. Let's say it was a real person."

Paula's torso lifts into straight posture, and her head whips around. "Ooh, is it?"

"I knew that would perk you right up," I say.

"Oh, stop it," she chuckles. "Look, it's okay for you to feel something. I even think it would be okay for *me* to feel. As long as I don't...hurt Gerard."

"Do you ever think about anyone else?" I ask.

"Of course I look and stuff," Paula says. "Of course." She rolls her eyes. "There even was this one time..." She bows her hand, as if to warn me that what she is about to say is insignificant, and shouldn't be taken too seriously. "This guy named Andy. He was in the same design group as me, at my first job in Portland. The ad agency, remember? We started having lunch together and the next thing I knew..."

"You liked him," I interrupt.

"It was a little more than that."

"Paula?" I interrupt.

"Ah, ah, ah—you're jumping to conclusions," Paula says. "Let me finish. So I grew to sort of like this guy, you know? He was so adorable, I just couldn't resist." She gives Erica another spoonful, wipes her mouth off with her already grimy bib. "But nothing really happened...I mean we kissed, but nothing happened."

"You *kissed?*"

"Yeah, but that's all." Paula seems calm about this kiss, as she cleans up her daughter's messy face, the baby who won't remember this conversation because she doesn't recognize the words, the subject matter. "We met on the beach once," she adds, her eyes gleaming. "Very romantic." Paula appears sad in a way, as if it has been forgotten until now. "And a very bad idea."

Even Paula I never suspected would do such a thing. I'd assumed that all her extracurricular desires had been fulfilled in those promiscuous years before she married, that she had gotten it out of her system. "I can't believe you actually kissed somebody," I say. "But was it really just a kiss?"

"Yes!" Paula grabs a paper napkin from the holder on the table, wipes her hands. "What do you think—I'd lie to you? Hey, *kiss* is where I draw the line."

I would hate it if I knew Seth had this same book of rules, if he felt no guilt after a kiss. "Maybe you shouldn't bother drawing lines," I say. I feel like a hypocrite, remembering how close I came to breaking my own rules. How quickly my life could have changed.

"You *should* draw lines," Paula says. "A person needs rules, a moral center."

"Paula, I was trying to make a point—that it didn't seem to do you any good, drawing lines."

"Hey, we didn't have sex or anything."

"Come on," I scold, like a mother. "But isn't it all about sex?"

"Hey," Paula snaps, "don't get all moralizing on me. At least I liked him, you know? I mean...I *knew* him." Perhaps she means as opposed to just wanting a body, a sweaty young stranger, as in my dreams.

My own views of sex and love have mingled and mutated so much over the years. When I was young it was all about love, and sex was a byproduct, as the textbooks described. Then when I married it changed—to love and sex, two different animals, that, in some cases, merged. Now that I'm alone again it seems more confusing and perhaps more discouraging. It seems more about sex than I originally suspected, and all the little things: the kisses, the innocent embraces—even in dreams—have much more implication.

"But *really*," I say, "what difference does it make whether you *liked* each other or not?"

"Hey, don't rain on my parade," Paula says. "You're one to talk."

"What do you mean?"

"You're always playing innocent."

I want to defend myself but don't have the right words; I know Paula will be quicker, snappier with her comebacks. "So, what happened to Andy?" I ask.

"He ended up leaving the agency. I never saw him again." Paula looks down as she cleans off the baby spoon with a paper towel. "He just sort of stopped talking to me. It was weird, you know? I think he felt guilty." She wipes Erica's face with the towel, a spot that seems clean already. "I always thought women were the ones who felt guilty, not men."

"Of course men feel guilty," I say. "But do you really think that's why he never talked to you again?"

"Why?" Paula snaps. "Do you think something else?"

"I wasn't saying that."

"You're implying," Paula says. "And anyway, why can't I believe what I want to believe? I like to think it was because he felt guilty." Paula's eyes suddenly appear moist, brimming with sadness.

"Why?" I ask.

"Because any other reason would break my heart."

Paula's emotional honestly rarely surfaces to this level. I remember Paula as being shallow, never looking for or realizing emotions, someone sheltered by tradition and religion, who rarely would think of *hurt*. Perhaps this emotional person is the real Paula, who pokes her head out from hiding every once in a while—and who rarely emerges into real life because it is much less painful below the surface. Maybe this is why I talk to Paula, to see the transformation, to witness the Paula Doctrine that first bewilders, then inspires me to turn my own beliefs inside out and reevaluate them.

This also may be why I don't tell her some things.

On my way home I drive slowly past the Jones's house again. I see the woods to the right of the house and the river deep within, down the hill. Through the trees I can see the blob of my own yellow house—three stops down around the curve but a straight route through the woods. I wonder how much has changed and grown in these woods where Hunter and I buried our treasures, try to imagine Angus's picture in the ground—the outline of dark hair, the hollow eyes. What did he look like?

He must still be out there, somewhere, amongst the young trees and sprouting poison ivy. There are a few spots I remember, landmarks in the woods where he might be. But to find such a treasure would take a miracle, or at least relentless, passionate digging.

As I pull in the driveway I notice the two figures standing in the road before the house, peering through the lilacs. One of them is Rick, red cap and all, and standing next to him is a taller, younger man with wispy blond hair. It is the man from the field, dressed in jeans and a white T-shirt, pointing at the house. They both look up as I drive up, watch me as I get out of the car.

"Hello," I say. "Can I help you guys?"

"Jenna?" The blond man says. "I'm Hunter...Hunter Jones. Do you remember me?"

So different from my dream, I think, and from what I imagined from far away. As a boy his hair was like wheat, and his eyes the color of Dad's metallic-blue Chevy. Now the hair is sun-bleached, the eyes not so bright-looking. He looks worn-out, old for his twenty-six years.

"Hunter," I say. "It's you." A rush of embarrassment moves through me as my dream flashes in my mind; but the picture quickly dissolves, as if it were some kind of joke I played on myself just to kill the time, the tension. A new feeling has overtaken me, one of childhood trust and understanding, of pure comfort. It is like twenty years has not passed between us at all and suddenly I am seven years old again.

thirty-one

The last time I saw Hunter was a strangely bright August day, the kind of bright that reflects off leaves and pavement like crystal. It was crisp and cool for mid-summer, and the sky was a gorgeous, saturated blue. It was a perfect day but a sad one, as we had just buried Angus's picture in the ground.

I felt so terrible for Hunter, and I wanted him to come back to the house to meet Aunt Adeline. But as we were walking toward the house I saw Mom pull up the driveway, her pale face, her hollow eyes looking out from the car window. She had come to pick me up.

"What's going on?" I heard, even before she got out of the car. The car door slammed and she stomped toward us. "What are you doing in the woods?" Mom scolded.

"Burying things."

"What kind of things?"

"Pictures of dead people."

"How morbid can you be?" Her voice was loud and sharp, and her eyebrows low and cross. "Playing in the dirt...where is your aunt?" As she spoke her head jerked about, loosening the hairs from her ponytail.

"In the house," I said.

"Not even watching you," she said, then looked at Hunter.

"Where are your parents?" Hunter pointed through the woods, to his house, and Mom's eyes followed.

"We were just playing," I said. Hunter looked too frightened to answer, and suddenly I was ashamed of my witch mother.

Mom grabbed the trowel from my hand and threw it to the ground. "What is this?" She took my upper arm and pulled me toward the car. "Let's go," she said. "We'll clean you up when I get home."

"I have to get my stuff," I said, "and say goodbye to Aunty."

"Your Aunty doesn't seem to be around," Mom said. "We can come back and get your stuff later with your father." She pulled me along, opened the car door. "Go on, get in," she said. I could see Hunter cutting across hill through the back yards of the neighbors' houses. Mom got into her side of the car.

"Who is that boy, anyway?" she said. "Does your aunt know you play with him?" She shook her head. "No, of course she doesn't...I'm sure she doesn't pay any attention to what you're doing."

"That's Hunter," I said. "Hunter Jones. I don't think she knows." I waited for the stern face, the screaming, perhaps another grasp of my upper arm. But it didn't come. Mom just stared ahead and didn't say a word.

"Mom?"

"He lives up the street, you said?"

"Yes."

She sat silent for a moment, then opened the car door again. "I'll go get your things."

I waited, watching her from the car—storming up the steps and slamming the screen door. Aunt Adeline still was inside, perhaps didn't know Mom was there yet. Then I heard the screaming—first Mom, then Aunt Adeline yelling back at her. Aunt Adeline's voice rose up and down, and it grew louder, loud enough for neighbors to hear. Mom tried to yell back, her voice spurting between Aunt Adeline's bellows. Then the screen door slammed and Mom stormed down the steps and back to the car. She got in and started the engine and quickly backed out of the driveway without saying a word. I looked back and saw Aunt Adeline at the door, her face smoky behind the screen. Her eyes were mean-looking, her mouth tight and serious, like Mom's. She looked scary.

It was not until we were up the road a bit that Mom spoke. "I don't want you going over there anymore."

She couldn't mean this, I thought, but I could tell by her thrusting chin and eyes steady on the road that she did. I was too scared to open my mouth; I knew she would snap back because I'd done something wrong. Or was it Aunt Adeline she was mad at for letting me roam free? I didn't know and was too scared to ask. Maybe this anger would just go away, and Mom and Aunt Adeline would be on the phone in a couple of days, making up to each other, and this would be forgotten.

I thought of earlier, what a perfect day it had been, how Aunt Adeline had seemed so happy and different. I especially remembered our talk over breakfast, when we'd made so many plans. She told me she would always take me to the beach down the road; we'd go in the spring and fall as well as in the summer. We could even go in the winter if I wanted, and make snow tracks along the shore. And definitely, she'd said, she would take me that very weekend because the pebbly Cape Wood beach would be alive with the smells and colors of summer for only a few more weeks.

But two days later Aunt Adeline was dead. How I longed to see Hunter again, to tell him that I, too, had lost someone dear to me.

———

We will meet in the Old Port section of Portland, where cobblestone streets are lined with specialty shops and galleries, and restaurants display their menus on the sidewalks. The ocean is just a walk down the street—boats and fish markets filling the harbor, condos towering over the shallow, murky water. The smell is strong: salt and fish and burning oil.

I get out of my car in the parking lot of the large boat-restaurant that floats in the bay, where Hunter is standing in front of the gift shop. He is dressed in a striped cotton shirt and tan vest, blue jeans. I have worn a skirt for the first time in months, my long, swingy daisy-print one, a white scoop-neck sweater. My hair is pulled back in a barrette; it wasn't until this morning that I realized how overgrown and shaggy it had become.

Hunter smiles as I walk up to him and reaches out a hand as if this is our first meeting. "How are you, Jenna?" he says as we shake.

"I've been better," I say, knowing *dead husband* will come up eventually. I might as well get it over with. Hunter doesn't even ask what I mean.

"Let's walk down to the pier," he says.

We walk down to the pier where boats are scattered around the docks. The water beneath where we walk is almost brown in color, and there is pleasant fried fish smell coming from within the restaurant. Hunter leans against a wooden pillar and points to a large tanker far out on the water.

"See that? That's a Navy ship." His face beams in the sunlight. "I spent four years in the Navy. It paid for my education."

"What did you study?" I ask.

"Agricultural engineering at Maryland State University."

"So," I begin, thinking how I'm not so good at small talk, "do you work in that field?"

"I do soil testing for the state of Maryland. But it's only about two-thirds of the year. I come up here for the summer. I like the job okay...good benefits."

"Does your family live here still?"

"Nah. They don't come here anymore." He leans against the wooden rail, bends down and looks at the water. "I really miss the Navy," he says.

"Do you?"

Hunter nods, doesn't say anything else.

"I'm a freelance artist," I say.

"Hey, good for you." He doesn't ask what my art is, what I do. I don't even know if I want him to ask, don't know whether I should elaborate or not. I'm not very interested in talking about what I do for a living; I have no passion for it right now. I'm just making small talk.

"How long did your parents keep coming up here?" I ask.

"Oh, a few years after you and I met." Hunter stands up straight again.

"Do you remember those days?" I don't know what else to say. Perhaps I should jump in with something about myself—he could just be nervous, waiting for me to talk.

"Oh, sure, a little bit." He smiles, a frowny smile with eyebrows to match, as if I'm silly to talk about the past, to walk down memory lane. As if he might be thinking there's nothing else in my life to talk about and he's bored with me already. He looks out to the water. "That ship out there," he says. "That's like the one I was on for a couple of years."

I wonder if I should just let him talk, take his own trip down his own memory lane. I let him list off his Navy achievements, one by one, many he noted just minutes ago. He continues with more technical details, his voice slightly monotone, buzzing in my head. There is a lack of emotion in his eyes, an apathy in his delivery. The words feel exhausted, as if he has given this speech before—to family, perhaps, to a father who requires it of him. I feel guilty about my lack of interest, but perhaps I'm doing the same thing, the obligatory small talk, giving little of myself. I want to barge in with something real, something with emotional credentials.

"My husband died in a car accident," I say. "A few months ago."

He looks at me, perplexed it seems, and runs his fingers through his hair the way Seth used to. "Jenna, I'm sorry."

I've caught him off-guard. I inhale, swallow air, widen my eyes so the tears won't form. I've caught myself off-guard, too. "I'm okay," I say. "I guess I just had to get it out of the way."

"It's okay, Jenna." Hunter's voice has come alive. His hand reaches to my shoulder, and I think of how we hugged when we were seven. "Are you sure you're all right?"

"I'm fine."

"Want to go get that lunch?" he says, his energy suddenly charged.

———

The Portside Diner is casual inside, with dark wood and warm tones and jazz music that is just loud enough to accessorize conversation. Hunter picks a sturdy, tile-top table near the bar, one decorated with a rust-colored glass candle holder. We order dark beers, and when the waiter brings them Hunter quickly gulps down half of his. I tell him about Seth and the accident, and he tells me about his fiancée, Beth, who is working up in Nova Scotia for the summer. It is all he tells me about her—perhaps just enough to let me know this isn't a date, in case I was wondering.

He talks again about his four years in the Navy, his studies in Maryland, how he returns to Maine the way he and his family did when he was young, to work on the farm. "Even though I love it," he says, "I couldn't just be a farmer. It isn't practical." He pours the rest of his beer down. "It wasn't logical to even try."

"Art is hardly practical," I say. "But hey, I did it anyway."

He is still, his eyes motionless, his beer in mid-air. He seems perplexed, as if this is an exciting new concept. Then he shakes his head, snaps out of it. "I say you were lucky," he says. "For me it was Navy first, then engineering." He puts his beer down and smiles, as if he is proud. "Gotta be practical."

"Oh...sure." His words ring in my head, *practical, logical,* buzzing like moths. I'd like to hear about his impractical, illogical side now, if there is one—a side that shoots from the heart, that does stupid, crazy, irrational things. I think of the time Seth rode his bicycle down Massachusetts Avenue with a pair of shorts on his head—shorts he could just barely see through, how he plowed right into someone's front hedge.

"Jenna?" Hunter suddenly says.

"Oh, I'm sorry." My daydreaming must be obvious. "So, you must have really liked the Navy," I say, trying to save myself.

"The military was a good education in discipline."

I chuckle. "Yeah, but did you like it?"

"I guess so." He seems stumped.

"You mean you don't know if you liked it?" I try not to sound too condescending.

"I'm not sure. I just know it was a really good experience for me."

"Did your parents make you go or something?" I can hear the sarcasm building up in my voice. I should stop now or I may get myself in trouble.

"No they *didn't*," he says defensively. "*I* wanted to go." He begins to peel at his beer bottle label. "My brother never got to go."

"Angus?"

"You remember," he says, and I nod. I think of the articles at the library, hope I didn't remember his name too quickly. "Rick worked with Angus," he adds, smiling. He seems to be coming alive now, perhaps because of the beer, or the topic. Even his posture has changed from upright and uptight to slouched and relaxed. "Rick's a good guy."

"He seems nice," I say. "Does he live at Stonybrook?"

"Yeah, he's our caretaker. He lives in the carriage house."

"Has Rick always lived there?" I finish my beer, feel a light buzz coming over me, a warm feeling. "Sorry I'm asking so many questions."

"No, that's okay," he says. "I like talking about the farm, about Rick. He hasn't always lived there. Just since eighty-one. See..." He readjusts in his seat, crosses his hands on the table. "After Angus died, my family didn't come up to Maine for a while. Not for seven years, in fact. That summer I met you—that was my first summer in Maine. Well, I also met Rick then. He had been good friends with my brother, and I guess that sort of made us instantly close." He pauses, taps his empty beer bottle on the table. "Rick...wasn't always like that," he adds.

"Like what?" I don't know why I asked, as I think I know already.

"He's a little slow. I guess the night Angus died, he almost drowned, too. And he had kind of a nervous breakdown or something."

"That's awful." I imagine Rick as a different person, alert and talkative, a businessman in a three-piece suit.

"Yeah," he says. "Hey, do you remember the woods between our houses?"

I nod, thinking of how earlier, when I spoke of the past I could have sworn he was snickering, about to laugh at me. Maybe he was, just out of insecurity, and this conversation has made him forget. I'm not sure now; maybe I was being paranoid, because he seems so alive talking about the past.

"We used to bury things," I say.

"My brother's picture. It must still be under there." His eyes are squinting a bit, dramatic. "They never found his body, you know."

I think of the articles at the library. "I heard that," I say. "It must have been awful."

"You know, it's weird," he says. "Every once in a while I forget about him. I mean I really forget all about Angus, so when I start talking to someone about him again it's a shock. All over again it's a shock."

"We don't have to talk about him."

"Oh, no, I want to."

I feel sad for Hunter. But I like this side of him—this side with the pain, the chaos of his life. "You never knew him, did you?" I ask.

"No. He died the year before I was born." Hunter plays with his spoon, pushing down on the scooping end so the handle moves up like a seesaw. "I've often wondered if my parents had me just because he died." Possible, I think, and shrug my shoulders. "Anyway, I got to see pictures," he adds. "And we had home movies of him." Hunter looks beyond me, squints his eyes. "Funny, there are no home movies of me."

"Oh, parents just get tired," I say. "Lazy, maybe."

"Angus was supposed to go into the Navy," he adds. "Did I tell you that?"

"Yes."

"And to college. He was going to do that afterward."

"To study?"

"Same thing," he says. "Agriculture."

There's something sad about a dead man bringing out passion, the genuineness in someone. About a brother following in the shadow of another who is dead. Angus is Hunter's hero.

And he must have been a hero to his mother and father, too. The Jones family never knew whether or not Angus would grow up to be a success, a wonderful man. His life stopped at nineteen, before he could commit too many evils, so they could only imagine; and what else would they imagine but a man who was a hero? So Hunter can do nothing else but go on living, trying to be as good as his brother was at the time it all stopped. And he will never succeed.

Because how does one compete with a dead man?

"When he drowned," Hunter continues, "there was a search—the Coast Guard and everything. But I guess after a few days they figured he wouldn't stand a chance if he was still out there." Hunter picks up his knife, twists it under the small lamp on the wall. Slices of light reflect and move on his face. "It's hard," he says, "never knowing someone who is your blood."

"I know." I think of Montigue, but hesitate to mention him. "I never really knew my grandmother," I say. "My grandfather died before I was born."

"I felt terrible when I heard your aunt died," Hunter says. "My mother told me."

I wonder if he knows about the suicide part, all the truth that came later. "Yes, it was a bad time for all of us."

"I met your aunt at the beginning of that summer," Hunter says, "before I met you."

"I didn't realize you'd met her," I say. "At least not before that day my mother blew her top."

"Yes, just once, when I was playing at the side of your—of her yard. I still remember the look on her face when she talked to me."

"Why—what did she say to you?"

"Well, she asked me who I was, and when I told her she got all upset, like I'd done something wrong. I'll never forget her face, probably because I was scared. I hope you don't mind me saying this, Jenna."

"No, it's okay. Aunt Adeline wasn't...very well."

"It's just that I was so young...I really thought I had done something wrong—that look on her face."

"Did she say anything else?"

"She asked me if my family would be living here all that summer. I told her yes, that my family hadn't come up for years, but that now we'd be coming back again." He pauses, seeming uncomfortable, like he's holding something back. Hunter must have heard the rumors about Aunt Adeline, perhaps saw the recent article about her suicide. I wonder if there could even be something he knows that I don't. "Sorry I didn't mention it," he says, "back then, I mean." I smile to reassure him it's okay, that I don't mind. "To be honest," he continues, "I was a little scared of her." He begins to tap his spoon on the table in a nervous manner. "I guess your aunt and your mother knew my brother," he adds, matter-of-factly.

A ball of weight drops into my stomach. "They knew Angus?" I ask.

"I don't know how *well* they knew him. They just hung in the same crowd or something. At least that's what Rick said. He remembers your aunt and your mother." He puts the spoon down again, lines it up with the knife. "Actually, I just found out all this stuff recently. Why do you think we were at your house yesterday? Rick knew who you were."

"I just figured you had gotten my message." Hunter shakes his head. "Oh, I just heard you were still around, and left a message for you..." I feel embarrassed telling him. "But...that's so unusual—to think of anyone knowing my mother when she was young. Or my aunt."

"Yeah," Hunter says. "It's fun to find connections where you least expect them." He reaches into his back pocket, pulls out his wallet and opens it. "I do still have some of Angus's things, at least." He takes out a shiny silver tie clip, hands it over to me. "This was his." I take the clip and flip it over, read the monogrammed metal.

Angus Montigue Jones.

part nine
the living

{renee

thirty-two

"The first few years of a child's development are most important," Renee will tell the class tomorrow. "This is a formative period for our personalities. The experiences we have as very young children, while we may not remember them, permanently shape our adult behavior."

This lecture never is easy to do. She must practice what she will say—the correct words, the right inflection—because the students could sense a lack of experience.

A lie.

And the class may have less interest in this subject than the last class—awareness, which included ESP and visual perception tests, all those fun little mind games. With this new subject their eyes will drift to the large sunny window that looks out to the spring courtyard, and Renee will have to find words that interest them. There are many that swim through her head, words like *nurture* and *love* and *critical*, phrases such as *trust versus mistrust*. And of course, *imprinting*, in which they will contemplate whether goslings have an inborn or learned tendency to follow their Mother Goose.

And there will be all those processes of cognitive development, all those theories of personality and morality, the things one often does not remember, but have formed them into what they are. Perhaps the students will find that fascinating.

She wonders what Jenna remembers about those first few years—about who was there, who did the caring, the nurturing. Perhaps Jenna remembers the earliest days, the ones that are mere flashbulb memories and said to be so formative. She hopes Jenna is selective and remembers the times when her mother did hold her, even if it was only for a second.

Sometimes she thinks about Jenna's older face, and sees that grimace she held for months after she lost her baby. She remembers telling her daughter it was for the best, even while it saddened her. "A baby would have changed your life," she said, trying not to expose her disappointment.

How the words must have translated.

Perhaps Renee was lucky to have Adeline when it was her time. Adeline was willing to race home from studies and life away from home—to give it all up for her little sister Renee, so that this little sister—the real mother, could be free to lose her mind, lose memories, even. Renee has always wondered why Adeline was so giving then, after what had happened—why she was willing to put her own life on hold to help her. But maybe Adeline didn't do it so much for Renee, but for the baby.

Because it was *his* baby.

This is the kind of thing her social science students are more interested in now; there is no need to learn child development, maybe not for a decade or two. Unless, of course, they are careless and impulsive like Renee was, and have the drive to delve into the world of the adult female too early. A world so exciting that getting pregnant does not cross one's mind—not in the midst of searing passion.

Getting to that passion was the easy part—the tickling, the teasing, the warm trembling hands on skin, lips wet and pliant and open; two bodies magnetized, melting into one. But after it happened, the image of eggs and tiny tadpoles entered her vision, and it no longer was ecstasy. It was like a torrent, a stormy end to childhood dreams, and she was transformed.

jenna}

thirty-three

There is something about a dead man. Something beyond mysterious, beyond unattainable. Perhaps it is a dead man's inability to love back. Because when one loves a dead man, there can be no worry about reciprocation.

Angus Montigue Jones is dead.

On a spring day much like the one today, Mom told me about a man named Montigue. It was the first day of the year when I could smell the ocean, where I'd spent all morning thinking of sand and colorful blankets, of cool, cobalt water. Even while Mom spoke his name I still may have thought of this ocean, because it was just a name.

Montigue.

When Hunter showed me his brother's tie clip he didn't seem to notice my reaction. It was a gut feeling I had—one that comes not only from connections I've made over names and dates, over letters engraved in brass. It was a true gut feeling, like I've never had before.

But is it truth? This is merely some dead man's name, I remind myself, a middle name at that. There are other Montigues in the world that Mom could have known.

And she certainly would have known if her Montigue had died; it would have been in all the papers. Dead, drowned, like

Hunter said. Mom would have told me for sure—she might even have been happy to tell me he was dead; there would be no chance of our lives revolving around a dead man.

What would Mom say about the thoughts in my head? She would somehow manage to smooth it over—turn it all into coincidence, make it into *nothing.* Even over the telephone she would be in control, manipulating the inflection of each word, of every breath. She would win.

And she would never have to talk about it again.

The old scraps of peach and green wallpaper lie in a heap in the corner of the bedroom. The once-soggy pile now is dried and crusty, and the white pile of letters lies separate from it, their ragged corners curled up toward the sunlight. They, too, finally are dry, and on several of them more random words and letters have appeared like magic. But there are no more Montigues, and no Angus Jones. Are they the same?

I lift the scraps at the top of the pile, see the photograph. And suddenly I wonder—is this a face I've seen before?

I run downstairs to the kitchen and grab my gardening apron, run out of the house through the side lawn past the shovel and bones, out back through the trees to the woods. I pull the trowel from my apron and begin to dig. I burrow into spots that seem familiar—next to large, rotted tree trunks, near long sections of stone wall, the old foundation of a house. Using my foot, I push down on the trowel and dig a foot or so deep in most places, more where the soil is softer. I wonder what happens to the things buried over so many years, in such a moist, eroding area of ground. Do they sink, move deeper into the ground? Are they lifted up by growing roots and heaving earth, then washed away? I think of how I buried rocks as a child, how I must have assumed it unique for a rock to be under the soil. I must have thought rocks only sat upon the surface, as in stone walls or paved roads. Many rocks are coming up—the smooth, rounded ones like the ones we buried, and I inspect them for paint or engraved letters, even though they could be washed or worn away.

But rocks are not what I am looking for.

My heart races as I dig, faster and faster with each shovelful, with each hope that I'll hit something significant. At times I do hear and feel metal-against-metal, but it is only a piece of scrap— a rusted bolt, a hinge or piece of framework, even a horseshoe. There are bottles here, newer ones that are cheap—thin glass bottles with seams and five-cent deposit letters. With every unsuccessful hole I dig I throw the dirt back into the hole, then cover it with soggy leaves. I wonder if I've disturbed the home of some innocent rodent, some slimy nest of worms or slugs.

Finally, the trowel scrapes against something—a metallic sound like the nails and horseshoes, but more squeaky and hollow. There is something here, something larger, flatter, and I hear my own voice chirp in excitement. I dig around and under the rectangular object, quickly because it is smaller than I remember: the tiny metal box with the medieval-looking engraving on the side. Using the edge of the trowel, I pull the corroded metal hinge off and pry it apart.

Inside is the small suede drawstring bag, now damp and dark with soil-stained water. But it is intact. I open the bag and pull out the rock: the engraved initials, letters Hunter and I sweated and cut our fingers over. I wish Hunter was with me now, as I recall how much time we spent doing this, for this dead man.

Beneath the bag is a piece of cloth—tan suede, like the bag. I lift it and there is the photograph of Angus, a face that has been cloudy, vague for twenty years. But it is the same face, the face under the wallpaper.

Angus Montigue Jones.

He is slender and tall-looking, with a crown of blackish hair that wisps over his forehead, and deep, shadowy eyes beneath a pronounced brow. His cheekbones are sharp and hollow beneath his eyes, and his lips are thin, in a half-smile. Wearing baggy military pants and a loose button-down shirt, he leans slightly against a stone plaque, atop a large slab of rock—part of a wall or a jetty—with the dark expanse of ocean beyond him. The picture is faded, almost colorless, except for the hint of blue background, the blend of ocean and sky—without a horizon, it appears. I feel a shiver as I look into Angus's eyes. Oddly, he reminds me of Seth, dark and puzzling, like a statue on his beloved slab of granite.

thirty-four

On a crisp autumn evening, Seth and I drove home from dinner at Mom and Dad's. The burnt-colored leaves separated before the headlights of the car like small rodents against the gray of pavement, scurrying to the woods.

Seth had a good time, he said, a slight hesitation in his voice, the hesitation he had for all of our years. Only this time he added to his comment and compared being around Mom and Dad to riding a roller coaster. "Lots of ups and downs," he said, "and turbulence at every corner."

I liked his honesty. "And you're stuck in your seat," I joined in, "and can't get off until it's over." Suddenly I felt guilty—for trying to be as funny as he was, for ridiculing my parents in the process. But Seth eased my shame when he smiled at me, his dark eyes understanding, reminding me of Dad.

"It's more like a Ferris wheel," he said, "A slow, calm ride, where you feel really safe and have this great view, but all you do is go around and around, and then it stops and you're stuck at the top. And you can't get off."

Seth must have noticed me staring at him; he turned toward me as he drove, something he hardly ever did. "Hey," he said, his voice turning soft, serious, "do you ever wonder what life would be like if we hadn't lost the baby?"

"Oh, sure," I said, but I was lying. Because for a little while at least, I'd actually forgotten about it.

As I stared out the car window I thought about the old Seth, the old me, how powerful we once had been together. I wonder what he really was thinking—how things maybe would have been better if I hadn't lost the baby, and how he had to live with my decision to never try for a baby again. We stopped at a red light, and Seth spoke again.

"That Ferris wheel thing," he said, "about being stuck at the top—you know I was talking about your parents, don't you?"

"Yes," I said. "I know." And I made sure to frown at him as if he was crazy, as if other possibilities have not crossed my mind.

And then I thought about how being around my family— myself included—was not at all like riding a roller coaster or a Ferris wheel. It was more like a funhouse, where everything was twirling and distorted, and we were are all masters of disguise.

The hum of a car wakes me, and I look out the bedroom window to see a Dodge sedan pull up close to the fence and park on the grass. Paula would do such a thing, I think, not care about a living thing as insignificant as grass.

I wonder if she can see my head, see me crouched behind this lower corner of glass on my hands and knees. I move quickly, scurrying across the floor to the hall, then squat at the top of the stairs. My legs cramp as I crouch here, hiding, as I peek around the corner like a spy to glance at the front door window, to hear steps up the walk, the sound of the bell. I hear a rapping from the side entrance to the kitchen, that irritating sound of the screen door hitting against the frame.

I don't want to answer it. It feels good to hide up here. But I can't just let her rap and rap; Paula would see my car in the driveway and know I'm up here somewhere. She would go for the windows, the basement, breaking in if she had to. *I was worried,* she'd say, but I think it's just nosiness.

I'll tell her the truth; Yes, *I was asleep in the middle of the day*, I think as I walk into the kitchen, where Paula is standing behind the screen door.

She has that skinny-lipped, guilt-admitting smile on her face, and in her arms is a brown bag full of colorful cellophane-wrapped food, chips or something. Her eyes open wide, anticipating a reaction from me. "Is this a bad time?" she says.

"I was getting ready to wallpaper," I say, my words sounding breathy and annoyed as they slip out of my mouth, uncontrollable. I don't know why I've lied, perhaps so she'll decide not to stay. I push open the screen door.

Paula steps up and inside. "I hadn't heard from you in a few days," she says. "I thought I'd come by, bring you some goodies." Her voice is high and shrill, ringing against the stainless steel pans that hang from the ceiling. She leans in close to me as she walks past. "Gosh, Jenna, you're looking a little pale. Are you okay?"

"I'm fine."

"Are you sure? You seem kind of...funny." She puts the bag on the counter. "Hey, this place is cute. You never did invite me over. I thought I was gonna have to just look at it from the outside."

I sigh loudly, so she'll notice. "You could have called first."

Paula thrusts her bottom lip out and pouts, looking like a clown. "I'm locked up in that house all day, so when I get the chance to get out I just go." She opens and closes the cabinets, looking for a place to put the groceries. "Anyway, what've you been up to?"

"Working on the house. Errands. I saw an old friend yesterday."

"A *friend?*"

My uncle, I think. *Hunter is my uncle.* If only she knew the anxiety and confusion I'm feeling. But could I tell her such a thing? "Don't start," I say. "Just a friend."

"Uh huh." Paula opens up one of the cabinet doors, begins to put away the chips and salsa she brought with her. "So," she says. "Just friends, huh?" She chuckles, probably to make a joke out of it, to give her license to say such things. Sometimes it's difficult to tell whether Paula is serious; she switches back and forth so quickly from concern to manipulation. She turns around.

"Paula, why do you have to say things like that?"

"You're right," she says. "That was pretty thoughtless of me." Her tone is sarcastic. "You always think I'm pretty thoughtless, don't you?"

"I just think you can be disrespectful, that's all."

"Disrespectful?"

"To Seth."

"To Seth?" Paula laughs, lands a hand on her hip.

"I know what you're thinking," I say. "Seth is dead and I'm being ridiculous."

"Come on, Jenna, that's not fair."

"You were thinking that, weren't you?"

"Fine." Paula lets out a huffy breath, throws her hands up in the air. "Yes. Whatever you say. I can't say anything around you." She stomps toward the door, leaving her purse behind on the table.

"Didn't you forget something?" I say.

Paula turns around, comes back. "Look, Jenna," she says, "if you have so many problems with me then why do you bother being my friend, huh? You're certainly not perfect, and I don't point out every little thing you do or say or *think* that I don't like."

"I never said I was perfect."

"No, but you do play innocent."

"What are you talking about?"

"Oh, don't give me that shit." Paula begins picking at her fingernail, the way she does before saying something more belligerent than usual, something she's been dying to tell me.

"What?"

"Okay," she says. "I'm gonna be honest with you. You've always played the moral goddess. You've treated me like I was lower than you, and like I was some kind of slut. And meanwhile you're always playing innocent."

"What is this?" I say. "Is this something to do with the other day? Did I say something wrong?"

"No, I..." Paula stops, puts her hand to her mouth. She is looking out the window now, past me, and I turn around to see what she's looking at. Nothing, it seems. She's just stopping, I guess, having one of those rare realizations, a Paula moment. Her eyes are wet, filling up. "I'm sorry," she says, her voice cracking, weak.

"Paula?"

"I'm just a little on edge."

"Is everything okay?"

She pulls out a chair from the kitchen table, sits down. Her cheeks and nose are flushed, her eyes wet. "I'm not pregnant," she says with a heavy sigh. "I was wrong."

"Are you upset?" I ask, and she nods. Of course she's upset, I think; *look at her*. But I'm surprised. I had no idea she wanted to be pregnant; she'd seemed tied down, exhausted, like another child was the farthest thing from her mind. I grab a napkin from the holder and give it to her, put a hand on her shoulder. "You can always try again," I add.

She chuckles. "When I tried for Erica it took forever." She blows her nose in the napkin. "Of course Josh just sort of popped out of nowhere...but when I decide I *do* want one it doesn't work."

"I didn't realize you wanted another baby," I say.

Paula looks up, frowning, as if such a statement is unfathomable. "Do we ever know? I mean, do we ever really know what we want? How many things do we let happen...but on purpose?"

"I don't know."

"I don't know either." Paula blots her face with the napkin. "But I was only sort of half-trying, you know? Not being extremely careful, if you know what I mean...but it wasn't until I thought I was pregnant that I knew I wanted another one." She laughs, a tear streaming down her cheek. "It sounds crazy, doesn't it? But really—lately I don't know myself so well. I'm not sure if I just sort of let things happen, or if I do things on purpose." She throws her napkin in the trash can next to the counter. "Who knows. Am I crazy?"

"Of course not."

"You know, Jenna—sometimes I feel like telling people *don't ever have kids*, because it takes so much out of you. Then I turn around and want more of them." I smile, thinking of how this is good for her, of how helpful and sane I feel right now, how minutes ago I was lying in the dirt, hiding upstairs. "If you were to ask me now," she adds, "if you should have kids, I don't even know what I'd tell you." She blows her nose. "Then again, I already know you'd never ask me that question."

"No."

"Well, it's wonderful." Her face lights up. "See? I'm just deciding this on the spot. Just being pregnant—despite its cons—can be pretty wonderful, too. Creating something of your own."

I've always wanted to tell Paula about my pregnancy. But it had seemed like too much of a coincidence at the time—that I became pregnant just weeks after her own announcement, that I also married within months of it. Paula might have thought I was trying to be just like her, finally getting and keeping a man. "Well, anyway," she says, "I'll be fine. It's probably my goddamn period that's making me so emotional. When I get my period it's like I'm drunk. I have no idea what I'm saying."

I laugh. "I know what you mean."

"No hard feelings?"

"Nah," I say. "But can I just ask you one thing?" Paula nods. "What did you mean when you said I was always playing innocent?"

"Oh, it's no big deal." Paula waves her arm and stands.

"No, really," I say. "I won't get upset. I'm just curious."

"I was just talking about what a flirt you were sometimes." Paula gives a quick flick of a smile, a furrowed brow. "It's funny, because you were so shy before Seth...but then once you were with him you really changed." Her face seems to be waiting for an answer—not in reprimand, but in mere curiosity.

Paula wants to understand me.

I don't have any explanations for her. I can only give her a quick smile back, one of embarrassment, perhaps shame—a guilty pleasure smile. And I can tell her only that she probably is right. "I remember so little about that time," I say, but really I'm thinking about what she said a few minutes ago.

How many things do we let happen on purpose?

thirty-five

On the morning of the accident, Seth and I were cleaning the apartment, a little junk-sifting before Seth went to the university for a few hours. This was a ritual, spring cleaning in the fall, something we did each October when Seth started dreaming about moving again. It needed to be done, he said, because we should start thinking about really getting settled—to look for a house, something permanent.

It didn't seem permanent, he always said.

While we were cleaning, I found a pile of satin sheets crushed into the corner of the bedroom closet, beneath a heap of mismatched shoes. Seth snatched it from me, unfolded the jade-colored satin and draped it over his forearm, then moved in front of the window and held it up to the light. Sun danced on the fabric, bouncing off cars two stories below. I thought of the clear, Caribbean water, the honeymoon we never had.

"How come we never use these?" he asked.

"I don't know," I said. "I guess because we don't have anything to go with them." Pointless, I thought, to use beautiful sheets on our old lumpy mattress, and with a rugged calico quilt. "Don't worry," I added. "We'll use them. Someday, when we have a house." For some reason, it felt like a lie.

Seth leaned against me from behind, holding the sun-warmed,

silky fabric to my cheekbone, placed a hand on my belly. He whispered, his breath hot against my neck. "Can't you just imagine this against your skin?"

He could always remind me why I shouldn't be so practical: his strong, knotty hands were careful, accustomed to my body; his deep, oaky voice was like sugar to my blood. "Nice," I said, thinking of the possibilities—our tangled bodies in satin on the floor, stripes of sun on hot skin.

Then *pills*, I thought—two days of forgotten pills. Take two to make up for it, the doctor had said, take another tomorrow. Make up for it, be careful, or there will be babies.

It had happened this way before.

For so long Seth had been hoping I'd change my mind and try for a baby again. For so long I'd punished myself, and I couldn't stop. I was sinful, undeserving. I could not be a good mother.

"No," I said. "Not now. Too much to do."

Why not? he might have asked me again, perhaps the next day, or the one after. And I probably would have stalled him, lied to him even—told him I'd change my mind one day. And while I'd tell him this I'd think about Mom and Dad, the epitome of obligation, of automated faith. Of purgatory.

Seth never did have the chance to ask me again. On that crisp, kaleidoscopic afternoon his life was vanquished, gone in a second. So *No* was one of the last things I ever said to him.

———

I don't remember seeing flowers around Seth's coffin, just a blurry frame of color around my focus on him, like bright Impressionist blotches. There was the smell, though—that pungent sting of carnations and roses that will always makes me think of death.

The roses especially.

He tried to comfort me with yellow ones when I lost the baby. He brought them to me one at a time at the hospital, and then at home, one for each day that I remained in bed. He would ask

Mom for a vase to put them in, and Mom would bring out the champagne flute she said was reserved for our wedding.

Then years later he still would bring me yellow roses for no reason but love this time. He would use the same champagne flute from our wedding, standing the roses in the center of the dining room table; and until each rose died, I would eat my dinner in front of the television. I didn't have the heart to tell him that yellow roses meant death.

I wonder if the bare, budding rosebush next to the porch is a yellow rose.

It's Saturday. I don't know what happened to Friday; it sort of dissolved into today—afternoon blurring, dimming into evening, then night, fading into a blank of sleep, the fog lifting, followed by the blur of morning. But the sun did not wake me; it was the screech of a crow outside on the lawn, on my unfinished garden plot.

One of Seth's seeds is peeking through the dirt. The anonymous plant is small, with hearty, rounded leaves. It could be eaten by a groundhog or a deer, or a heavy spring rain might drown it. Or worse—it could die for some unknown reason. Maybe I should get it over with, kill it now rather than wait for natural causes. I could let my own plants die that way; that would be acceptable, but not Seth's. I couldn't bear to watch.

Our years together are a blur. Seven years that seem like one—days and months and seasons I can't distinguish. Which birthday did he give me the diamond birthstone earrings? Which Christmas was it that we didn't go to Mom and Dad's or Seth's parents, and stole away to New Hampshire? I can't remember.

I do remember when he began to teach—when he got the job at the high school. It was something he had always wanted to do, but it was still scary for him at first—the sophomores dissecting him with their eyes, not sure; testing him, he had said. Until they finally began to accept him and to look up to him as if he was a god, the way I once had. That was when he stopped teaching me.

It was as if there was no more to teach, nothing left to say. But now I wonder if it was all because of me—if I just stopped seeming interested, stopped giving him the signal.

I'll never be sure how much it bothered Seth that we never tried for a baby again, but I know how it bothered Mom. She always managed to find a way to bring up the subject, even though I had told her that I never intended to try again. In her subtle and skillful way, *reproduction* inevitably slipped into most conversations. And she didn't stop, even while she knew how much it hurt me. Perhaps she kept pestering because I didn't tell her my reasons. *Why not?* she would always ask, but I never could seem to answer. Then over the years Mom's heart seemed to shrivel away, as if watching my independent, childless life with Seth was draining the life from her. I'll always wonder in what way it was painful for her—if she felt bad for me, if she was jealous; or if she simply was confused by my lack of an explanation. Maybe it has been my fault all this time, and all I need to do is to tell her *why.*

Maybe she would have told me things, too.

I sift through the coffee-ground soil surrounding the tiny plant, my fingers spaced apart to act as a colander to weed out roots and unwanted growth. Soon there will be dandelions, and those fleshy weeds like the ones in front of the porch. Then the spearmint—all that spearmint that smells so wonderful, but is so deadly, because it will eventually take everything over.

It too must be killed.

I hold my breath, pull at the roots, and Seth's tiny plant lifts up, pulls out, so smoothly, so easily toppling over and shedding deep soil beneath it. What have I done? I think. But then when I breathe out, the air feels cleaner, sweeter smelling somehow; it feels better for his plant to come up this way, lifted out by another's roots instead of my fingers. As if I did not do it myself.

I grab the shovel from the shed that's broken and splintered, its handle wrapped with duct tape like a mummy. I dig deeper this time, more vigorously. Scooping the soil is difficult; it's still cold and solid in places, filled with weeds and little rocks. I have to stand on the shovel to push down with each scoop, to slice through; sometimes it won't go down. Or sometimes it does go down but gets stuck, and I have to yank at the old dead grass and dandelions—some of whose roots are thick as carrots, and throw them onto the side of the large dirt plot. I think about how well Aunt Adeline did this—how she rooted and planted and gave life to things in a different way from most women.

As I step down on the shovel this time it drops down fast to a sharp, resistant crash, hitting something hard—another rock, it sounds like. Lifting the shovel and slicing at the dirt from another angle, I cup the blade under and around something.

There is a rock here—a long piece of slate, which I pry up and lift out. Below it is something else: wood and metal, charcoal gray, water-soaked boards with metal buckles or strapping, like on a door. I clean the dirt away, digging trenches on both sides until I can see the rectangular shape about a foot long and a little less wide. Scooping the dirt away from both sides, I see a small wooden box or trunk, a tiny treasure chest.

The structure is warped, wobbly, its wood fibrous, like tiny threads of dried pot roast, stacked and shaped and held together by the rusted metal. I touch the shovel to a wooden corner and the wood crumbles, becomes part of the dirt. I take another shovelful from each side and scoop beneath the small trunk, lifting it out of the ground. Tilting the blade, I slide the shredding box off the blade and onto the grass. It caves in as it lands, and balls of dirt roll into the new cleft in the lid. The tiny balls of dirt continue to move as the structure crumbles more, as if exposure to the elements has brought it back to life.

As I try to lift the rusted metal latch, it pulls off, and the trunk completely collapses. What is left of the top deteriorates in my hand, turning to dirt—small, dark crumbs like rich coffee grounds. Beneath the shredded wood is something else; I shudder at the unmistakable color.

Bone.

They are fragments of ivory—slivers, limbs, it appears, and rounded pieces of what appear to be a skull. When I touch my finger to the round pieces they splinter; the bone is delicate, so thin—like a broken light bulb, an eggshell. Smaller pieces are scattered around these, many rotted down to tiny knobs and splinters, vivid against the dark dirt. The display is gruesome, like some child's prehistoric creature model, only real.

I wonder if this could be a kitten, a baby puppy; it is that small. Mom's cat, I think, Aunt Adeline's. But this does not look like a cat.

I think of the last tenants, who seemed to have kept a garden here. But they would have found this first—unless they did not dig deep. Or perhaps they did find it and reburied it. Aunt Adeline's garden may have been here, too, years ago; although what I recall is another forsythia bush right about here, in the center of her lawn. Her garden could have been anywhere on this lawn; things grow over so quickly. I wonder how many years this tiny grave has been here, and how close others came to digging it up. To think, that all this time it was just below the surface.

But what is it?

Whatever this body is, someone cared enough to package it so, to rest it here on home property. If only there were teeth on this skull to help identify. Seth would have known—he was good at bones. What would he have said? A tiny skull, so undernourished. Underdeveloped, even.

Not fully formed.

My stomach contracts. I hold it tight with my arm, rock back and forth on the softening ground; it is comforting to do this. Looking up from the bones I see the houses around mine—people I have not met, their windows dark, their lives a mystery. How many of these people, who otherwise seem so happy, have had pain in their lives?

I am dizzy as I stand, and feel unstable, scatterbrained. I fumble across the lawn and up the front steps of the house, then through the door and into the bathroom. The sink is a support as I buckle over; my red, bulging face in the mirror the last thing I see before my eyes are down at the drain.

There, in the reflection of the stainless steel plug, my nose and chin are distorted, bulbous, like a fetus. I reach up to the faucet and turn on the hot water, then close my eyes and rest my elbows on the side of the sink. I will stay here until I relax a little, until I can stand up again. For now I just want to breathe, to take in this clean steam and not think about it.

A pain enters my abdomen, like electricity moving into my stomach, and then my chest and neck and up to my head. I think of Seth's face—that same face from last October when I said no to him.

If I could go back to that day I would say *yes* to Seth this time. I would take a chance—gladly take a chance, perhaps even hoping it would happen. I wish I'd taken advantage of such an opportunity, this wondrous control over my own body; I might have a piece of him with me now.

I have realized this before, this control.

I think back to the one time in my life when I did allow it to happen, when I missed those three days of pills seven years ago, and replay what the doctor had said to me about missing pills: miss one, and take two the next day; miss two, take two for two days; miss more than that, and they are unreliable. When I missed those pills I wasn't as careful as I could have been. I was perhaps hungrier for Seth on those days—unusually hungry, and there was no worry, no desire to be careful. I didn't know what was happening to me; I was a feline in heat. And I had stopped thinking, stopped agonizing over the fact that I could get pregnant. There even might have been a few moments when the thought of bonding with Seth forever gave me a safe, sparkly feeling.

So for that week or two when it was not safe enough, I took my chances and awoke each morning with a smile. Until one day it finally happened; the seed was planted, and this different behavior of mine suddenly stopped.

And on the day my baby died, I felt my soul was lost too— the soul I had swallowed down and lost before, the one I wanted back. Now it was gone forever. And to think, that just moments before on that day I had been in a realm of tranquillity. A goddess in sweeping rayon, summer green, a flower amongst the black and navy-dressed men. A blur of wind-blown hair and carnations, champagne and chardonnay, fluffy white frosting.

Tall green grass.

part ten
a fertile green

{renee

thirty-six

Renee followed Adeline to the youth center all that spring. But it seemed like every time, after following her sister around like a puppy dog for three hours, she had to walk home alone because Adeline had left with some boy. Until one day the boys began to talk to Renee, and she realized she could get their attention, just like Adeline could. Even the attention of the new boy, a boy Adeline had yet to conquer.

Angus was nineteen, four years older than Renee. Mother would never allow her to be with a boy his age. Nor would his parents, he told her on that night they met. But Renee and Angus couldn't help it when they clicked eyes and souls that night at the youth center, and took that long walk together.

It had to be their secret, at least for now. No one could know, especially Adeline.

———

The first morning after Renee was out late she awoke to singing birds and warm, clean air outside her bedroom window. A ragged-looking Adeline was hovering over her. "Where did you go last night?" she asked, accusation in her voice. "You were supposed to come home with me."

"You're always leaving without me anyway," Renee said.

"Don't get fresh," Adeline said. "Where were you?"

"Nowhere." Renee wouldn't tell her, even though there was a part of her inside that wanted to, that wanted to prove that she could get boys, too. Instead, she decided she would talk back to her big sister. It was a scary thing to do. "Adeline," she said. "You probably didn't notice I was gone until two in the morning. You were probably too busy with Mark Fisher, in the bushes or something."

Adeline grabbed Renee's upper arm with tight, bony fingers. "I said don't get fresh!" she shouted.

And what would Adeline say if she knew Renee had been talking to a grown man? To a man who didn't leer over *her*? She probably would say he was a nerd or a gay boy—something to discredit Renee's success. If she did believe it she would get angry and tell Mother. Or she would be jealous, and would find a way for Renee not to have him. She might even try to get him herself. Adeline always got what she wanted, especially when it came to men.

"Let go," Renee said, thinking of how aggressive her big sister had become since she went away to college. "Anyway, I just walked home."

"I'm never taking you there again," Adeline said.

Renee would be devastated if she couldn't go back. "I can go by myself," she said, hardly believing the words coming out of her own mouth.

"Don't even think about it." Adeline finally let go of Renee's arm, which now was sore and red. "If you go on your own, I'll tell."

Adeline always said things like that.

That afternoon, while Adeline practiced her piano, Renee went upstairs and put on her best summer outfit, a short, fitted-waist sundress in tropical colors she had bought with her baby-sitting money, and a pair of ankle-strap straw sandals. Adeline caught her as she was walking out the door.

"Where are you going in that clown outfit?"

Adeline's face turned red when Renee didn't answer. It felt powerful to not answer for once, to actually have some control over her big sister.

———

Renee and Angus would meet secretly, usually in front of Healy's Ice Cream or the pizza parlor. Each time Angus would stand outside with his hands in his pockets, his feet taking turns kicking up sand, trying to act casual. And each time as she approached his eyes would stop on the road in front of his feet, then slowly glide toward her walking up it—as if his eyes were pulled in that direction, as if afraid they might move too fast and be disappointed to not see her. But he did see her, because she had managed to get away, to once again sneak out of the house. His face would blush, and she would think of how beautiful an older man was when he blushed. His words, however, showed no restraint.

"Let's get out of here," he would say.

She thought of the men in movies, how they always said such things with confidence—as if they knew women would want it and obey. She thought of how, in the movies, this meant they would steal away to some private nook and make love. Angus must have said it just to get out of sight of any curious onlookers. But it felt good hearing it; it felt warm and tingly, so she imagined he was stealing her away somewhere, too.

They would walk down the street to the pier near the jetty, and he would show her the yachts and fishing vessels, the rafts and canoes they could take out on the water if they wanted to. They wandered over a grassy hill and down a staircase made from railroad ties, past pink-gray granite bluffs to the beach area, which was covered with pebbles and soaked driftwood. They hiked across the lower rocks next to the water and inspected mussels and snails in the tide pools. When the tide came in they jumped away from each wave just in time, strands of kelp wrapping their ankles. Angus would talk about fishing, about how his father went deep-sea for swordfish and bluefins, how he had spent much time with his father on the water.

"I feel closer to the ocean than to the land," he said, and Renee suddenly agreed. She felt close to this man named Angus with the bright turquoise eyes.

———

Sometimes during breakfast the phone would ring, and Father or Mother or even Adeline would answer. No one there, they would say after hanging up, and Renee knew that Angus would be in front of Healy's or by the docks or some other place they had most recently talked about.

They managed to see each other, discreetly leaving their meeting places to walk on the beach or take the boat out from the jetty to Mackerel Point. Renee would go to Tucker's Pizza and just run into him, and they would casually leave at the same time. They didn't speak much at the youth center, except for in big groups, or when Adeline was not around. Renee knew if Adeline saw her with him, she would inspect her face and recognize her falling in love with this older man.

But he hadn't kissed her, not yet. She hoped he would soon because in two days he would be leaving for Carbur in Aroostook County to work in the potato fields. He would be gone for ten days, then back for three, and then he would go out again. "I'll write," he said, but what she really wanted was for him to kiss her before he left.

———

The first letter arrived on a Saturday morning. Postmarked Carbur, Maine, potato farming country. Renee knew what it was, even without a return address. There could be no address, no last name, even. Even the letter should be signed with an alias; he'd come up with something.

Renee was the one to get the mail that day because it was the weekend, because she wasn't at her summer job at the golf club. Her heart pattered as she walked back toward the house with it.

I can't wait to see you again, it read.

Mother was standing in the front doorway, still in her bathrobe, as Renee walked up. "Anything for me?" she asked.

"Nope."

"Anything for Dad or Adeline?"

"No. Nothing." Because this was the routine.

But on Saturday it was Adeline who stood on the front steps, and saw the letter in Renee's hand. "What's that?" she asked.

"Nothing."

Adeline gave Renee a squinty-eyed look, a look that admitted she could be devious, that she would find out about it eventually.

The letters came, and with each one Renee wrote back immediately. There were two or three each week waiting for her when she arrived home from work at the end of the day. Only on Saturday did she make it to the mailbox herself, and on this Saturday, she tried not to blush as she read the words right in front of Adeline.

I want to kiss you.

But this also saddened Renee, reminded her of how they didn't even hold hands like other couples. His hand only lightly touched her back a few times, as he was guiding her over the rocks or helping her step out of the dinghy. Angus's actions, in many ways, did not imply they were anything but friends. But she knew. She knew there was something beyond comprehension between them, and that one day they would gather this energy they had reserved and come together full force, like converging storms.

jenna}

thirty-seven

I have wanted things dead.

I did not realize this until I was thirteen years old—the year I discovered the oils, when two frantic, late-summer houseflies landed upon my freshly gessoed canvas, and I quickly, almost unconsciously, decided to stun them with the muscle of my palm. And instead of their usual escape from the slow metabolism of my flying human hand, they lingered in a stupor, their twiggy arms rubbing, their wings twitching. It was late summer; they were slower, dying, and had found something wonderful, so I slapped them—both of them, and did not miss, so their black mealy bodies were spread upon the white background, the mica-like wings twitching. I thought of control, of independent creation. Of wanting things dead.

And I thought about it years later, when Seth brought me yellow roses, that once again I had made such a thing happen. I had wished for it, prayed for it—not about the insects that landed on canvas or nibbled at me, but about my own flesh.

My baby.

I wonder what Paula would say about such a thing, had I told her. Your own blood, she would tell me; *how could you?* she would say, disgusted, or perhaps amazed.

It was an accident, I told Seth, but now I see it again: a different angle, a different light. The summer picnic, where I laughed and tumbled because the grass was tall and safe and cushiony, and because blue eyes in a green meadow had invited me.

There had been many faces there—faces I had never met, people who did not know me. Women were dressed in wild, exotic patterned skirts and dresses, silver accessories; men in linen and colorful ties, with long hair and beards, and strong facial bones. They were from different programs and years, different schools, and as I began to talk to them I realized I was in another world—somewhere unlike my days at school and nights with Seth, or those tense moments with my family. I felt uncomfortable and shy, and I spoke only to the few people I did know. I made sure to always have some food or drink in my hand, made sure I was always on my way to or from some other table, some other venue, so I wouldn't look as awkward as I felt.

A jazz band was playing in the center of the lawn, so I walked over with my sweet-frosting cake and decided to watch. As I stood there I could feel eyes watching me, and looked around to notice that many were—mostly men; young men, older men, and the husbands of female professors. Maybe it was the dress, my green-and-black rayon that showed off my shoulders, or that silver anklet I spent twenty minutes contemplating over, which sparkled against my tanned skin, flashed in the sunlight. I felt like a woman, soft and sweet-smelling in the heat, a woman who came alone to this party, to walk amongst the flowers and crisp wine. It was not until the waiter walked by with the tray and I took my first glass of chardonnay that I remembered. Something was growing inside me.

Suddenly it was as if all could see through me, and see the throbbing, pumping heart in my uterus, see me as something different: mother of someone, lover of someone. Untouchable for always. These faces, these men, the boys whose eyes penetrated, whose attention fueled my spirit, were there only for display. And I knew that I could never wonder, never imagine, because wanting and not knowing could destroy one's soul.

I blinked hard, then saw they were not staring at me after all, but were back to their talk about artists and galleries, about the latest in independent film. They tipped their heads and waved their glasses and beer bottles, while their partners nestled tightly next to them, secure.

I took another sip of wine, wondering how it would make me feel—not my head, but my mind. I was conducting an experiment: would I be scolded for each sip, would I get away with it and feel nothing? The wine went down smoothly, cool and buttery, so I took another sip and then another, waiting.

Then I felt something next to my bare arm: cloth—crisp, loose white cloth was what I saw, and I turned to see the young men standing close to me, so close. The one next to me was young, a freshman or sophomore, by his smooth, dewy skin and blinking, insecure blue eyes. His hair was dark, over-gelled, his posture stiff. He held his beer awkwardly, as if for the first time. Next to him was another man, also blue-eyed, fairer, perhaps even younger, drinking a glass of champagne. The two of them were dressed in more conservative attire than the others—ironed white shirts and two-color ties, pleated dress pants left over from the last family wedding or graduation, and shiny black slip-on dress shoes. They didn't look like art students; they didn't appear to belong at all, so I gulped down my second glass of wine, turned to them and spoke.

"Are you in the art program?"

The dark one, who swayed a bit, told me the truth. Freshman, he said, looking to his friend for approval. Undeclared freshman. He smiled with bright white teeth, the corners of his eyes wrinkle-free.

We heard there was this party.

Ah, I said, making sure to display my approval. My head felt fuzzy. "I am an art major," I said. "And I don't feel like I belong here at all." I lifted my empty glass. Another, please.

I had thought I would go to this party to expand my mind, to speak to people of my own kind, to escape my little world. But

I liked these two young men who spoke simply and didn't want to stand around and interpret art, who wanted to small talk and be open and natural and free their identities with me.

The dark one lifted his hand to my cheek, fingers brushing. I felt myself flush, tremble, felt the vein in my neck pulsing. My stomach felt empty, convulsing, and as I reached up to take his hand away I couldn't seem to reach it, didn't want to reach it as it slid down the back of my neck. He pressed his fingers against my skin, his thumb kneading my tendons like soft dough. I closed my eyes and he spoke.

Want to take a walk through the arboretum?

I followed him and his friend, but at a distance, through acres of apple and pear trees, through the hedge maze, the rose gardens. The sky seemed more open, bluer than ever. The air was crisp and delicious, and feeling good helped me forget.

We dodged around bushes and ran down hills, and it didn't matter. When we jumped down from four-foot stone walls, tumbled in the thicket of tall grass and milkweed, it didn't matter. And while I played with those fresh young blue-eyed boys, I made sure not to think about what was growing inside me.

Not until I felt the pain.

When I tumbled down that final hill all was silent—there was nothing but grass around me, green and late-summer brown—tall as corn, it seemed, then the empty blue sky above. I waited for a cloud, a bird, a sun—anything to move into the cold, blue space. I thought about the spiders and ants and other creatures that might burrow into my hair—how for the first time, I welcomed them. And as I lay there I saw the blue-eyed boys again, this time their faces hovering, asking *Are you all right?* But now they were faces without eyes—only holes to look through to that blue sky beyond. Then the pains came, and I hated them, and prayed Seth wouldn't think badly of me. For the very first time I prayed for our baby, but I was too late.

An accident, I later told him, a simple trip and tumble.

What I didn't tell him was that I had frolicked in grass, played and jumped because two strangers had asked me to. They were boys I knew nothing about, except that their eyes were blue and their hands were warm as they guided me through tall, caressing grasses. Their simple touch had consumed me, and I had melted. And they were not beautiful or deep-voiced or perfect—they were not husbands-to-be. They were no one.

Only touches, nothing more. But how destructive a touch can be.

"No baby," the doctors at the hospital told us, and Seth's face caved in, eyes melted like wax. But he never had to feel that surge, that vacuum of pain. He never had to lie in that strange, sweating meadow like I did.

Was it the wine that made you fall? he asked as I lay beneath the bright white hospital lights, and I wondered if he was angry, if it was something else he was saying with his eyes. *What were you thinking?* he must have been saying. But I could only think of my empty soul now, and I didn't answer.

It wasn't the wine, I finally told him. And don't you worry, Seth, I added. We'll marry anyway, just like I promised.

part eleven
buried things

{renee

thirty-eight

There was one night after Angus came home when he didn't speak to her at all. There wasn't the usual *Hello* and *How are you?*, the pretending they weren't boyfriend and girlfriend. On this night, neither of them needed to speak.

As he smiled at her from across the room the music seemed to vibrate and shoot up through her legs to her stomach. And her eyes teased as they moved in his direction, passing over the salmon-colored fake-marble tile, the clusters of folding metal chairs. He smiled just barely, and slowly glided away from his group of greasy boys without being noticed. His black bangs parted away from his face as he approached, as if wind was blowing at him, and suddenly he was standing in front of her, so close that he almost was hovering above.

He rested his hand gently on the back of her bare arm, and his head motioned for them to move on, somewhere—away from the crowd, toward the darkness beyond the glaring red exit sign.

Without hesitation she went with him, and as she left through the door she turned back to see Adeline in the corner of the room, her eyes flicking here and there while she talked to some man—perhaps checking for other men, checking to see who was watching her. For a second it seemed Adeline's eyes had stopped on Renee and Angus, and that her brow had furrowed, lips grown concerned. If she had seen them, Renee wondered, would she have even acknowledged it? Would her ego take over and make her believe she had not?

Renee hoped no one else saw as Angus led her out through the door and down the walkway, toward the grass outside the building. He didn't speak, and when she began to say something herself—something about the beautiful late-evening light or the air or the moon coming up, he turned and hushed her with his gentle finger, not against his lips but against hers. A thing she saw in movies, the man hushing the woman, telling her to wait; the woman obeying, succumbing, waiting for something. For what? she always had wondered.

For something good, she knew now—to be taken into their powerful arms, into their mouths. This was real, no fairy tale— the fact that her words could stop at his command, that her questions could wait, that her body would obey. What lay ahead didn't matter, except that it be his wish.

And then she did not think. She only followed, gripping his strong hand now, over the lawn and through the gardens in back of the youth center, through tall bushes to a path beyond the light of the building. There was a different light ahead of them—from the moon, over the water beyond the woods, slivers of light through the trees.

They stepped beyond the trees and into this new light. He stopped, taking her upper arm again with one hand, then reaching for her other arm, turning her toward him.

She could see the silhouette of his hair blowing around his face, and just the bluish edge of skin, the gloss of his eyes. His arms pulled her toward him, and she could feel the ruffle of her blouse touch against his shirt, then her body, her abdomen, all melting together and with the earth below her feet. She heard the ocean, louder and louder, as if they were in it, the water as warm as their blood.

His face moved toward her, and his mouth was there somewhere in the darkness; it came in warm and soft like a flower petal, not to her lips but to her cheek, pressing in with suction then pulsing to her mouth. His mouth opened and grappled with hers; hers fought back, welcomed back. She thought of the sea and them in it, underwater creatures tangled with each other, mouths open to let in salty water. Through her half-open eyes she saw his in the moonlight, the whites glazed, shiny like eggs, the blue iris paler, icier—a frozen pond, half rolled into his lids, abominable and enticing. She saw the sea creatures, the octopus—all arms and a mouth, tightening, engulfing; her own body wrestled in its grip. And she did not want to get away.

He pulled his face away from her and took a long breath, pointed to the water. She did not want to leave this spot in the moonlight, but she followed. They ran down the path through the woods, her heartbeat frantic, her body a life of its own. At the bottom of the path was the dock across from the jetty, a small boat. They got in it and pushed off, onto the calm water, away from the lights of the dock.

He rowed to a dark spot on the calm ocean, just below the trees where there was a hint of moonlight—just enough to see the edges of skin, the gloss of eyes. The air was cool, but his hands were warm and supple against her skin, and the flat, blanket-covered bottom of the boat was soft as a pillow. The dark, starlit universe was above her, and as his body moved she unexpectedly opened and heaved, as if giving birth. She breathed in the raw, salty air, and was no longer inside her body. She was a ripe, freshly split fruit, opened beneath a sky of pulsating stars, and a moon that occasionally hid behind a thin, milky cloud.

jenna}

thirty-nine

I lie in the master bedroom, in the double bed in which Seth and I once slept, keeping my eyes open to the swirling patterns in the plaster ceiling, because if I close them I see Seth again. I look to the top of the bureau, where the photograph of Angus stands, just next to another dead man. Angus and Seth, both staring out at me, crying for me to save them.

Seth's picture was taken early last fall from the small balcony of our Cambridge apartment, and in it he looks directly at the camera with steely, shadowed eyes. His face is stark white, over-exposed—with a creepy focus that seems to follow me when I move. He appears tired, a bit agitated in his tight, impatient posture, constricted by the white railing surrounding him. The photograph was never one of my favorites while Seth was alive; I always thought he looked cross, impenetrable, as opposed to other photos in which he's all soft shadows and warm eyes—the sweet, more innocent Seth. After he died, the sweet photos changed to sad, vulnerable ones; suddenly he was a pitifully abandoned man. Now I prefer this photo, this tired, aggravated Seth whose eyes don't leave me. The eyes staring hard, as if he knew when the picture was taken that I one day would look at it and feel this pain. He seems watchful, fighting back at the world.

At me.

A portrait of Mom and Dad is also on the bureau, and Elisabeth's glamour shot, in which she looks glossy and strange and ten years older than she really is. Angus doesn't belong here, but oddly his face seems no more foreign than the others do: a pseudo psychologist mother, a father with his dream world in the basement, and a little sister who—unlike me—is high-powered, confident, and ready for the thrill ride of life ahead of her.

I move into my old bedroom, where the new wallpaper will go up today. I have picked out a lovely paisley print in rust-on-vanilla, so different from what used to be in this room. Different is what I need.

I lie on my back, look up to this ceiling. There's a whole world in here; I could get lost in all this pine, in its knots and crevices. There's an eye in the wood, a mouth even. I think the mouth may be moving now, speaking to me. It tells me how Mom would lie terrified in her bed in this very room, perhaps praying there was no baby growing inside. Baby Jenna—developing in this very room, feeding off of her insides, and off any residue from these walls, these floors, any breeze that might have blown through the window. Maybe Mom was thinking what I sometimes think—that suffering is enough to make it better. Suffering, the thing that makes one a martyr.

These are the same knots of pine Mom looked at as her belly grew, as she thought of love and death, as she thought of her destiny. What was it like for Mom as she lay in this room? Did she have doubts and fears at the tender age of fifteen? Did she ever hear from Angus again? And when Angus died, what was that like? Was something new born inside her, as guilt was born when Seth passed on?

There are things I want to ask her, things I want to tell her. I'm not sure if it's because I'm confused and seek answers, if I want to shock her and shake her, or if it's simply because my head is swimming. I just know I can't remember ever feeling this way before.

I'm drifting; I'm not focused. I keep straying from the memory, trying so hard to forget how all the ethics I knew and firmly stood by could be tested, slaughtered in a heartbeat. Trying to forget what weakness I am capable of, what horrors. I had thought that suffering would do the trick—that guilt plus suffering equaled redemption.

But this one won't go away.

I need to tell someone—not just the conscience inside of me, but someone who might understand this level of pain. I need to talk to my mother.

I lift my head and see the telephone back across the hall on the nightstand. I imagine myself dialing, Elisabeth answering in her not-a-care-in-the-world tone, my nerves getting the best of me. "Just wanted to say hello," I end up saying to her. Can I do this or not?

I feel dazed, hot. I don't know what time it is. My fingers feel numb, and my hands are smothering, as if in rubber gloves. There is a fuzzy sensation within the bones of my arms, my legs, a buzzing in my skull. I sit up and see the scraps and glue surrounding me, hear the breath of a quick laugh, my own.

I pick up the brush. It is the only brush I can handle now, one to coat heavily, to make things stick. I slather today's canvas—my once-peach, once-green wall, with my fresh can of glue. But there are no flies to land on it, no mosquitoes even—anything I would feel indifference about killing, adapting into my artwork. So I simply slather it on—light here, a bit heavier there; I'll spread it around. The smell of glue is sickening as I press the paper flat to the wall.

I feel faint. Outside the window there is sun, a blue, rippling heat—or is it just the curvy old glass? It is only spring, I tell myself. Can there be such heat in spring? Sweat pours down my forehead, down the back of my neck, between my breasts, and my hands are full so I cannot wipe. I need to open a window.

I open the one next to me, move across the hall to the master bedroom, to the other one, to get some air flow. I moved too fast, because my vision is black around the edges, my head throbbing with pain. There is the window in front of me, the nightstand phone in front of it. My hand lands on the receiver, but it doesn't feel like my hand because I can barely feel anything, but it is on the receiver, as if acting on its own, without my brain commanding it. I pick it up and dial the first number I have pre-set, the one that comes well before 911 on the list, and the voice that answers isn't Elisabeth at all but is that soft, motherly voice I sometimes confused with Aunt Adeline's, asking over and over, *"Hello? Hello? Is anyone there?"*

part twelve
the umbilical

{renee

forty

In his next letter Angus wrote that it must not happen again, not for a long, long time. He could be arrested, he told her, thrown in jail. But she had known this already. They both had known. Why, she wondered, had they not been so practical before?

They would still meet, he promised, when he came home. The same places, the same times, as if nothing had changed. He would be back in two and a half weeks, and he would be with her. In the meantime he would keep writing. He would give her the address of the new farm at which he could be reached. It wasn't at all like Adeline had said, that they leave afterwards—that they take advantage and move on. Angus would stay.

Perhaps he loved her.

At the beginning of July, Renee's period didn't come like it should have. Never before had she wanted so badly to see a little bloodstain, a little tinge of color on white. But her panties stared back at her with their whiteness. For nights she panicked, lying in bed staring at the pine ceiling in her bedroom. So all she could do was wait for his next letter, wait for this new address, and for her period to come.

She wondered what she would say to him if it never came. He would be as terrified as she was. And he would be in trouble.

So while she prayed for a stain on her clean white panties, she waited for her letters. And suddenly, Adeline also was interested in the mail.

Each day as Renee left for her kitchen job at Sable Oaks, Adeline sat down on the front doorstep, waiting for it. She would make sure to say what she was doing—just sitting there waiting, each day while Renee left for work. And Renee would always miss the mail truck because she didn't arrive home until three in the afternoon. Anything for me? she would ask as she walked in the front door, and Adeline would chuckle and just say no. She would just sit there with her smirk and a chuckle, just so Renee would wonder.

So she never would know for sure.

The letters from Angus had stopped coming. Letters that had arrived twice a week, sometimes three times a week no longer were coming, and Renee could feel a heavy weight in her stomach pulling her down.

The world was caving in on her; so she prayed it was a mistake—that her period would come and her letters would come, while she waited for Angus to come home again. But after eight more days the panties still were clean. She was fifteen years old, her whole life ahead of her. All alone and in need of help.

It was time to tell Adeline.

"Do you have any idea what you've done?"

Adeline was like a dragon, a hissing sound coming from her mouth as she stomped back and forth from the night stand to the doorway, her spindly fingers running through her hair. Renee sat on the edge of the bed while Adeline yelled about how this incident would shame the entire family, about how Renee was a slut.

"No worse than you," Renee said.

Adeline stared down at her, an abrupt, sharp glance that lasted only a second. Then she continued on her lecture, her face flushed, eyes wide and fierce, and her words sharp with consonants, words like *stupid* and *slut,* then long and exaggerated, groaning *whoooor-rrre.* Renee watched Adeline's tall shadow move back and forth on the pale wall in back of her, like some angry tree.

"Are you listening to me?" Adeline yelled.

Renee burst into tears, nodded her head. Of course she was listening. How could she not listen to this ranting and raving? But what was she supposed to do, plead for forgiveness? Bow and kneel at every word, every slam? Adeline wanted reaction, obviously—perhaps an apology for each crime she named. Renee would not give in to this rage. She would only give answers, she decided, if there were questions.

"How could you do this to me?" Adeline said, slapping her hand to her forehead. Renee was confused.

"Do what?"

"He was going to be mine."

Renee at first wanted to laugh at such a smooth delivery of nonsense. "What are you talking about? You think that about everybody in town." She waited for Adeline's reaction, but there wasn't one. "And how can you—you don't even know him."

"Oh yes I do." Adeline raised her brows, squinted her eyes in analysis, a look that had worked on Renee in the past—convinced her she was nothing but an immature, undesirable twit. It wasn't working this time.

"You're crazy," Renee said.

Adeline stepped closer, so to stand high and directly above Renee. She lifted her arm in the air in back of her, as if to slap, her face boiling. "What did you say?"

Renee ducked, threw her hand up in front of her face, then slid off the edge of the bed and slumped to the floor, rupturing into tears. She felt the lightest touch of Adeline's hand against her hair, knew she was close. She very carefully lifted her head and turned it, still imagining the flying hand and Adeline's puffed, mean face. She had never seen her so ugly. But Adeline was sitting on the bed now, just staring into the fiery bulb of the lamp.

"He's coming back tonight," Renee said. "I'll talk to him then."

"Maybe he'll finally tell you about us."

"What are you saying?" Renee asked. This had to be a joke, a game.

"They'll arrest him," Adeline said. "Just because you're so young, they'll arrest him. Did you know that?"

"What did you mean—us?" Renee asked. Adeline said nothing.

It couldn't be true; it had to be one of Adeline's little power games. And she couldn't let it get her down, not now. "Adeline," she said, "I'm asking for your help. Can you help me?"

"I'll tell you what you can do," Adeline said. "You can get an abortion; that's what you can do." The words were delivered with such ease, such nonchalance. They had slipped out of her mouth like any other response would, as if she was telling her how to wash and clean a small wound. *Put a Band-Aid on it.*

"I can't kill my baby."

"Look," Adeline said, "there are many things you don't know about Angus, or about me." She paused for a moment, and her eyes seemed to moisten. "And there are many things he never knew about me. Maybe it's time he knew."

Renee was afraid to ask what Adeline was talking about, but the words suddenly came out. "What do you mean?"

"He never knew about my baby."

"Adeline?"

"Do you have any idea what is going to happen to you?" Adeline said, her eyes fixed on the bright white wall.

"What did you mean?" Renee asked. "Baby?"

"I mean...a baby will change your life."

"I know that. But Angus and I—"

"Angus and you *nothing*," she said. She appeared to be in a daze as she spoke into the blank white wall, as if each word she said hypnotized her directly into the next one, as if she was making it up as she went along.

"But what did you mean?" Renee asked.

Adeline didn't answer.

"Adeline—"

"You can't be with Angus," Adeline interrupted. "Do you know why? Because he's nineteen years old, that's why. Because you're just a baby." She laughs. "You're not even allowed to be together."

"I'll be sixteen when the baby is born."

Adeline covered her ears, shut her eyes tight. A strange groaning sound came out of her, as if she were trying to scream with her mouth shut. Renee couldn't stand the sound, so she thought of other sounds—pretty sounds like the ocean, and birds in the morning. It worked; the sound of Adeline screaming and all her silly words quickly went away.

Renee could not eat. The beef stew felt lumpy, fatty in her stomach. She felt full already; there was no more room in her growing belly. While her mother talked about the upcoming craft fair at the church, Renee watched a vision in her own head, in which she was telling Mother about the baby. In this scene Mother's face turned from its usual smiley, round peach to one with creases and ripples, dimples of anger. Dark, angry, pit-like eyes. But as her mother went on and on she wondered if there would be that kind of reaction. Any reaction.

It was more likely that her mother would get up from the table without stumbling or sighing, and place her soiled silverware into the empty bowl, the folded napkin on top, then quietly glide over to the sink, where she would look out the window and say in a calm, steady voice, *Now what are you going to do about this?* There would be no yelling like Adeline, no comforting either. There wouldn't be an opinion about the whole thing, only the request for a prompt solution.

Mother had always been practical, so self-sufficient, so free from emotional and physical want. Except when Father died, when Mother did open up for a while; suddenly she *needed.* Renee and Adeline cared for her while she lay in the master bedroom, staring out the window, whispering to herself that he was not coming back. And one day a few months later, on the first day of spring, she suddenly got up out of bed and planted her flowers, and everything went back to the way it was before, except that Father was gone. Adeline never was the same again. After Father's death she became hungry for men, then went off to college as planned.

It was seven-fifteen when Adeline returned. She rushed into the kitchen, her wild curls frantic around her flushed face. She grabbed a soda from the refrigerator and headed upstairs.

"Aren't you going to eat?" Mother asked.

"No time," Adeline said. "I'm going out again." She nodded to Renee. Upstairs, she was ordering her. *I want to tell you something.*

jenna}

forty-one

Getting here was a blur.

First there was the fall to the floor, the splits in the pine like fault lines. It didn't hurt when I landed, although I did hear the knock of something, perhaps my head hitting the wood. But the floor that sounded hard seemed like a soft, giant pillow, and as I flopped onto my back the warmth of sun hit my forehead, and then I saw black. It seemed like it only was seconds before there were voices, a siren, and the colors white and red.

I am in recovery, a woman in pale blue tells me, and a jowly, gray-bearded man stands above. He wears white over his blue shirt and navy-striped tie, and photo badges, beepers, a stethoscope. The doctor smiles. "Hello there," he says, as if I am five years old. Beyond him, in a corner of this sterile white room, is Mom, from over hundred miles away.

I must be dreaming.

"Jenna," Mom says, the vinyl-seated chair squeaking as she stands. I think of her voice on the other end of the telephone before I chickened out and hung up.

"What happened?" I ask the doctor.

"You passed out."

There's a pasty feeling in my mouth, a floury taste. My head is throbbing. "Where? When did you get—"

"Paula found you," Mom says. Her eyes look swollen, as if she's been crying. "Upstairs in the bedroom. She said she rang the doorbell but you didn't answer. You're lucky she found you."

It seems surreal, the thought of Paula coming back for me, me not remembering any of it. "Have I been here long?" I ask.

"A couple of hours," the doctor says.

"*What?*"

"You've been in and out for a while."

"Am I okay?"

"You're going to be fine," the doctor says. "The CAT scan showed you have a very mild concussion. You'll need to take it easy for a few days. But you should be able to go home after we take care of a few things."

"I had a CAT scan?" I suddenly remember a room filled with colorful machines, the strange humming sounds. "Is Dad here?"

"He took Elisabeth to the ladies' room," Mom says. "And Paula is here."

"Jenna," the doctor says, "have you been under any stress lately? Your mother explained a little bit about your history, that you lost your husband."

"Yes." I look at Mom, who gives a quick smile, and suddenly I remember. Angus Jones.

The doctor leans over and holds a light to my eyes, one at a time. "I don't suspect any neurological goings-on," he says. "I do suspect your body couldn't handle something, though. When your friend found you she said you had been wallpapering in the next room. There were heavy fumes."

"I remember I was going to open another window."

"I think those fumes may have gotten to you. But then that floor got to you—a bit of a bump on the head." He pats me on the arm. "Now, is there anything else I need to know—what you ate, what else is going on...could you be pregnant?"

"No." I chuckle. "But did my mother tell you I lost a baby once?"

"She did not. Recently?"

"No. Seven years ago."

"Ah," the doctor says, as if I'm crazy. Mom's eyes are wide and vulnerable-looking, and her forehead is full of lines and folds—not the usual, tense, pressed-down kind; these are a different shape, more afraid. "She did say you were seeing a psychologist for a while," he adds. "What happened with that?"

"I moved."

He tilts his head, raises his eyebrows. Disapproval, perhaps. "You need to take it easy," he says. "I'll be back to check on you."

I close my eyes for a second, try to remember the last things before I fell: wallpaper, glue, a hot room. A wave of nausea hits me; I am dizzy with my eyes closed. I open them again and Mom is standing closer to the bed. "The doctor didn't ask about your full medical history," she says. "That's why I didn't tell him about your miscarriage. It was so long ago."

"Sometimes I wonder," I say, "if you realize that I almost had a baby."

"Of course I realize."

"But you've always punished me for not having kids." As the words come from my mouth I relax, as if these words have been trapped within my body, like a gas.

"What—" She chuckles, not seeming to take my words seriously. Her mouth curls into a cynical smile. "How can you say such a thing?"

"Because it's true. You've always told me how difficult I made your life."

"Jenna," she says, "you're not feeling well."

"You've always criticized me."

"I said you had choices," she corrects.

"Choices? Mom, I miscarried. I couldn't help what happened—"

"No, I mean Seth," she says, and stares at me with steady eyes, without a blink. I've seen this look before—the one that says I already know what she means, the one that is threatening to tell me in case I don't. "You didn't have to marry Seth," she adds. "You had a choice. You know that." She smiles, a strange, warped smile, as if her real mouth is in there somewhere, behind a cancerous one that controls it. I wonder why I ever wanted to talk to her, and remember why I hesitated to for all those years.

"What did I do, Mom?" I say, my voice echoing in the high-ceilinged room. "Did I really make your life so difficult?"

Dad and Elisabeth come into the room, followed by Paula. Elisabeth and Paula are talking, but Dad gives Mom a steady eye, as if he has heard every word we have said. "Hello, hon," he says, moving in front of her.

I see the facial features that aren't mine—the gentle, downward curve of his mouth, the convex nose, the deep brown eyes. But this is my father, my true father, not the sperm or blood or DNA of that Montigue person. "The doctor says you're gonna be okay," he says. "You had us scared there for a minute."

Elisabeth and Paula move around to the other side of the bed and hug me, one at a time. "Thanks for finding me," I say to Paula.

"I left my pocketbook at your house."

"Good thing."

"You were half-awake," Paula says. "You don't remember?"

"Not really."

Paula smiles, that forced-looking smile of hers, and I think how if I were to analyze her face and its many layers I could peel her apart, find the passion beneath, and find a truly dissatisfied woman. A woman who has yet to awake, who chooses to sleep through and settle with life as is. This is the woman I see once in a while, the one who makes me think, who emerges unexpectedly but just as soon goes away again.

Elisabeth approaches the bed, puts her hands on the rail. "What happened to you?" she asks. Her fingernails are polished in a fluorescent, glittery pink.

I pat her on the arm. "Oh, let's just say your big sister's been a little stressed out. There's some weird stuff going on."

Elisabeth's eyes illuminate. "What kind of stuff?"

"Stuff about Aunt Adeline." I look at Mom, who is staring out the window.

"About her suicide?" Elisabeth asks.

"You know about that?"

"Yeah, Mom told me."

Mom does not turn. "When did she tell you?" I ask, loud and clear.

"I don't know...after you left, I guess."

"Pretty awful, isn't it?" I see Mom's neck tighten, her chest move out and in as she takes a deep breath.

"Well—" Elisabeth shrugs her delicate shoulders. "I didn't know her. I feel bad and everything, but..."

"It's okay," I say, and pat her on the arm. I think of Hunter, how much he feels for the blood he never met. "Hey," I add, "can you stay with me?"

"She's got school tomorrow," Dad says.

"And I don't want to miss school," Elisabeth says, then leans over the bed, close to me. "There's this boy named Joe," she whispers. "I think he likes me."

"What happened to Tommy?"

Elisabeth grins, as if proud of herself, and shrugs her shoulders. Dad moves next to her. "Your mother's going to stay with you for a few days."

His words feel a little like he's joking, as if he, too, is thinking this could never happen. But it is happening, he's telling me with a sober gaze, and he doesn't look away until he's sure I understand. Mom is looking away, pushing aside the polyester-crepe curtain and looking out the window—to a big cement parking lot, I figure.

"Yes," she says, her voice soft, timid-sounding. There is reluctance, but it's not the usual kind that wants me to know how cool and unaffected she is, how disconnected we are. Mom is actually afraid.

She will be coming to the house. We will be stuck together, and while there are so many things I want to ask, I don't want to ask. Maybe all of my thoughts should not come out, and I should only give half-answers, half-questions. Maybe I should be careful not to cry, because it could make Mom cry too, and then all kinds of emotion could just spill out of me, and I don't want that.

Perhaps this is what it feels like to be Mom.

Another rush of dizziness comes over me, and suddenly I want to go back to sleep, to that strange, cushiony wood floor where I remember only the sun on my forehead, and where—for a few seconds—I thought of nothing.

It takes two hours to get out of the hospital. I am poked and prodded; nurses scuff in and out the room, then wheel me down the hall to fill out paperwork outside of the emergency department. One by one I watch the injuries come in: the stomach aches and cut fingers, a branch in the eye, a heart attack.

An automobile accident.

The man who has been hit head-on has blood all over his face and arms. It is difficult to tell if he is conscious or even alive as they pump his chest, pumping, pumping, as they wheel past me. Twenty-five to thirty he seems, his family most likely not knowing yet, not suspecting anything. A mom, a dad, a wife just waiting for him at home. Hot food on the table, waiting for him.

At three-thirty they finally let me go. Dad wheels me out to the car while Mom and Elisabeth walk beside us, then I stand myself up and get in. A dizzy spell hits me, and I take Mom's arm for support. Mom, who will be staying at her old house. What can she be thinking right now?

As we drive back to Cape Wood I feel a pressure in my head and ears, the kind of pressure I sometimes feel before a storm.

Elisabeth sits next to me in the car, pointing to cows in a pasture, a barn where llamas peer out from behind a gate. Mom and Dad are quiet in the front seat, perhaps considering the change in the landscape over twenty years. Considering something.

As we pass by the Jones's house I see Mom flinch to the left— only for a second, though, before her hand moves up to meet her brow, her elbow coming to rest on the car door. Dad looks at the house, too; how odd the way he closely observes this house, and only this house, along the route. Or perhaps he simply saw Mom look at it.

When we arrive it takes Mom a few minutes to get out of the car. She sits in the front seat, and I can't see her face behind the tinted glass of the car. Out on the lawn are the bones, still hiding beneath the blade of the upside-down shovel. More scattered than before, more ravished. Perhaps birds have picked at them, or a neighborhood dog has stolen a limb or a splinter and buried it somewhere else. No longer a whole body.

Mom finally opens the car door and gets out. She grabs her small suitcase from the back seat. "I brought it just in case," she says. "I didn't believe I actually would stay." She says this with a chuckle, a half-chuckle of fear, as if she's got to be out of her mind. For the first time I feel terrible for Mom, who seems afraid of what is on the other side of the front door. She is back home again, out of her element, out of control.

part thirteen

undertow

{renee

forty-two

"I can't sleep," Renee hears from her daughter, an aching voice. Jenna lies on her back in the bed, her eyes on the bedroom ceiling, perhaps following the swirls of plaster with her eyes. *Like little hurricanes,* she used to say whenever she slept in here.

Renee wonders what Jenna is thinking when she's staring at the wall or out the window. Others might look at her and think she has no thoughts as she lies here hardly blinking, her lips occasionally moving to form silent words. They do not understand this state of mind.

Your eyes are the ocean, Renee used to think when she looked at a young Jenna, *deeper than I can reach.* She should have told Jenna her eyes were like oceans, but she knows the words would have translated to something else. She should have told her something.

She brings her milk and juice in a colorful glass with a straw, and makes her sharp-cheddar grilled cheese. Jenna props herself up onto her elbows and eats, giving little smiles here and there, and when she is done with each bite lays back and stares at the ceiling again. Renee has to tell her to sit up higher while she is chewing. "You'll choke," she says, and Jenna obeys.

Don't move around, the doctor had said. Lie down for the rest of the day. Renee knows Jenna will be all right, but still she helps her, the way she used to when Jenna stayed home sick from school. Because she can.

Renee washes dishes, gathers magazines and half-emptied glasses from the living room. The house is half-stripped, half-painted, except for her old bedroom, which Jenna supposedly has wallpapered. Being back here is not as difficult as she imagined. She had thought it would be more painful, as if evil would jump out from each doorway. But there is a calm feeling instead, one of reassurance. It may be all right.

It has been a long, stressful day: first the phone call from the hospital, the panic. "Your daughter's had an accident," the voice said, and it doesn't make a difference now that she's fine; that voice will always be with her. Then the drive, the two and a half hours that seemed like eight, the patter of her heart, the anxiety. Only for once it wasn't about what she would say to Jenna; it was about whether Jenna would be okay. It has been a long time since she's had such a feeling.

"Mom?" she hears from the bedroom. It's good to hear Jenna speak.

Renee moves to the doorway. "Yes."

"I don't want to lie here anymore."

"The doctor said you shouldn't move."

Jenna sighs, stares at Renee for a few seconds. "Do you think maybe I was supposed to die?" She sounds like she is drunk. "When Seth died."

"Jenna," Renee says. "You don't believe that, do you?"

"If I had gone with him and was sitting in the passenger seat I would be dead."

"But you didn't go with him."

"No." Jenna looks out the window for a moment, then looks back to Renee. "Do you believe in fate?"

"I'm not sure. No. I think people create their own destiny. I don't believe fate rules anything."

"You believe in so many other things," Jenna says.

"I do? Like what?"

"Like God."

"God is different." Renee wonders what she really feels, how much she believes simply because she always has. "Fate seems more like chance to me. Like luck. Hocus pocus."

Jenna turns her head to the side, rests her cheek against the pillow. Her dark bangs are matted to her forehead. "Anyway, I'm not dead," she says. "So I guess I wasn't supposed to die."

"Jenna, you shouldn't talk this way."

"Do you know what happened to my baby?" Jenna closes her eyes tightly. "It was my fault."

"Don't be silly," Renee says. "There are many things we think are our fault, but aren't really."

"Are you being a shrink now?" Jenna opens her eyes, smiles. "Mom, my baby would be seven now."

"Jenna—" She wonders if Jenna's medication might be making her a bit loopy, making her say things. "Look...do you need anything downstairs?"

"Mom, are you listening? It was my fault."

"Stop saying that, Jenna."

"It's okay, Mom. Really. I *know* it was my fault. I should have taken better care of myself, of the baby." She looks out of the window. "I loved Seth, really I did."

"Of course you did."

Jenna sits up higher, props her pillow up in back of her. "And yes, yes, he loved me. But did he want to spend the rest of his life with me?" She throws her arms up in the air, lets them fall onto the bed. "After all, we had to get married. I guess he was just doing his duty."

"We all do our duty once in a while," Renee says. "We spend a lot of time making up for what we've done wrong." She thinks about Adeline, a life unfinished, a death she can't stop blaming herself for. Suddenly the doorbell sounds downstairs. "I better get that," she adds, and heads toward the door. "I'll shut this," she says, and as she begins to close the door she sees the door across the hall, open to just a crack. She remembers what Bill said about the wallpaper, something about letters. "Oh, Jenna," she says, "would you mind if I had a peek at your new wall?"

Jenna's eyes spring wide, and her eyebrows move down sharply. "Oh..."

"What is it?"

"There are things I need to tell you." There is a youngness, a tenderness to Jenna's voice; she sounds afraid of telling whatever there is to tell. Renee thinks of the possibilities—something about the house, about Adeline. Perhaps something even worse, a long forgotten thing or person.

She is prepared for anything.

Renee breathes in, smoothes out the wrinkles in her mind, the little bumps and obstacles that make her brain skip around and justify things or make excuses. There can't be any of these things anymore. She must be calm, and whatever it is, she must tell her daughter the truth. "I'll go get the door."

She goes downstairs and finds no one at the front door, then goes to the kitchen, sees someone behind the screen door. He is a small man with a plain, chubby face, dressed in a green nylon windbreaker and a red hat. He wears blue pinstriped gardening gloves that are ripped at the tips, his fingers sticking out.

"Hello," he speaks, a childlike voice. "Any birds today?"

"Excuse me?"

"Is Jenna here?" he asks. It must be a friend of Jenna's, she thinks, she hopes. Or maybe she should shut the door right now.

"Jenna's not feeling well today. Can I tell her who's looking for her?"

"She gonna be okay?" The man seems slow in his speech, dramatic in his eye movements.

"She's going to be fine."

He seems confused, uncomfortable. "Who are you?" he asks.

"I'm her mother."

His eyes revert to curious slits as he leans close to the screen, takes a closer look. His small mouth drops open. "Renee..."

Renee is startled at first, hearing her name; Jenna must have spoken about her, perhaps told people she used to live here. Yes, there could be people who do remember her, remember her name. "Yes, I'm Renee," she says. "Do I know you?"

"I remember you. Renee Winslow. But I know everybody's name."

"It's Renee McGarry now. And who are you?"

"Rick." He frowns, as if thinking hard, then adds, "I'll come back when she's feeling better." He steps down to the porch, with a strange, mechanical walk.

"Please, stop—" she says, and he turns around. "Your last name?"

"Holmes," he says as he walks away.

Ricky Holmes.

She remembers him, amongst the clinking of bottles, the young boy on the docks with his spy novel and his AM radio, who always turned up Led Zeppelin. This boy, this fifteen-year-old boy, young like Renee, always following his elders, always watching in the sidelines, learning about life. He couldn't swim as well as some of the other boys, but he jumped, sprawled out in mid-air, a snapshot in Renee's memory. Then seconds later, he was tangled in slimy weeds like olive green satin tassels. He choked as his foot caught on something, then treaded water; but he was getting nowhere, panting like a dog.

His face was red, showing horror and hopelessness as he waited, as he held tight to the red and white buoy bobbing up and down. There were shouts as he went under, as another man dived and splashed. The shouts turned to whispers and gasps as they pulled him to shore, as they looked back out to the water. Then all was silent as they all waited.

Angus Jones was not coming back.

Ricky was the one. It was a shock to find out it was he who'd jumped in after Angus, to learn that they'd had been best friends. Ricky had been the short, quiet kid who sat in the corner at the pool hall, who waited his turn. The one who, on this night, ran up from out of nowhere, up to and through the crowd of boys at the end of the pier. Angus must have fallen from his boat, was what the police would hear from all of them, and no one would know any better than anyone else. No one had been close enough to see what really happened, perhaps not even Ricky. The police even came all the way to the hospital to talk to him, but he'd been frozen, unable to speak.

He is so different now—so blank-faced and impassive, so childlike in his speech. Renee tries to remember if he was like this before, or if twenty-six years have taken something from him and turned him into a scared, shaking, forty-two-year-old man.

jenna}

forty-three

As Mom approaches the door from the hallway, I see Angus.

I've forgotten about the photograph on the dresser; only moments ago it was half-concealed by a stack of magazines—hidden—before I grabbed a couple from the top of the pile and hopped back into bed, before I heard Mom's steps and looked up again and realized. Now I can see the dark mop of hair and sculptured face, the thick black lashes like a female's peering over the shiny edge of *Art & Antiques*. When she enters the room, I know it's too late.

Her eyes flick to the side for a second, then move back to me and stop. She has seen something unexpected, something shocking; perhaps she doesn't believe what she has seen and is afraid to look back. My own eyes bounce involuntary back to the dresser, the photo, then back to Mom, whose eyes flick back to the picture and stick.

She does not blink or move; her eyes seem without lubrication, the dull sheen of hard-cooked eggs. Her mouth pulls down at the corners, into a bitter frown, and the tendons in her neck surface like the thin, parallel roots of a tree. There is pain behind her taut face in all that pulled muscle and skin. A lump rises in my throat and I swallow, hoist my head higher on my spine.

It's all true.

Mom reaches up to one of the photographs, the black-and-white face. "What's...this?" She has said it; there can be no escape. She can't take it back, can't suddenly act calm or pretend she didn't see it. She probably wants me to answer this second—to tell her what's going on before she has to begin talking about it herself. I could say nothing if I wanted. I could wait for the maximum two or three seconds required before a question requires repeating, clarification. I can't recall coming to this point in any conversation with my mother before, where Mom has to wait for an answer, with me in control. How powerful I feel right now. But I decide to save her instead.

"Angus," I say.

Mom's mouth is open, just suspended there and still dropping. Her fingertip brushes across the photo, but she doesn't pick it up. "Angus," she says softly, no longer pretending. Then she walks toward the window next to the bed and looks out. "Where did you get this?"

"Hunter."

Mom looks at me, her face relaxed from its tightened state, her eyes watery, appearing greenish in the sunlight. She shakes her head. She doesn't know, doesn't remember who this is.

"His brother," I say. "Do you remember?"

"Yes." Her eyes drift past mine to the wall behind, her eyebrows lift in recognition. "Your little friend...at Adeline's. Did he tell you?"

"Tell me what, Mom," I say, but not as a question—more a statement of what I want her to think I suspect, what I want to confirm. But I can't do this to her, no matter what she's put me through. I can't torture her like this. "No," I say. "He didn't tell me. I figured it out." She just stares at me, waiting for me to say more, then speaks the words herself.

"Angus never even knew he was going to be a father."

How strange it is to hear the words, the truth, coming from Mom. "Mom," I say, "did Dad tell you I found letters under the wallpaper? The green wallpaper?"

Her face seems to pull backward, away from her body. "Your father did tell me...but he didn't say much." Her sentence ends like a question, and she looks at me, asking me to tell her more.

"The letters were addressed to you, Mom," I say. "And that photograph—was with them."

Mom's neck grows tight and stringy, her mouth pursed, as if she is holding her breath. She puts her hand over her mouth, and her eyes shoot to the floor. "Oh my god." This is a look of realization, of a brain that is tapping into archives that have been stored away and locked, which never were supposed to be opened. I know about such things.

"Mom?"

"The green wallpaper," she says. "Where are they—the letters?"

I motion my head across the hall to the other bedroom. "In there. All over the floor."

Mom stands, moves across the room as if to go out and into the hallway, but then stops in the doorway. The door across the way is shut tight; I see diagonal dark stripes of shadow upon it. She turns around again, and her cheeks and nose are flushed, her face bloated, ready to burst. She puts her fingers against her lips, perhaps to suppress her own words. "Letters," she says. "I wonder..."

"Why don't you go look?" I ask. "I think there are some things you need to know."

Mom looks away from me, then walks past the bed, back to the window, and sits down on the chest in front of it. She looks out, pressing her forehead against the glass, looking like a teenager in her jeans and sweater, her hair trying to escape from its ponytail, the wispy bangs suspended over her forehead. Her eyes appear sad and glazed as she stares out.

"I don't know if I want to know," she says.

What could she be thinking? Mom seems in a trance, her eyes in a wide stupor, her lips apart, dumbfounded. It's that strange, stoic face from my childhood, the ghost face in the living room window. Watching her weakens me. The room spins a bit, and my heart is beginning to palpitate, the aftermath of trauma.

Mom moves over to the bed, sits down on the end, near my feet. She leans over, bends down so her head touches her knees, and wraps her arms around her legs.

"Do you remember that day," she says, her voice muffled by her body curled around her, "when I said you couldn't play at Adeline's anymore?"

"Yes."

"I broke Adeline's heart, did you know that?"

"That's *not* why she killed herself."

"No?"

"What did the date book say?" I ask.

"It was only one page of writing," she says, still leaning over to her knees. "Just that date. She didn't even bother to write until that day."

"Mom," I say, "I think that date book was for me. It was found in the alcove at the base of the chimney—my old hiding place. Aunt Adeline knew about this special hideout of mine. She knew I would find it."

"Someone else found it."

"It took two decades for someone to find it. If we had lived there, I would have found it. Maybe even right after she died."

Mom is silent for a moment. "I'm sorry we moved away."

"It's okay." I want her to sit up and look at me, to know that I mean it. "But the date book, Mom—what did it say? Why didn't you want me to see it?"

She finally sits up, her hands near her mouth, in a praying gesture, almost. "Angus was in that book."

"He was?"

"*I will drive into the ocean,*" she says, in an almost musical tone, and I realize she is reciting from memory, *"where a lost father's soul lies at the bottom."* She looks at me. "That was all it took for the police to spill out to everyone that she killed herself."

"Mom," I say, trying to be gentle, "why couldn't you tell me the truth? Why couldn't you at least have told me my real father was *dead*?"

"I never told anyone, at first because I promised Adeline I wouldn't—I told her I would make something up. So I did make something up, and then eventually—by the time I got to know your father—I think even I may have started to believe it."

"Dad doesn't know that Montigue is Angus?"

She straightens up. "I've never said anything to him...because he already knew. He's always known."

"You didn't tell him?"

She looks at me solemnly. "He knows."

"Are you sure?"

"Jenna, your father understands me in ways that no one else does, and that's why I love him. And because he came back into my life at just the right time."

"Did you always love him?" I ask.

Mom shakes her head, as if she's telling me I have much to learn. "Your father came back at a time when I was most desperate. In the end I loved him, so it didn't really matter."

"And you never talked about Angus? It never came up?"

"Your father knew how much I loved Angus. He knew I wanted to forget. So he forgot, too."

"Just like that?" I wonder if Mom ever loved Dad as much as she loved Angus.

"Just like that."

"Why was it so important to never tell?" I ask. "Why would you promise Adeline something like that?"

Mom takes my hand. Hers is warm and sticky, and her eyes appear to have pressure behind them—a pleading, as if I am not her daughter right now but some judge, a jury. "It all happened so fast," she continues. "I don't know why..." she looks around the room, as if some evidence will appear to show her the truth. "I didn't mean to do it."

"No," I assure her, curious about what she is talking about. "You didn't."

"But it was Adeline who started it." Mom lets go of my hand, runs her fingers through her hair. "Adeline was so used to getting what she wanted. Not getting him...it nearly destroyed her."

"Maybe it *did* destroy her, Mom."

Mom sinks into her chest, slouching, and her exhausted brows fall, relax over her eyes. "I'll never know for sure." She reaches over to me again, but her hand doesn't make it; this time her arm falls and rests limp on the bed, palm up. "Maybe I destroyed her," she says.

"Mom," I say gently. "What about Angus...and Aunt Adeline? Can you tell me what happened?"

"The accident." She brings her hand to her mouth, to her lips. "It wasn't..." Her eyes jump around my face, as if searching for something.

"You don't have to tell me."

"No, I want to." There is revelation in her eyes, a look of relief. "Why on earth *wouldn't* I tell you?"

part fourteen
in the wake of green

{renee

forty-four

The words from Adeline were like a knife in Renee's side. *Angus is meeting me tonight.*

"What?" Renee asked. "Angus is—"

"Nine o'clock, at the jetty."

Renee's heart fluttered wildly, and her forehead grew hot. "No," she said. "He isn't back from Carbur yet." Or was he? After all, he was due back that night. But Adeline had to be making it up. The jetty was where everyone went; it would be easy for Adeline to fake it, to go there anyway. "Is he?"

Adeline nodded yes.

Renee wanted this to be a lie, needed to know that this was only her big sister scheming again. "Adeline," she said, making sure to look at her directly, holding her gaze. It was difficult for her to do, even now; she could feel the pull, her eyes begging to withdraw. She expected Adeline's eyes to cast her own away. "Why are you doing this?"

"I should say—" Adeline let out a single chuckle. "Why are you?" She shook her head. "You are not going to get away with this."

Renee was confused. "Get away with what?"

"With *him.*"

"I don't understand." Renee felt the tears swelling, blinked to keep them back. "What am I supposed to do? There's nothing I can do now but tell him." She wasn't even sure why she was crying—if it was out of despair or out of helplessness about being pregnant. Or was it for Adeline, who no longer seemed in a right state of mind? "Why are you meeting him?" she added. "Are you going to tell him about the baby?"

"I'm certainly going to tell him about *a* baby. But not necessarily yours."

"What?"

Adeline sat on the edge of the bed, took off her sandals. "Do you know what will happen," she said, "if anyone finds out about your baby? They'll take him away, Renee."

"It's not that simple."

"You'd be surprised."

"I'll just tell him," Renee said, "and then we'll wait...to tell everyone else."

Adeline chuckled. "Don't be silly, Renee. You can't have this baby."

"I don't...really have a choice."

"Look," Adeline said, "I couldn't have my baby. You are not going to have yours."

Adeline wasn't making sense. "What are you talking about?" Renee asked.

Adeline stood and brushed off her jeans. "I tried to tell you the other night, but you refused to listen."

"Tell me what?" Renee remembered part of a story, something about a baby, but nothing real. There was something about Angus in there, too. It had been a quick rush of words, another blur of Adeline nonsense.

"I was pregnant," Adeline said, looking to the floor.

Renee wasn't sure whether or not she wanted to hear the rest of the story, at least not from Adeline's lips. Perhaps she could learn it from some other source. This was a story she preferred to hear without witnesses so she could toss it back into the trash if she chose to. She didn't know what to say.

"I lost it," Adeline continued. She had a wild look in her eyes, the pupils small in the lamp light, the color like bright jade. "Or you could say I gave birth and lost it. He was a stillborn."

He. Renee thought of the word, how it suddenly brought an image to mind: a rubbery, living thing, a tiny baby boy. "But how could…" she began. "Adeline, we would have known. Were you in a hospital?"

"The bathroom. At college." Adeline's words emerged so calmly, so smoothly, as if this was not a significant announcement. "It was a few months ago. In April."

Renee's stomach turned; she felt nauseated, dizzy. She waited for Adeline to say something else, to take it back or explain what she really meant, and she didn't. "Don't say things like that," she said. "You're scaring me."

"But it's true."

"Adeline—what are you saying?" Renee suddenly felt like the big sister, trying to make sense of this. "I saw you at Christmas...you weren't fat."

"I was only three months at Christmas."

"But—" Renee would not hear this nonsense. She knew what would come next, feared hearing his name. She wanted to block her ears and mind from it. "You couldn't have been."

"Are you saying I'm *lying*?" Adeline snapped. "You heard me. My baby died." She crossed her arms and turned away from Renee, toward the white wall. When she turned around again her eyes were hard on Renee, as if she had been recharged. "And Angus and I—"

"No!" Renee yelled out, afraid of what Adeline would say next. A lump rose in her heart and her body went heavy; she shut her eyes tight to hold back the tears. "You're lying!" she shouted, and covered her ears. She did not want to hear Adeline's voice, or even her own. "You're doing this just to—"

"To what?" Adeline leaned down close, and Renee could no longer look her in the eyes. "Why would I play games about something like a baby?" She picked up her jacket off the bed. "Now get out of my way. I'm going to meet him."

Renee could not move her body, she sat slumped on the floor. "I don't believe you," she sobbed. She thought about Angus's letters, how they just stopped coming.

"Renee," Adeline said, her voice gentler now. "If you don't believe me you can come by tonight, see for yourself. Come see if he really is meeting me."

Renee didn't want to believe Adeline. She would prefer this was just some cruel joke; Adeline seemed capable of something this extreme, only using nonspecifics, only hinting at things, to lead Renee down a path to madness. It was something Adeline was good at.

Renee looked up at her big sister, saw a woman both frightening and sad. For a mere second, she believed what she had said. "Your baby," she said. "What happened to it?"

"He's buried in the yard," Adeline said, "beneath the forsythia bush."

———

At eight-thirty Renee told Mother she was walking down to Healy's for a soda, then maybe to Cherine's house. *Take your windbreaker* was all Mother said. It was cold this time of night down by the water.

The sky was clear, with only a slice of moon showing, but the stars were bright. The road was gray-green in the overhead street lights, and the trees at the side of the main road looked like a tall black hedge. The hedge seemed so long, so endless as she walked as fast as she could, but it didn't go by fast enough; it was a good mile and a half. Renee was frantic to get there—no longer just walking, but trotting, running in spurts. Walking felt too much like she was wasting time, like she'd miss something. But what would she see when she got there?

It took her only fifteen minutes. She could hear the surf as she approached, crashing hard against the rocks and the pier; the tide was in and the wind was strong. The lights from the wharf reflected on the water, and on the boats that rocked within the cove. In the distance she could see silhouettes on the brightly lit docks, long legs dangling over the edge, and could hear the clinking of bottles. The jetty, about two hundred yards across from the docks, blended into dark, and all Renee could see was the dim yellow glow of the lighthouse lamp above it.

She walked down Mackerel Pass and turned onto the cement slab step entrance to the jetty. She passed through the rusty iron gates, by the commemorative plaque, onto the rocks, and stepped into sudden cold and dampness. It was difficult to see the size of the cracks between the large slabs of granite, so she was careful jumping from rock to rock. The wind was strong and cool, but the stone felt warm beneath her sneakers. Over the loud rush of surf she heard voices, probably the youth center kids on the docks far across the water. She wondered if they could see her, as they were tiny silhouettes to her.

As she moved farther down the rocky pier she saw something in the distance—two figures in the dark, moving toward the left side of the jetty. It could have been anyone—two fishermen going for mackerel when they weren't supposed to, or perhaps two creepy men waiting for a fifteen-year-old girl to wander out there alone. She stopped for a moment and was quiet, listening to the voices. One was low-sounding and barely audible amongst the crashing of waves against the rocks. But after the water rushed out again she could hear the other voice, higher and soft, unmistakable.

Adeline.

Renee felt a panic in her heart, a turn to her stomach as she moved closer, more slowly this time. She crept in, stopping about ten yards from where the figures stood, and could clearly make out their silhouettes beneath the yellow glow of the lighthouse. It was too dark to see features, but the strong profile and angular build of a man looked familiar, too familiar. She saw wisps of hair above a high forehead, blowing in the breeze. When the figure spoke, she shuddered. "Give me a second," the man said, and she knew it was Angus.

Angus and Adeline.

They were moving over to the left side of the jetty and down the steep decline of rocks, toward the bottom. In the murky water at the base of the rocks sat a small dinghy roped to a wooden pillar, waiting for them. It rocked gently as a crest of whitecaps rushed in, reminding Renee of their night together under the stars. How it seemed like a dream now, a nightmare.

She blinked hard, opened her eyes wider as she moved closer. They were in dim light now, from the lighthouse lamp that hovered above. Adeline's face looked stern, impatient, as she waited for Angus to step toward the boat. He stopped at the bottom and looked back up the rocks, then to the left, toward Renee. It seemed for a second that he was looking right at her, but then he turned back toward the boat, where Adeline was already stepping in.

"Come on," Adeline said, her voice muffled by the wind. "You said you would."

Angus seemed to hesitate, then continued down the rocks. As he reached the water, Adeline put out her hand and he took it, supporting himself as he stepped into the dinghy. It hurt Renee to watch, his skin touching Adeline's.

From her seat in the boat, Adeline leaned over the edge and grabbed the rope and began to untie them from the pillar. Renee imagined Adeline leaning too far over the edge, her neck catching the rope as she plunged into the water, her arms flailing while she pleaded for help. She imagined Angus just sitting there, watching her die, because he was not there of his own free will; like Renee, he was captive of Adeline's power and madness. But in real life Angus wouldn't just sit there; he would most likely plunge in after her—and not because he was a good guy or a man of duty, but because he cared about her. *He cared about Adeline.*

Renee fought the tears swelling up inside. Her anger was strong, perhaps strong enough to overpower the tears. She couldn't cry now; crying would only weaken her, diminish the anger she needed to get through this. How awful it was going to feel, she imagined, to confront them, to be defeated; how humiliating it was going to be to admit herself a victim. But it was better than waiting in agony for a confrontation that might never happen, for subtle innuendoes from Adeline, lies from Angus. She had to face it now, before this anger could melt away into pure sorrow that would crush her completely. She wanted to step into the light above so they could see her, and explode right now.

As Renee moved forward, her heart pounded against her chest and a surge of heat rose to her face and neck. She had no idea what she was going to say and didn't care; there was an energy inside her like nothing she'd ever felt that would be speaking for her. She saw Adeline with the rope in her hands now, the boat slowly drifting, rising high in a wave. Angus looked tense, holding tight to the sides of the boat, jerking as waves lifted them and water crashed. As Renee stepped into the glow of the light above her, Adeline's mouth dropped open and Angus's head whipped around, his eyes wide with surprise.

"Renee," he said, his voice in decline, heavy with breath. She expected him to say something more, but it didn't come.

Adeline gave a quick nod to Renee, a haughty glow upon her face. She seemed satisfied with this outcome, this ultimate humiliation for Renee. But there was also a daunting look behind her eyes, as if she'd never truly expected her little sister to show up. The confrontation was no longer just between Adeline and Renee; now it was the three of them, and Adeline seemed as though she might actually be afraid.

Angus suddenly grabbed the rope from Adeline's hands. "Wait!" he called out. He flung it out toward the rocks. It missed, landing in the water. "Take it, Renee," he said, his voice trembling, desperate. The boat was rocking hard in the water now, moving away from jetty. Angus reached for the oar to his right, but Adeline grabbed his wrist to stop him.

"No," she snapped. Her mouth was tight with threat, her eyes serious.

"Adeline!" he shouted, shrugging her off. "Let me talk to her!"

Renee moved down the steep slope of rocks to the base of the jetty, slipping on the greasy moss-covered rocks and clumps of seaweed. The surf crashed against the rocks as she stepped into the water, over her shins and knees, spattering her face. The water was cold, but she could barely feel it. The boat had moved back toward the jetty again; still, it teetered hard in the waves. The rope was within reach, writhing just below the surface of the water. She grabbed for it, managing to grasp the frayed end in her hands. It was difficult to hold, as Adeline was tugging from the other end.

"Stop it!" Angus demanded. "Let's go back."

"There's only room for two of us in this boat!" Adeline shouted back.

"No," Renee said, holding tight to the rope. "Apparently, there's room for three." Her voice had emerged with such strength and sarcasm, it did not feel like her own. She plodded toward the boat, each step an aching push against the heavy water, which rose higher and higher as she advanced. Her jeans and windbreaker were soaked. She looked at Angus. "Isn't that right, Angus?"

"I can explain, Renee," he said.

"Yes," Renee said. "*Do* explain why you are here."

He continued to paddle the boat toward the shore. "Adeline asked me to come," he said. "To talk."

"Oh, I see," Renee said. "Did she *make* you come here?"

A larger wave was rushing in, moving quickly; the dinghy tottered and splashed, and the wave pushed Renee onto her back and into the water. As she stood up again the wave was pulling out, and pulling the dinghy boat with it. Angus was paddling quickly. "I think we should get out of this boat," he yelled over the crash of water, "and then I'll explain."

"Tell her the rest, Angus." Adeline said.

"You shut up!" Renee shouted to Adeline. She could yell as loudly as she wanted; the roaring surf demanded it, and so did her anger. Her right hand burned, and as she looked down she saw that her palm was raw and chapped, and the rope was still in her hold. She felt like crying, wanted to stay angry instead. She had to stay angry, so she could bear to listen to the rest. "Angus," she said, her voice garbled by the waves. "Why did you stop writing to me?"

"I didn't." Angus's eyes grew wide with innocence, complete surprise. "I sent letters twice a week."

"Well, they stopped coming."

The watery wind spit hard and raw against her face. She wondered if he could be telling the truth, and she remembered Adeline, so interested in the mail. But Adeline would only get pleasure out of such an accusation, at the mere thought of causing more paranoia and confusion for her little sister. It wouldn't even matter if it were true or not; Adeline could make Renee go mad just looking for the truth.

At this point, Renee didn't know who to believe. "Just tell me," she said, "why you had to come here tonight."

Angus shook his head. "There's so much to explain."

No explanations would make sense now; she wanted a simple, clean answer to make her feel better. But she knew there was no such thing. Her mind raged with thoughts and images: their stolen moments, their nights in the dark; always hidden, always in disguise, using lies and aliases—no real names for now, he'd said. *Not yet,* he kept saying. Of course he showed no fear about taking her out on the water that night—no concern about consequences, the possibility of creating new life inside of a woman who still was a child. How many women had he done this to?

"I suppose," Renee said, "you think you can just have both of us." She threw her head back, laughed to the sky. The stars were fuzzy and looked like they were moving. "That's what you think, isn't it?" Inside she knew the suggestion was ridiculous, that this wasn't exactly true. But the power she felt at speaking so freely, so sardonically, encouraged her words. When she lowered her head again she could see the stunned look in Adeline's face; her big sister seemed amazed, horrified at Renee's words. "What is it, Adeline?" she said. "Isn't that what you want, too?"

Adeline didn't speak, and Angus raised a hand up, as if asking her to remain silent. He turned back to Renee, his eyes steady, gentle. "Renee," he said, "there's nothing going on." His voice was mild yet urgent-sounding, dedicated to the words. "And I do not want Adeline." Sacrificial words, Renee thought, bold enough to hurt Adeline.

Adeline lifted her chin, turned her head away. "Tell her about before," she said.

Angus's body seemed to tense up, and his eyes lowered quickly, as if he'd been caught. A wave swelled, lifting the boat. He grappled the side and leaned back, then forward again to counterbalance. "Let me talk!" he yelled, his voice drowned out by the roar of the sea. "But we have to get out of this boat. This is not good."

"You don't have the guts to tell her!" Adeline's shouted, her voice trembling a bit, sounding frantic. "You just feel sorry for her. I mean, look at her. She's so pathetic."

Angus was shaking his head.

"And you're crazy," Renee said to Adeline.

"Yeah?" Adeline chuckled. "And you're a little slut."

"*Excuse me?*"

"Maybe," Adeline said, "I should tell Angus how you've been sleeping around. Mark Fisher, Rob Wetherbee. There are probably more."

Adeline really was crazy, Renee thought. She would stop at nothing, go as far as she could to win. "Angus, she's lying," Renee said.

Angus looked sternly at Adeline. "Look who's calling who a slut." Renee felt a tinge of relief, waited for his words as he looked back to her. "Renee," he said, "I did go out with Adeline. Last year."

Hearing the words was worse than she ever imagined it would be. Even after this buildup of anger and preparing herself for truth, Renee was not prepared to hear it. It was better to view Adeline as maniacal, only a liar. It was better to pretend.

This felt so much worse than anger, just as she'd feared it would. It was no longer about the fight; it was about defeat, total loss. The words were painful, stabbing her all over her body. They could tear her heart out, even destroy her or the baby growing inside. The baby, the tiny life that was all her own, the one thing only she could control. But she had to know more, even if it killed her. "You and Adeline?" she asked.

"It wasn't like that," he said. "Nothing happened."

"He's lying," Adeline said.

"Lying?" Angus snapped back at her. "And should I tell her *why* I never went out with you again? Should I tell her all about your little escapades?"

"Angus," Renee said, "why didn't you tell me?" Her words felt lost, drowned in the noise, as the tide moved in again.

"I was going to tell you," Angus said. "It's the truth."

"But you didn't."

"Renee," he said, "it was only one date."

One date, she imagined, under the stars. There were stars above them now, blurring into tiny blobs of light. She felt dizzy, and Adeline and Angus looked fuzzy to her, as if a fog had settled between them. She was waist-deep in the water, close enough to the dinghy to touch it. Delirious, she reached out her arms, put her hands on the side of the boat, couldn't feel it. She thought of Adeline's stories earlier that night, her angry shadow against the white bedroom wall. *I was pregnant too*, she'd said.

"What about the baby?" Renee asked, the words coming out without a thought, on their own.

"What?" Angus grimaced, as if what she'd said was implausible. "What the hell did Adeline tell you?"

"Don't listen to him," Adeline said. "He'll say anything to get out of this one."

"The baby," Renee said, and thought of her own, growing inside. She broke into a cry, collapsed on the edge of the boat. She was leaning over it now, her chest hard against the side. Angus leaned down and took her shoulders, and she lifted her arms to him. The rope was still in her hands, and she thought of how she could take him now—just wrap it around his neck until he choked hard, until he begged her to let go. She would not kill him—*no*, she thought, but she could show him, yes; *he will never hurt me again.*

"Are you drunk, Renee?" Adeline quipped.

Or Adeline, Renee thought, feeling her sister's eyes on her, but unable to look—how easily she could wrap the rope tight around her, squeeze her until she popped. But she may not be able to stop. Yes, she could kill Adeline right now.

A wave crashed against the boat; the sharp edge thrust against Renee's chest. She fell back, splashed into the water. Angus took her shoulders again, then her arms. "Renee," he said, his voice wavering, lost in the roar of the sea. "Let me help you." She looked into his eyes—so blue, so sincere, like she'd seen before, and lifted the rope again, in front of his face and in a ring above his head, like a halo. She could not hurt him; she could only play, pretend to take him captive—forever—hope he never got away. The rope looped over him, slid down the back of his head and to his shoulders. Angus smiled and let it tumble down to his waist. "It's going to be all right," he said, then nodded to Adeline. "Pull her up. I'll paddle back."

As Adeline took her arm, Renee flung a hand at her. Adeline snapped back, then leaned forward and tried again, but Renee thrashed and shrugged her off, then lifted herself onto the edge. The boat tipped slightly, then more as the ocean grew loud behind them. Water crashed against rock, stinging her face, and there was a sudden pull on her legs from under the boat, then a wall of wood in front of her, tangled paddles and rope, arms and legs toppling over her. She heard muffled cries as the boat turned—not cries of fear but more of surprise and excitement.

This was shallow water, after all.

But then she was under the boat, scraped against sand and rock as the tide sucked her out against the surface. She swam up quickly, straightened her body out, but now could barely reach the ocean floor; even on tiptoes she bounced to touch the bottom. They had been pulled out a bit, perhaps another ten feet or so; but when she turned toward the shore she saw no one. As the wave calmed, she regained her composure and breath and senses, began to tread water—a frantic dog paddle. Her body only buoyed, now as weightless as it had been heavy in the undertow; she was bobbing aimlessly in the wave. She saw Adeline's tiny head surfacing just a few feet away, a quick gasp of breath from her mouth. And there, not ten feet behind her, was the dinghy, upside down.

Where was Angus?

There was a quick splash next to it, then another. A hand, a foot, trying to reach the surface. The upside-down boat wiggled violently, and Angus's head emerged—just the top of it, then went down and popped up again. His head bobbed simultaneously with the rocking boat, and finally his mouth made it to the surface, letting out a gurgle of words, a scream.

"Oh my god!" Adeline cried as she dove into a desperate crawl toward the dinghy. "He's stuck under there!"

Renee paddled behind her, as fast as she could—imagining him under there as she tried to keep the water out of her mouth, to keep breathing, to not be pulled out by the tide. How long could he last under there? And why couldn't he get out from under the boat?

The rope.

She cried out as she swam, heard her own voice emerge like an injured animal, a cry of desperation. Her body was numb, breath running out, her mind so clear now; what a state of confusion she'd entered just moments ago. Adeline was close to the dinghy now, but there was no more splashing next to it. The surf was approaching again, as Renee could hear the crash against the rocks beyond them, at the very end of the jetty, then moving closer, closer. Adeline yelled out as the waves approached; her body rose and plunged toward the shore, then slammed against Renee. The dinghy seemed to defy the incoming tide somehow—moving only a few feet toward the shore, but as it pulled out again the boat quickly went with it, as if destined to move away from land.

The strong current pulled at Renee's limbs and she imagined Angus under there, tangled in her rope, running out of air and strength and life. She and Adeline were even farther from the boat from before, and a second wave was rushing in. They could attempt to swim against it, or let it take them back to shore. Adeline must have known this was hopeless too, as she was frantically swimming back toward Renee, crying out a horrified *No*. They both knew they couldn't get to the boat.

They swam back toward the jetty, their splashing bodies not moving fast enough, their breath wheezing, gasping for air. They reached the base and scrambled up the slippery rocks, their ankles scraping on the sharp mussels embedded in moss. Finally they reached the top and looked out to the water, and Renee could see the small boat drifting out. Near it was something else—a buoy, it appeared, a round object. Was it Angus? The object wasn't moving, though; it just drifted slowly along. When the next wave moved in, the object moved toward shore again, but further away from them to the left, toward the docks parallel to the jetty. As the whitecaps rushed in Renee lost sight of it again.

"There!" Adeline pointed to where the thinnest light skimmed the surface of the water.

It appeared to be a face—arms sprawled out around it, bobbing up and down amongst the buoys scattered between the docks and the jetty. A wall of foam pushed him inland, closer to shore. On the docks the silhouettes under the lights were beginning to stir, take notice. They appeared to be yelling, but Renee could not hear over the water.

"Can they see him?" she said. "Do you think?"

Adeline grabbed Renee's hand and they ran down the jetty, back toward the junction where it met the road. Renee followed in her sister's exact steps—a couple of feet in front of her was all she could see, Adeline's lengthy calves and feet. She tripped as they leaped over a wide gap in the rocks, scraping her knee. There was no time to stop.

Renee looked out to the water and saw the silhouettes on the docks, more of them now, all racing toward the water, the foam rushing in, rushing out. One of the figures jumped—sprawled out—into the water.

"Did you see that?" Adeline asked.

"Yes—can you see Angus?"

"I think I see his head."

They reached the gates and cement embankment, and stepped up onto the road and into a thick cloud of warmth and calm, away from raw wind and ocean spray. They moved quickly, jogging down the road toward the pier, closer to the muffled cries that echoed across the docks. A crowd of silhouettes had gathered at the edge of the docks, just next to the water—perhaps from the Wharfside Café or youth center, Renee thought; perhaps those she'd seen just a short time ago, laughing and clicking beer bottles. She felt dizzy, and the lights towering above the docks appeared blurry and yellow. A voice shouted out.

Someone is out there!

Chaos erupted over the dock. Bodies moved and voices shouted. A rope tossed from a dinghy. "Throw it in the water!" a man shouted.

Renee began to move forward, but Adeline's hand clutched her shoulder and pulled her back. "Don't get too close," she said. Renee tried to pull away, and Adeline tugged at her again.

"Look at us!" she scolded, a shouted whisper, her eyes stern with caution. *The wet clothes, the soaked hair.* "Stay back, out of the light." She took Renee's hand, and Renee could feel her rigid palm, the trembling fingers.

"Why?" Renee asked. "He's out there." It was scary that Adeline could be hiding at such a time. But Renee felt it too, that gut-wrenching fear that someone had seen them out there with him. But why bother to hide? Angus would tell what happened anyway. He would be back to tell. "They'll save him, right?" she added. "He's there, right?"

Adeline stared ahead, didn't answer.

Renee looked beyond the crowd of silhouettes, saw a wash of greenish light on the water, a buoy bobbing, the lights of a fishing boat moving out, a smaller boat beside it. A splash sounded next to the docks, a cry from the crowd, and suddenly a dark spot of a man was moving through the water, swimming furiously toward the buoy. He stopped and treaded for a moment, then began to head right back again, this time with something, or someone.

"Do they have him?" a woman yelled. "Who is it?"

Adeline's grip tightened on Renee's hand as the dark shapes moved back to the docks and the man pulled himself up. "Get an ambulance!" he shouted, and two men helped him pull another from the water. One of the men leaned over and began to resuscitate what looked like an unconscious man, while voices chattered throughout the crowd. "What happened? Who is it? Is he dead?"

Ricky Holmes, a man's voice said. *He tried to save that boy.*

Renee's heart thumped hard, her head flushed. She knew the name, a boy from the youth center. But where was Angus? "I can't stay here," she said to Adeline. "I have to go up."

the one true ocean 335 }

Adeline shook her head. "Don't."

"Why not?" She wanted to believe Angus was alive, that he would be all right and there would be nothing to explain, nothing to fear. "It was an accident…wasn't it, Adeline?"

Adeline's head turned steadily to Renee's, her eyes without discernible expression. She still held tight to her hand. "Was it?" she said, her words sounding weak, defeated. This wasn't a threat; it was a declaration of something, an upcoming penance for both of them.

This couldn't be happening, Renee thought. She couldn't believe that just a blur of a minute ago the three of them were speaking, arguing. Such stupid things, it seemed now. Even the baby growing inside seemed inconsequential, so easy to deal with. And her state of mind—how murky and out of control it had been just moments ago. It seemed fabricated now, the way she suddenly snapped out of it and was now remembering everything. It was scary to think she was capable of such sudden change. This had to be a dream.

Out on the water she saw the fishing boat moving out, and a small bright spot on the water next to it. It was pale and round, like a small face lit by the moon, swirling in the current; just a face, without arms or legs, no splashing or reaching out. Then it vanished, like nothing had ever been there.

"He's okay!" the man called out, still hovering over Ricky, who still lay flat on the dock. *The other boy must be dead,* a hushed voice said.

Renee put her hand to her mouth, felt her throat close up. She looked to Adeline, who was motionless, her mouth agape, her eyes emerald-colored in the yellowy lights.

A large wave came in and the crowd seemed to inspect it morbidly, and they let out a moan of disappointment as the surf cleared and rested on the shore. Renee saw only the white foam of a leftover wave. And heard more voices.

He must have fallen from his boat. Was he alone out there? Seemed so. Did they lose him?

Renee felt a brief rush of fear again—for herself this time, wondering if someone may have seen her out there, the rope around his body. What a horrible feeling it was, to think—even if only for a moment—that she could worry only about herself, that it was possible she could lie if questioned by police. *We barely knew him,* she could always tell them.

And how horrible it was to know that the tide was moving out, and would not come in again until early morning. Perhaps six hours later Angus's body would return, white and plumped and slimy with sea life.

She was numb.

————

But later she would feel everything. She would feel him growing in her belly, and would try to convince herself that it could have been worse. He could have died even more senselessly, she thought, perhaps in the war. Because like so many who died in the war, his body would never be coming back.

As her belly grew she found it more and more painful to remember that he once existed, so she tried hard to pretend that he hadn't. Then the sharp, green waves would come crashing in, and she would think of him again.

forty-five

I found some bones, Jenna says.

Renee looks out the window to the lawn, skims it with her eyes. She sees the bugleweed, notices it has taken over the grass near the garden, where the forsythia bush once stood. It grows so fast, she thinks as she listens to Jenna's description of the delicate skull fragments, about the crushed wooden chest with metal strappings. She imagines a baby's bones, wonders if it is possible they could exist today, and appear as they do. After all, this was not some indistinguishable blob that tore away from Adeline and was washed away; it was a life with features and fingernails growing, almost seven months along. Anything could be under there now. "All I know," she says, "is what your aunt told me."

"Mom?" Jenna is waiting.

Renee doesn't want to remember—the story she'd doubted then and doubted for years after. "There was a baby," she says.

It had happened in the spring, Renee tells Jenna, at least that was what Adeline had said. Her aunt gave birth to a seven-month still-born baby in a college dorm bathroom; a boy, she said, now buried in the yard. As Renee tells the story, she thinks of how Adeline hadn't looked as if she'd been through such a loss. In fact, that spring and summer she'd been her usual, playful self—perhaps even more play-ful; rosier, prettier, more ravenous for the boys. It couldn't be true.

She never knew what to believe. Adeline had even been home for the holidays earlier that year. She hadn't appeared fat or unusually radiant; she hadn't said anything. When she arrived back home in March she wasn't carrying any strange bundles or a coffin in her arms. How could it be true?

Still, while Jenna grew inside her, Renee would look out at that lawn every morning and think of the night that Angus died. She thought of Adeline telling the story about the baby buried in the yard, and imagined the poor thing dead and wrapped up and carried home on a bus. How did she do it? she would think. It had to be a lie, she would tell herself, each time she looked out at the lawn, because Adeline had not sounded rational that night. Because Adeline was a liar, or so Renee had hoped.

The father of the baby could have been anyone. There had been many boyfriends—several names in the letters she sent home from the dorm. Adeline had dated before, but after Father died that summer she'd grown hungry for boys, gone wild at college. And she was quick to tell Renee all about it.

And after all that happened, Renee certainly wasn't allowed to have anything Adeline could not. Because Adeline's baby would have no real father, neither could Renee's. If Angus was named as the father, Adeline would tell everyone what really happened that night on the water.

Renee would abide by her big sister's rules and come up with a name they both could agree on, one they could use that wouldn't be recognized, but wouldn't be a lie either. But in the eyes of anyone who might ask, he would never be a legitimate love; he would be nothing but a one-night stand. Renee knew she would acquire a new reputation; she would be a casualty of a promiscuity that never truly existed.

Montigue was a disguise, but barely; much like the letter *M* on Renee's letters, something she didn't think Adeline would ever figure out.

"You didn't lie, Mom," Jenna reassures her. "Montigue was real."

"But I could have told you," Renee says. "Later on, after Adeline died...I could have told you everything."

But telling Jenna would have reminded her. For so many years Renee tried so hard not to think of Angus, not only because of what Adeline had said, but for herself. Even after Jenna was born she didn't let herself think of him. Each time his face and name would come to mind she'd quickly erase it. She found she was quite good at this, too, and even wondered if one day he would go away completely.

"I think I tried to convince myself," she adds, "that your biological father really *was* just some man who passed by in the night, who never stuck around. It was easy to hate him for this, and hating him—this man named Montigue—was so much easier than loving Angus."

How powerful the human mind is, this made her realize.

"Adeline changed after that." Renee looks back out the window at the garden. "She became so engrossed in her work that she never had time for friends or for love. I don't think she ever was with anyone after that. And we never spoke about Angus again. At least not until we saw Hunter playing with you. I think our worlds sort of came apart that day."

Jenna looks saddened, disappointed. Perhaps her aunt's suicide all makes sense now. "She must have been so alone."

"Yes," Renee says. "It was her penance, I think."

"And what was yours?"

Jenna's words are like a blow, a cold wind up Renee's spine. But she is somehow relieved to have someone ask her this, such an honest question. She wonders how to answer it, though. She wonders if indeed she has suffered enough, or if she has only made others suffer instead.

"Sorry," Jenna says.

"No," Renee says, telling her it's okay. "I should have reached out to her. In the end, I think plants were her only friend." She reaches out her hand, touches Jenna's arm. "And you were too, of course."

———

Rick is the first to arrive after Jenna invites him and Hunter over to the house.

He seems uncomfortable without Hunter at his side, peeking anxiously out the window. He removes his hat but not his coat, and leans awkwardly against a delicate ladder-back chair that doesn't support him and only tips forward. Jenna hands him a cup of the coffee she has made, invites him to sit at the table.

Renee knows he most likely will not speak until they speak first. "I knew Angus," she says.

"He—" Rick says, "he was my best friend." There is a warmth in his eyes that says this still is true today.

In his slow, stuttering speech, he talks about how he knew Angus, how they worked together. He talks about the night Angus drowned, how he was there. He recalls Renee amongst the crowd as the coast guard searched the night waters, how everyone stayed for hours. And he recalls Adeline.

"She came by Angus's house that night," he says.

Renee leans into the table, a little closer to Rick's face. "She did?"

"Yup." His eyes wander upward, up the wall behind Renee, trying to remember more, perhaps. "I was at his house. I was waiting for him to get back."

"From Carbur?"

He nods yes, enthusiastically, as if he's getting it right.

"Do you remember—" Renee looks at Jenna, wonders what else to ask, how much to ask. Jenna gives a slight nod, approval. *You need to talk about this, she is saying.* "Do you remember why she came by?"

Rick's eyes squint a bit, and the lines deepen between his brows. There is something on his mind, something that isn't right or shouldn't be told. Or perhaps he simply can't remember.

"It's okay," Jenna says. "It was a long time ago."

"She said," he begins, but hesitates, tilting his head to one side and looking beyond Renee again. Then he looks back at her, dead on. "She said she wanted to give him a message…to meet her at the jetty."

"Did she say why?"

"Nope." Rick purses his lips a bit in contemplation. "But she said he had to meet her or else."

"Or else what?" Jenna asks.

"Just or else." He smiles, as if proud to recall everything correctly. "So I gave him the message."

Renee imagines Adeline, her flurry of words earlier that day, the confrontation later that night, just before Angus died. What drove her to be so cruel? And could it be true that the child was Angus's? She would have conceived the child in September, she'd said—mid-September at earliest.

"Rick," she asks, "was Angus ever in Maine any time except during the summer? Did he ever stay through the fall?"

"His family always went back in August," Rick says.

"Back to Maryland, you mean?"

"Always in August. He never stayed."

Perhaps Angus had told the truth. Perhaps he'd only been there that night to fix things, to explain. Or to keep Adeline from going to the police.

"I wonder what Adeline really wanted," Renee says, "or what she expected she would really get."

Rick looks off for a moment, considering the comment seriously, as if required to answer it like a question. "I think she wanted Angus to love her," he says.

She thinks of her big sister, how she once had sparkled with life, how her pain and loss turned into a small madness. But then Renee had a madness of her own.

She hopes Jenna understands all the pain she endured, living with such questions. *Please forgive me,* she thinks.

jenna}

forty-six

As Hunter steps up the walk and through the door, I watch Mom's face. I think of what a gift of immeasurable greatness he must be to her. His face, his bones and skin—the same blood as Angus, the same DNA. This matters.

And perhaps she is a gift to him. Someone who knew his brother—how must that have been? he's probably wondering. He shows it in his furrow-browed smile—anticipation—and in his trembling words.

"Hello, Mrs. McGarry."

"Hello, Hunter," she says, with a release of air as she speaks, a collapse of her chest, and the tension in the room suddenly dissolves, the way air clears after a storm. "You can call me Renee."

How much more powerful would this meeting be, I wonder, if Hunter knew about the blood connections? One day he will need to know that this woman and his brother bonded, that I am his niece and part of Angus. Odd, that just days ago I was confused about how I felt about him—before he was a real person, when he simply was a shadow of a boy I used to know.

"I remember when I first met you," he says to Mom, and I think of it—the backyard at Aunt Adeline's, he and I with dirt on our faces, trowels and buckets in our hands, Mom's stern eyes as she approached. And then finally to Hunter, as she pulled me away by the hand, *Do your parents even know where you are?*

She'd had no idea who he was. Not until we got into the car, and I told her his name and where he lived.

"I wasn't very nice to you," Mom says. She rests her head on her cupped hands, then glides her hands over her face and sighs into them.

"Are you all right?" Hunter asks.

"I'm fine," she says, her hands sliding down her face and over her jaw. "I was just thinking about my sister, how that day...was the last time I saw her alive." She looks up to Hunter, shading her eyes from the sunlight. "She died just a couple of days later."

"Yes," he says. "I know." He puts his hands in his jeans pockets. "I'm sorry."

Does he know the rest of it? I wonder. He could know; he could know and not come right out and say it. Perhaps his apology says that he does know. People don't usually talk about such things twenty years later.

"She killed herself," Mom suddenly says.

It's strange to hear her say it, strange especially when she looks to me afterward with a half-smile—perhaps searching for support, for approval of the bittersweet confession. I smile back, but wonder what Mom is getting herself into.

"Why?" Hunter says, shaking his head, his shoulders collapsing. It seems a hypothetical *why,* from the inert lift of his forearm—hand flopping back, fingers extending to nowhere. It's a helpless hand that, along with that baffled expression on his face is saying *Do we ever really know why?* He may have known all along about my aunt's suicide, but like me, he'll never stop asking the question.

In the afternoon Mom sits on the warm bedroom floor and reads through her letters again. She reads the bottom of the last one over and over, tears in her eyes.

I love you, Renee.

"He never had a chance to tell me," she says.

I take her outside to the garden, where the fragments of bone lie beneath the shovel. Perhaps I should have reburied them, I think, and paid respect for whatever soul may have passed from them. Or maybe it was right to let them be, to let them harmonize with the earth. I squat down, put my fingers on the blade, but can't move them to lift it. The shovel will rust if I leave it here, and while this rusted steel blade will survive, the wooden handle will turn to pot roast, like the tiny coffin. Let the rains come, I think, and quickly melt them back into the mud, so I won't have to bury them. So I won't have to ever look at them again.

Mom reaches down and lifts the shovel, gently touches the bones. Perhaps this really is the body of Adeline's stillborn baby boy, or some other ghost, a shadow of what could have been. We can't know for sure without asking Adeline. These are unnamed bones, and they rest here in place of another body that never came back. We will name this unknown grave Angus.

We carefully wrap the remains, arrange the slivers of the wood box around it as best as possible, and put it back in the ground beneath the forsythia bush, where Adeline's garden used to be. As we shovel the dirt and pack it onto the grave I imagine the tiny skull pieces crumbling, crackling more. Nothing but white chips of a shell, a life that was once. Perhaps this tiny life existed for only minutes, seconds, outside of the womb. Or it didn't make it into the outside world at all, and simply washed itself out of its mother too early.

Because this happens sometimes.

Mom says she doesn't want to be angry with Adeline. She wants to forget all of this. She wants to remember her as the complicated, sentimental woman that Adeline was capable of being, the Adeline who could give out warmth and love as well as she could dish out anger and hostility. She was someone who *felt* so much that it must have boiled her blood and burnt her brain, and she just couldn't take it. Then there was Mom, who after a complete collapse willed herself back with denial, trained herself to handle things fine. All the lying, the self-control—it worked after all. It became the much less painful way to live.

What was it, I wonder, that really killed Adeline? Which pain drove her heart and mind inside out? Was it the baby? Was it Angus's death? Or could it have been a guilt that came from the subtle torture of her little sister? Mom and I will never know. No written word, no date book, ever could explain it.

forty-seven

A self-portrait never is easy to do. There is a tendency to draw oneself in a safer, more ambient light, perhaps with fewer lines between the brows, more lift to the eyes. In each portrait from my high school classes, I have a cautious rigidity to my face, as if I am holding my breath.

The one I've attempted today seems amateurish, a fruitless attempt at dark and light—the shadow over my eyes has too much transition; there is too gentle a blend from dark to light, as if I fear definition, the true dividing line. And the detail within the shadow is too visible, the outline of my eyes still too vivid— each lash a stroke of thin horsehair bristle. Even the color of my eyes seems too bright—a sudden green emerging from the black- ness, like glowing emeralds.

But I will try again.

Mom and I look at my painting, and Mom observes how while there is no Dad in my face, I have over time developed his dimpling frown and plummeting brow, not to mention the ten- dency to cross arms tight across my chest. How did Angus stand? I wonder. One day soon we will talk about him again, and I will not be afraid to use his name.

There is so much in this portrait which is Mom: the mouth, with its deep curve above the upper lip, its tight corners, the eyes deep and smallish, hiding within thick brows and straight black lashes. The color of my eyes is brighter, though, where Mom's have only a hint of green in their kaleidoscope. And Mom's cheekbones and jaw are strong and sharp, while mine are a bit more delicate, perhaps from Grandma or Great-Grandma or someone else I don't remember.

I wonder how difficult it was for Mom to lie all those years, to tell everyone that her baby's father had been a stranger, that she had no connection with the young man she loved, who died in the ocean. Perhaps it was easy because it was worth saving her dignity—sacrificing her sexual reputation to save her moral one.

Because she, too, had killed.

I will continue this portrait for now. Perhaps it will end up looking more like Mom than me. Then after I am done I'll get back at what I'm good at—drawings alive with green and dew and living things. I may start with the wall in the small bedroom—the one now masked over with paisley, a pattern Mom says is drab and morose. Maybe I'll just paint right over it.

As Mom and I look out to the water from the stone jetty, we see dark patches on the water—shadows from clouds, schools of mackerel, perhaps. Or something else. There could have been a dark patch in the water on that day Angus died, or the day after. Someone may have seen it, mistaken it for the school of fish, and moved on. How many were that close to him and didn't know? How many people saw his body and didn't know they were looking at a body? What a shame that would be.

It's just a body, I think. A shell.

But unlike Seth's, it's a body never found. What was it like for those who knew Angus? To never have closure, to never even know for sure? It's the stuff of Sunday night movies—all those missing bodies. Except in the movies the missing often have done this intentionally; they've pretended to die so they can escape their life and emerge someplace else as some new person.

If Angus were alive today and I were to run into him on the street, would he know me? Would it be better to know? Does blood mean something after all? Cells join, DNA tugs. I used to be glad he never knew about me. Until I heard his name, and saw his face.

The breeze is crisp and fresh. I feel Mom's fingers brush against the palm of my hand, dangling, then searching, then her palm cupping, and remember the last time we held hands. It was just before we moved away nearly twenty years ago: we stood on this very spot in a cold, raw November wind. I was amazed that Mom had taken me to this spot—to the ocean she despised. And when I looked up and saw her red eyes and face streaked with wet, I knew that it was her last look at the Maine ocean, that we never were coming back. I just hadn't realized then that Mom was leaving part of me behind too, and that she had no choice.

But today, as I look into the eyes of my mother standing next to me on these rocks where lives and love ended, I know where the pain comes from. I can read the words in Mom's eyes because they are thinking the same thing I am right now.

Where is he?

Angus is in the sky, I tell her in my mind—with the pollen of flowers and the breath of birds, carried by wind around the earth, around again and again, swirling oceans and dusting up storms, flowing through clouds and rain and with all the others— Grandma and Grandpa, Aunt Adeline, Seth, and the tiny babies who didn't make it into this world. All those lost souls, whatever a soul may be.

But then I imagine Mom asking *Where is he really?*, because Mom is Mom, because she needs to know. *What do you believe, Jenna?*

I believe that his body is out there somewhere, beneath the glass surface of green. No longer bones—just salt and minerals, the crust of a rock or reef. Food for plants, the silky, swirling algae. He is the metal dust on the bottom, burying the treasures.

Or he is on part of some crystalline shore, as some powdery quartz—part of a lonely child's sand castle, the mortar of some great stone precipice.

Part of me.

And then there is Seth, buried in the earth one hundred miles away, mixing with the soil, fertilizing some growth around him. An experiment he would have loved. It's sad to think there's the possibility I won't be lying next to him there, that my own life is subject to evolve with love—some other love, perhaps even children. But Seth's soft voice in the wind reminds me it's okay.

Just a shell, he says.

Mom smiles, as if she can hear me thinking, all these thoughts swirling around. Her hand feels warm and good in mine, protective like a mother's should against this raw, fertile air. We look out at the swirling, dark green ocean that is alive with fish and shadows and souls, and together wait for spring to turn into summer.

about the author

Sarah Beth Martin began her writing career with a story published in *Mostly Maine: A Writer's Journal.* Since then, she has been published in *Pearl*, *West Wind Review*, and *Animus*, among others, and ran the literary journal *Foliage*. Martin lives in Yarmouth, Maine, and is currently at work on her second novel.